Ivy Pembroke is a law professor who specialises in copyright and trademark law, with a focus on fanfiction. An enthusiastic writer all her life, she loves the backspace button, overuses italics in emails with friends, and thinks there is little better than a story that makes you smile. She splits her time between Mississippi and her home state of Rhode Island.

A House in Provence

Ivy Pembroke

sphere

SPHERE

First published in Great Britain in 2020 by Sphere

1 3 5 7 9 10 8 6 4 2

Copyright © Little, Brown Book Group 2020
Written by Ivy Pembroke

The moral right of the author has been asserted.

A CIP catalogue record for this book
is available from the British Library.

ISBN 978-0-7515-7366-4

Typeset in Palatino by M Rules
Printed and bound in Great Britain by Clays Ltd, Elcograf S.p.A.

Papers used by Sphere are from well-managed forests
and other responsible sources.

Sphere
An imprint of
Little, Brown Book Group
Carmelite House
50 Victoria Embankment
London EC4Y 0DZ

An Hachette UK Company
www.hachette.co.uk

www.littlebrown.co.uk

For Peyton, the newest little one, and the rest of our merry gang: Jordan, Isabella, Gabriella, and Audrey

Prologue

If Jack the Christmas Street dog were to tell you this story, it would be full of new smells and new people and brand new squirrels. It would be a story full of things to be curious about, to learn about, to get to know.

Actually, that's what the story would be about from the human perspective, too. Sometimes everything aligns.

Chapter One

Once you find the tree that looks like Winston Churchill, find the third cow path. Be careful of things that only look like cow paths but have really been created by humans. Cow paths will look like cows should be on them.

'These directions,' Sam remarked, 'could be better.'

Considering that the directions consisted of things like *Turn right at the third green stile only they may have painted it red now*, and *Bear left at the old Savoir house that has been abandoned and is a little overgrown*, Libby saw his point. 'It's an adventure,' she said gamely. Only it was an adventure that had gone on for a while now, through various wrong turns and backtracking and pit stops for Jack, and they were enjoying the long summer twilight but darkness was eventually going to catch them, in the middle of the French countryside, still hoping to stumble upon a house.

3

'We're probably going to have to sleep in the car tonight,' said Teddy morosely. 'And it's tiny and we won't fit.'

'We're not going to have to sleep in the car,' Sam said.

'You'll probably kick me with your feet all night,' Teddy continued.

'We're not sleeping in the car,' Sam insisted.

Libby looked out at the miles of countryside stretching all around them and wondered where exactly they would sleep other than the rental car, if they didn't find the farmhouse.

Sam must have had the same thought because he amended, 'Probably.'

'*Dad*,' Teddy whinged. 'I'm telling you, how are we going to fit in this car? I refuse to share the backseat.'

'Well, that's not very—'

'Oh!' Libby exclaimed suddenly, cutting off the burgeoning argument. 'Wait! I think that might be the tree that looks like Winston Churchill.'

'Really?' said Sam. 'It's just a tree.'

'No, no, if you squint a bit, it looks like Winston Churchill's profile. See, it's even got the cigar.'

Sam stopped the car so he could squint at the tree and then said, 'Huh. You're right. I suppose that tree looks more like Winston Churchill than any other tree we've seen.'

'Exactly,' said Libby confidently, consulting the directions. 'So now that we have located the Churchillian tree, we have to find the third cow path past it.'

'The third cow path?' Sam echoed. 'And then we're driving down that?'

'No, then we're taking the driveway just beyond it. That's

the house's driveway!' Libby couldn't help the little squeal of excitement she gave. She'd been looking forward to this for so long, and now they were almost there!

'Locating cow paths,' remarked Sam, as they all squinted into the lingering golden dusk, 'would be easier if we were actually cows.'

'I guess we've got to think like a cow,' remarked Teddy.

'Moo!' Sam replied.

Libby glanced back in time to see Teddy roll his eyes.

Sam sighed.

They located what they thought was the third cow path, and then the driveway beyond it. It was nothing more than an expanse of sandy dirt, just wide enough for a car to pass between the overgrown grass waving on either side, and Sam drove slowly. He was probably worried about coming upon holes or ruts, or maybe turning a bend and finding a cow blocking the way, but Libby liked to think that he was going slowly just to be sure she could truly savour this first approach.

The driveway wended its way through the cow pastures, seemingly without any meaning or purpose, and then abruptly ended in a little cleared farmyard. It stood empty at the moment but Libby could envision it, in some past time, with a goat or two, and a barn cat for keeping out the mice. It was that sort of farmyard.

And sprawling comfortably beyond the farmyard was just the sort of rambling old French farmhouse that Libby had imagined in all of her dreams.

It was clearly very old, made out of a weathered stone

that had been whitewashed at some point in its very distant past. Night-time was quickly making a full approach, and the dulled ivory colour of the farmhouse caught all of the last rays of the sun and glowed a burnished gleaming bronze in places.

The house looked like lots of bits and pieces cobbled together, dripped on top of each other and sewn up in odd ways. Libby felt like she could count all the centuries in which each of the sections had been built. There was a section with a door so short Sam would have to stoop to get in, and small windows with curious little arches to the top of them, and then another section with an incredibly large and gracious set of doors, with equally large windows flanking it symmetrically, and then another section where the door looked like a serviceable afterthought and windows had been haphazardly punched through the walls. All of the windows were closed up with shutters that had once been a pale blue colour and were mostly flaking into grey. The inky thickness of the darkness creeping in meant that the shutters looked flat and stark against the stone of the house. The closed-up nature of them was the only thing uniform about the house they were looking at, and Libby *loved* it. This house didn't even look the same from window to window. It was *marvellous*. Just the sort of adventurous change of pace she'd been looking for.

'Is this it?' Sam asked, peering through the windscreen at it.

'It has to be,' Libby said excitedly.

'How would we even know?' asked Sam.

'We'll see if my key fits.' She held up the key.

They dutifully scrambled out of the car and stood in the farmyard looking up at the house. Jack kept close to them, tail wagging very slightly, as if he was trying to determine how to feel about this new place. Libby had no such qualms: Libby was in love.

It was a gorgeous evening, the warmth of the summer day kissed with the coolness of the evening rushing up, and the air around them felt hushed with expectation, like everything waiting to happen. Libby inhaled deeply, the scent of grass and warm earth and lavender intermingled. She wanted to remember this moment *for ever*.

Sam said, 'Which of these doors do you think we're meant to enter through?'

Which was a very unromantic thing to say, but Libby supposed pragmatism was important at the moment.

'Good question,' she said. 'Our first task: finding the right lock!'

They started with the nearest and smallest door. As they examined it, Jack went sniffing around the farmyard, getting his bearings. His tail was wagging a bit more steadily now. The first door had a very ancient rusty lock that they all decided their key wasn't going to fit into. The next door was the very grand door. That lock was scrolled and filigreed and elaborate but also not right for the key.

'It's like Goldilocks,' Libby said. 'The last one we try will be the right one.'

'It's always the last one,' Teddy said, heaving a sigh, with great world-weariness.

Jack came up to join them as they walked to the last door, bounding around with his usual enthusiasm and barking.

'I think Jack likes it,' said Libby fondly, and curled her hand into Sam's. 'What about you? What do you think?'

'It's certainly been an adventure getting here,' Sam said, and smiled at her.

'I love it,' said Libby. 'I think it's perfect. It's exactly what I was hoping for. It's exactly what I envisioned.'

'We haven't even seen the inside yet,' said Sam, laughing.

'I don't need to,' Libby announced grandly. 'It's *perfect*.'

'You're drunk on France,' Sam told her. 'French-drunk.'

'Hey!' Teddy called to them from where he was standing examining the last door. 'This looks like a regular lock!'

'Well, that's a relief,' Sam said, slinging his arm over Libby's shoulders to tuck her in closer against him. 'Otherwise we'd be breaking the shutters down.'

'No,' said Libby, 'we can't destroy the house.'

'Do you think you really could break the shutters, though, Dad?' asked Teddy sceptically.

'Probably,' said Sam carelessly.

Libby peered at the nearest shutter. They might have peeling paint but they seemed pretty solid, which they would have to have been to have withstood all these years of apparent neglect. She had her doubts whether Sam could actually break through those shutters but she decided to let him have his fantasy.

'Yeah, this looks like an ordinary lock,' Sam was saying. 'Would you like the honour, Libby?' He gestured to the lock with a dramatic flourish.

Libby grinned and stepped forward and held the key up. It caught the very last of the dying sun, and Libby felt like the heroine in a fantasy novel. And then she inserted the key into the lock – it slid in without any resistance – and turned it.

And the door opened.

Inside smelled musty in that way of houses that had been empty for a while, and it was pitch black, as all the windows were shuttered up. They stumbled over the threshold together, Jack running ahead of them and barking with discovery.

'I wish I could see like Jack,' Teddy commented.

'Where are the lights?' Sam asked.

Libby felt along the wall for a switch.

Sam held his phone up, letting it shed some bright white light over the wall Libby was feeling against. There was no switch anywhere where there should have been one, and Sam kept playing the mobile light across the plaster, until they finally spotted a switch, further along on the wall.

'Watch your step,' Sam said, as Libby headed towards it.

The floor seemed sloped and uneven and Libby tripped a little over the trailing edge of one of the dustcovers that had been thrown over the furniture, but she made it to the switch, and flipped it on . . . and nothing happened.

'Uh-oh,' said Teddy.

Libby flipped the switch a few more times, just to see.

'Is the electricity off?' Sam asked quizzically.

'I don't know,' Libby admitted, at a loss.

Teddy said, 'See? Told you we were sleeping in the car. We are *not* all going to fit in the car.'

9

'If we could find candles or something ... ' Libby said, trailing off, because she had no idea where to start looking in this huge maze of a house they were stepping into for the first time.

'I think sleeping in the car makes somewhat more sense,' Sam said. 'It's fine. It'll be an adventure, right?'

Libby knew he was saying that for her benefit, because she kept saying she wanted an adventure, but getting all three of them – plus a dog – sleeping in a car their first night seemed extreme even by her standards.

She flipped the switch again, futilely, and looked around her at the dark house. The darkness grew deeper and more absolute, stretching off into the distance, and who knew what lurked there? They couldn't possibly go traipsing around in the dark. It was a much safer idea to get Teddy settled in the car. She and Sam would ... figure something out.

Chapter Two

Remember to pack for all sorts of weather!! We'll be there a long time!!!

It had started like this: Libby wanting to go on holiday; and a grey, dreary day in the staffroom, Libby with her hands cupped around a mug of tea, letting the warmth seep into her.

Mrs Dash, also seated in the staffroom with her, heaved a heavy sigh.

Libby glanced across at her. Mrs Dash looked very mournful indeed. 'Would you like to talk about it?' Libby offered kindly.

'It's just that the things you think will be wonderful never quite turn out to be as wonderful as you think,' said Mrs Dash. 'I'm going backpacking in Brazil this summer.'

'Oh, dear,' said Libby. 'And that's not going to be as much fun as you hoped?'

'No, no,' said Mrs Dash, 'I'm very much looking forward to it. Except.'

'Except?' prompted Libby.

'Except for Great-Aunt Clarissa.'

'Is she ... supposed to go to Brazil with you?' asked Libby, confused.

'Oh, goodness, no,' said Mrs Dash. 'She's dead.'

'Oh, I'm sorry,' said Libby.

'No, no.' Mrs Dash waved Libby's condolences away. 'She died ages ago. It's just that, because of Great-Aunt Clarissa, I've this great big house in the French countryside being entirely neglected.' Mrs Dash sighed heavily again.

And Libby stared at her, sure she'd heard her incorrectly. 'You've got what?'

'A great big house in the French countryside. One of those rambling old farmhouse affairs. In Provence. Near lavender fields. And olive groves. It's quite lovely. But, alas, it will be abandoned for the summer whilst I am in Brazil. And it's not like I ever find any time to visit in term time. So, really, poor Great-Aunt Clarissa.'

'So,' Libby said slowly, 'to clarify: you've got a massive house in a charming part of the French countryside you're worried is going to be empty all summer?'

'Yes,' said Mrs Dash. 'If only I knew that someone might be able to pop in and make sure it's okay. I mean, naturally I have a local doing it, but he's very *French* about the whole thing. *You* know. I can't really trust him to make sure the house is kept up.'

'Well,' said Libby. 'I might be able to help you out there.'

Teddy was settled sulking in the car, and Sam turned away to find where Libby had wandered off to. The moon had emerged, bright and full, and Sam was surprised how much light it cast over the farmyard. It was enough for him to see that Libby had wandered over to the edge of an old, shallow basin that was full of water that reflected the moonlight and gave her a spooky mournful quality.

She looked at him as he approached, and the moonlight was definitely strong enough for him to make out the anguish on her face.

'How is he?' she asked.

'Fine,' he said casually. 'Don't mind him. He's just been sulking. And he's overtired from all the travel. He'll perk up and be fine and cheerful in the morning.' This was wishful thinking, since Teddy had been deep in his sulk for a while now, but Sam was deciding to be optimistic in France.

'After sleeping in the car?' said Libby sceptically.

'Oh, yeah, he'll be fine,' Sam assured her heartily.

It didn't work. 'I'm so sorry,' Libby cried.

And Sam was tired and frustrated and experiencing a bit of foreboding about their time here, but he felt terrible to see the disappointment on Libby's face, when she had been *so* excited and *so* looking forward to their French holiday. 'For what?' he said. 'You've nothing to be sorry for.'

'You didn't really want to come here. I convinced you—'

'That's not true,' Sam said. 'I was of course excited to go on holiday with you—'

'And now your son is sleeping in a *car*.'

'He's fine,' Sam insisted. Then, 'Come on.' He took her hand and led her back to the car. 'Let's stargaze. It'll be romantic.'

'How?' asked Libby morosely.

'Now, now,' Sam said, trying to be playful to alleviate the mood. 'No sulking.' He kissed her cheek briefly, then went digging through the luggage in the boot until he found what he was looking for. He walked over to Libby with an armful of sweatshirts.

'What are those?' Libby asked, eyeing them.

'Our clothes,' Sam replied. 'Well. All of the warmest clothes we brought.'

'I can see that.'

'It isn't much,' Sam continued, spreading them out in a patchwork on the dusty ground of the farmyard, 'but I think we've got just enough for a bit of a blanket of sorts. There.' He stepped back to survey his handiwork.

Libby lifted an eyebrow at him. 'That? That doesn't look very comfortable.'

'Shh,' said Sam, finger to his lips. He sat on his makeshift blanket. It wasn't very comfortable. But . . . 'Come here,' he said, reaching his hand out.

Libby, after a moment, came. She sank down onto the 'blanket' with him, settled against him, and sure, it wasn't comfortable, but it wasn't unbearable, just the two of them snuggled up like that. And . . .

'Look at that,' Sam whispered into her ear, and pointed up at the sky over their head.

So many stars. An astonishing amount. So many more than they could see in London.

'Wow,' Libby breathed, and Sam could tell it was working magic on her.

Sam said, 'It almost seems fake, doesn't it? How can there be that many stars?'

'I feel like I understand *Starry Night* better,' Libby remarked, snuggling against him.

Sam said, 'All those stars there, all the time, and we never really get to see them. I feel like that's a metaphor for . . . something.'

Libby laughed. 'It might be a metaphor for *everything*. Everything we're bad about remembering is there.'

'Yeah,' Sam agreed reflectively.

Libby turned closer into him.

After a moment of silence, Sam said, 'France doesn't have bears, right?'

'I don't think so. Why?'

'Wondering if I have to worry about defending us from a bear attack.' Sam was only half-joking. He was not and never had been a caravanner; sleeping in the open air like this was full of hidden perils he had no idea about.

'I shouldn't think so,' Libby said, 'I think our main issue is going to be how dusty all our clothing will be,' and then, 'Really, though, thank you. You've been great about . . . all this, being . . . so not what I'm sure you imagined.'

'Well, I imagined a rambling old farmhouse,' Sam said. 'It's certainly that.'

'Emphasis on the "old".'

'A bit,' Sam agreed. 'I admit to being a trifle concerned about the Wi-Fi situation. I'm glad I've got a couple of days off work to start with so I can figure that out.'

Libby groaned. 'And I mocked you for worrying about that. I'm so sorry.'

'Please stop apologising,' Sam said. 'I'm doing a horrible job of not making you feel guilty about this. It's fine. New things are always bumpy in the beginning. You should have seen how bumpy our first few days back in London were. We'll be on track before you know it. I just can be . . . bad, a bit, with new and unexpected things.'

'I don't think you're bad at all. I think you've been an understanding dream about all of this.'

Sam thought of how he felt like he was flailing, uncertain, and trying to keep his irritation at bay, and wasn't so sure about that. But he was glad Libby didn't seem to be reading all of that in their interactions. He said lightly, 'I'm an excellent husband.'

'You are,' Libby agreed gravely.

'We've a lot of new experiences ahead of us this summer.'

'We have.'

'We'll have to be sure to manage them properly so as not to overwhelm my delicate system,' Sam continued.

Libby laughed and kissed him and said, 'We'll see what we can do.'

Chapter Three

Sam was in the process of doing a dismal job of tying his tie – because it had been a while since he had had to wear a tie – when Libby came galloping up the stairs, Jack at her heels, barking excitedly at her energetic entry.

'Hello,' Sam said in surprise, because that was hardly the way Libby usually came home.

'Sam,' Libby said breathlessly. 'I've got the most amazing news.'

She did indeed look thrilled about something, her cheeks flushed extra-pink and her eyes extra-bright. Sam was charmed and bemused. 'I can't imagine what, but I can't wait to hear.'

'How would you like to honeymoon in France? In *Provence*?' Libby asked it dramatically, with a little flourish.

'Is that where you'd like to go?' Sam said. 'I thought you were going to be keen on an island getaway but Provence sounds lovely. All the websites I've looked at recommend Paris for a honeymoon, but Provence would be—'

'No, no.' Libby shook her head. 'You're not understanding. I want to go to Provence ... for the *summer*.'

'The summer?' Sam echoed.

'I don't want it to just be a getaway, I want us to take Teddy and immerse him in French culture. Immerse *ourselves* in French culture. We'll have so much sun. And cheese. And croissants. And sun. Just think of it, Sam. *Think of it.*'

'I ... ' Sam felt confused. 'You want to go away for the entire summer?'

'Why not? I don't have to work with the summer holidays and all, and you can work remotely from anywhere. Why shouldn't we?'

'Because spending weeks in Provence costs a great deal of money I haven't been saving for?' suggested Sam. 'This idea came out of nowhere, didn't it?'

'What if I told you we could stay somewhere for free?'

'Somewhere like where?' asked Sam, wary of the answer to that question.

'Mrs Dash's Great-Aunt Clarissa's old rambling farmhouse,' Libby answered in an eager rush.

'Mrs Dash?' said Sam. 'How did I know that Mrs Dash *had* to be involved in something so foolhardy?'

Libby looked vaguely offended. 'It isn't "foolhardy". I think it sounds *wonderful*.'

'To leave Christmas Street for the whole summer?'

'*Yes*,' Libby insisted. 'Look, you know I like Christmas Street just as much as everyone else, but it would survive the summer without us.'

'Yes, I'm not really concerned about Christmas Street. What about Teddy?'

'What about him? You don't think he'd like France?'

'I think he's—' Sam cut himself off, hearing Teddy come dashing through the front door.

'Dad!' he shouted up the stairs. 'Hurry up! Everyone's leaving without us! Hi, Libby.'

'Hi, Teddy,' she said to him warmly, then turned back to Sam. 'Leaving to go where?'

'Max's gallery show. Remember? Our artist neighbour Max who's having his first gallery show since he and Arthur adopted Charlie?'

'Oh, my goodness!' exclaimed Libby. 'I completely forgot.'

'Why'd you think I was wearing a tie?'

Libby lifted one shoulder in a shrug. 'To look fit?'

Sam laughed. 'Don't get any ideas, we promised we'd go.'

'Yes, yes, of course we'll go. I'm excited about it.'

'Look, we'll talk about this later,' Sam promised, leaning forward to kiss behind her ear, because Libby loved to be kissed in that spot.

'Just think about it,' Libby said, catching his hand and

looking earnestly into his eyes. 'I think we could make it work, and I think it would be *wonderful*.'

Sam had never been to an art exhibition, and he had no idea what he was supposed to do at it.

He was hoping it was going to be obvious. Probably you just looked at the paintings.

Luckily, he was right. There was wine and cheese and paintings everywhere. Sam made sure Teddy and his best friend Pari were going to behave themselves and not act as if the evening was boring, and then he fetched himself some nibbles and found Libby and the rest of Christmas Street in among the paintings.

Some of Max's paintings were aggressively bright, with colour palettes that were practically neon. Other paintings were muted, almost gauzy, washed-out and pale. But no matter the colour scheme, all of them seemed like snatches of objects. As Sam walked along, glass of wine in hand, studying the paintings, he could recognise some of the images. That one looked like Arthur's profile, seen through a blurry mirror. This one looked like Charlie's chubby hand, grasping a toy of some sort, but somewhat out of proportion. There was one that seemed like a dog's perked ear, waiting for someone to come home, that made Sam think of Jack. And Sam thought one particular painting could have been Christmas Street, the tidy terraced houses looking like they stretched into infinity, but they were slightly lopsided and rendered in the brightest of colours that had never been seen on a London street.

'Is that the street?' Millie, the street's newest inhabitant, asked beside him. She was studying the paintings very closely and thoughtfully, with a little frown of concentration.

'I think so,' said Sam. 'A bit skewed.'

'Everything's a bit skewed,' said Millie. 'It's interesting.'

'It's dreams,' said Arthur, Max's husband, from behind them. 'It's meant to be dreams.'

'Oh, hence the title of the show,' Sam realised. 'Life Is But A Dream.'

'Exactly,' said Max, arriving in their little group. He was holding Charlie and looked immensely pleased with how things were going. Sam couldn't help smiling at him, as he launched into a tumble of words about his art, about how it was meant to be both aspirational and very familiar, like everything you could imagine when you closed your eyes and all the things you could never imagine but happened anyway, all the things from your everyday life that showed up in dreams in oddly wrong ways and all the things that showed up in dreams that you'd never even seen before.

Max talked for so long that eventually Arthur said, gently and fondly, 'Okay, that's quite enough, you're boring everyone.'

'Not at all,' Millie said warmly. 'It's so lovely to hear someone talk about their art. Jasper talks about wood that way sometimes, about how it speaks to him, and I love to hear it.'

'And that's the way you talk about baking,' Jasper, Millie's boyfriend, said, smiling. 'So, you see, we all have our arts.'

'Hmm,' mused Pen, another Christmas Street resident who had wandered over during Max's lecture. 'All the different arts we can have, with all the different artists. I feel like there might be a story there.'

'You think there's a story everywhere,' said Libby, laughing, as she joined the group.

Sam said, 'I'm not sure what my art is. I don't think I talk that passionately about my job.'

'No one understands your job,' Libby pointed out.

'Least of all me,' said Sam.

'I want to show you something,' Libby said, sliding her hand into Sam's and giving it a gentle tug. 'Actually, Max, I want to ask you a question, too. About one of your paintings.'

'Oh,' said Max brightly. 'I would be delighted to answer any and all questions about my paintings.'

'Try to confine your lectures to less than an hour,' Arthur joked, provoking light laughter around the group, and Max tweaked at Arthur's tie as he followed Libby and Sam across the room.

'This one,' Libby said, pausing in front of it. 'What's this one?'

It was one of Max's technicolour paintings, all impossibly vivid yellows and other-worldly greens, with a splash of electric blues and shining glints of silver threaded here and there. Up close, it looked like nothing but a swirl, like a storm had overturned all of Max's paints and they had run chaotically together into the painting. Sam studied it in vain, looking for one of the familiar snatches he'd been able to spy in the other paintings.

'Oh, this one,' said Max, as if Libby had chosen his favourite painting, but Sam had the impression that Libby could have expressed interest in any painting and garnered the same reaction.

'Can you tell us what it's supposed to be?' Libby asked.

'In my head,' said Max, 'it's this magical ideal place, this fairyland of bright sunshine and beautiful meadows and the bluest sky you've ever seen. It's that place you go to in your dreams when you wake up in the morning and think, I don't know where I was but I know I'd been there before. But even as you think that, you know you can't possibly have been there before because it was too perfect, too beautiful, too wonderful. It's that place.'

'What's the silver?' asked Sam.

'In my dreams there's always a flash of silver in a fairytale place,' said Max. 'It complements the gold of the sunshine, and always it's something that winks at you from the next valley over.'

Sam tipped his head at the painting, seeing it through Max's eyes, and now he could see it. Instead of senseless chaos, it did seem like a beautiful landscape, shimmering in an eternal dusk, when the sun had hit everything just so to make it seem fuzzy around the edges. The flashes of silver did look like something winking at you from the next valley over, beckoning you to keep exploring. Sam wanted to step into the painting now. He couldn't imagine why he'd looked at it before and not seen the seductive welcoming of it. No wonder it was Libby's favourite.

'What do you see when you look at the painting?' Max asked.

Libby said, 'I see the French countryside.'

'Okay,' said Sam, 'it's not that I don't want to spend the summer in the French countryside. I mean, who *wouldn't* want to spend the summer in the French countryside?'

'Exactly,' said Libby, beaming, as if she'd already won the day. She disappeared into the bathroom to continue getting ready for bed.

'But,' said Sam meaningfully, raising his voice to be heard over the running water.

Libby's head poked back out of the bathroom. 'But?'

'This is a major new proposal. Spending the entire summer abroad. In a house we know nothing about. Who even knows what this house looks like?'

'It's a rambling old farmhouse in the French country-side,' said Libby. 'How bad could it be?'

'It could be a falling-down barn. Do you even know if it has plumbing?'

'I'm sure Mrs Dash's Great-Aunt Clarissa saw fit to put plumbing into the place,' Libby said. 'A woman named Clarissa doesn't sound like the sort of woman to ignore plumbing.' She disappeared back into the bathroom.

'I'm just saying,' said Sam. 'Plumbing is fairly important to me. I wouldn't want to have to spend the entire summer without plumbing.'

The water turned off and Libby came back into the bedroom. 'Where's your sense of adventure?' she chided him.

'The house could be infested with mice,' said Sam.

'Or bats,' Libby grinned at him. 'And we know you're an expert when it comes to bat infestations.'

'Hardly,' Sam said. 'That was a disaster.'

'I'm sure there'll be a lovely fresh market we can go to,' said Libby, climbing into bed, 'and we could buy lots of carrots and beetroot.' She beamed at him.

The problem was that when Libby beamed at him just that way, it was difficult for Sam to remember why he was resisting her. He tucked a tendril of her red hair behind her ear and said, 'No more subpar supermarket produce for us?'

'We could have had a French meet-cute,' Libby said. '*Très chic.*'

Because they'd met in the supermarket, over carrots and beetroot, and yes, later she'd turned out to be Teddy's teacher but the whole thing had started over supermarket produce and Sam thought it had been the luckiest supermarket trip of his entire life.

'You said we ought to go on a honeymoon,' Libby continued. 'What could be more romantic?'

Sam sighed. 'Look. I take your point. I really do. My real objection to it is Teddy.'

25

'What about Teddy?'

'I'm always worrying about Teddy. His mum died, I moved him across an ocean, I made him create an entirely new life for himself, and then I married his teacher. It's maybe rather a lot to stuff into the life of a little boy who's not yet lived a decade. And now I'm going to tell him we're going to go and live in a completely different country for the summer? When I've barely given him enough time to get used to *this* country? He doesn't speak French – I mean, none of us *really* do, aside from tourist French, but he grew up in America, where they don't believe in teaching children other languages, and I had other things on my mind when Sara was sick so I never corrected that. Which is off on a tangent, but the point is, it's a big decision for me to make about Teddy on a whim.'

Libby was silent for a long moment, and Sam felt as if he'd been melodramatic and over the top.

But Libby just said in a soft voice, 'I get it. I do,' and snuggled close to him. 'All we have to do is think about it. We don't have to make any decisions right now.'

Sam let out a breath, relieved. Libby was . . . the *best*. He could think of no other way to describe her. This was, after all, why he'd married her. He might feel melodramatic and over the top but she always acted as if he wasn't, made him feel like he was being reasonable, or at least that there was time for him to find his way back to 'reasonable'. Libby just always gave him time, soft, understanding, sweet.

26

'You,' Sam said, wriggling down so their faces were level in the bed, 'are very lovely to me.'

Libby smiled. 'Well, *you* are very lovely to *me*.'

'Isn't it nice how that works?' said Sam.

'Fantastic,' agreed Libby.

Chapter Four

Dear Pari, This house doesn't even have LIGHTS. It's
the worst. I miss you and Christmas Street lots.

Libby dozed off but Sam did not. He stared up at the impossible number of stars over their heads and Libby snuggled closer to him, snoring lightly, and he tried to spread his warmth over her as much as he could.

He wished he'd been able to drop off to sleep as easily as Teddy and Libby and apparently Jack, who was quiet in the car. But he felt too tense and uncertain. Libby was off on a grand adventure, but Sam felt like he had to be the one worrying about the practicalities of this adventure. Sam felt like he'd done nothing but worry about practicalities for the past decade of his life, ever since Teddy had entered it, and then Sara had got sick, and then he'd moved them to London, and there had just always been so much to worry about, so many balls to keep in the air. He never felt like he had the luxury to just fall asleep. What if there *were* bears?

What if there were a million things that it was his job to protect everyone from?

Sam wanted to just be spending the summer in France without worrying, the way Libby seemed to be doing. He wished Libby could teach him her knack to greet this with enthusiasm. To look at the falling-down rubble of this house in front of them and see a romantic adventure instead of a nightmare that probably wasn't going to have the Wi-Fi Sam desperately needed for his job.

Then again, Sam considered, that was probably why he'd married Libby: because she balanced him, made the adventures in life seem like *more*, and when he embraced them he didn't feel like he was just going through the motions for Teddy's sake, keeping up morale.

Change could be a lot, and Sam was always trying to pretend it wasn't overwhelming him, because he had to. But Libby made him feel like it genuinely *wasn't* overwhelming, like there would be something steady to hold onto through it all: her.

Sam let Libby sleep next to him and watched as the stars seemed to wink out, the sky lightening almost imperceptibly at first, and then suddenly it was no longer dark velvet but blue silk rippling overhead. High streaks of clouds above him glowed pink and yellow with the promise of a sunrise. The birds were a loud, cacophonous army all around him, winging to and fro, and the air warmed with the scent of lavender, and Sam smiled suddenly. It was beautiful here, a fantastic change of pace, and Teddy was totally going to come round. How could he resist something as magical as this?

Libby was right: France was going to be a grand adventure, and things no longer seemed so bad.

When Libby was a child, she was afraid of the dark. *Things*, she always told her mother, *are just better in the daylight.* When Libby, curled up next to Sam, opened her eyes to the sight of their beautiful French farmhouse glowing pink in the new light of a fresh day, she remembered that childhood motto of hers in a way she hadn't in ages.

Sam was already awake, watching her with a faint smile playing around his lips, and she said, '*Look* how gorgeous it is.'

'It is rather pretty,' he allowed.

'"Rather pretty"?' she echoed. 'It's *amazing.*'

'I'm glad it's a bright sunny day,' said Sam. 'It'll give us time to explore.' He sat up and rubbed at his neck, wincing. 'I might be getting too old to sleep on the ground any more.'

'Did you used to do a lot of that in your younger days?' Libby asked. Sam helped her up, and she spent a few moments walking around the farmyard, working the stiffness out of her muscles. Sam did have a point about being too old for this.

'No,' Sam admitted, 'and now I know why. I think what we should do is find a bedroom to make sure we don't have to do this again.'

'And a bathroom,' Libby added.

'Good point,' said Sam, and opened the back door of the car.

Jack came bounding out, paused to stretch extravagantly, and then continued bounding over to Libby, barking an excited good morning.

'Well, Jack looks bright-eyed and bushy-tailed, at least,' Libby laughed.

'Jack always does,' Sam replied. Teddy was sitting at the edge of the car seat, blinking blearily. 'And what about you?' Sam asked him. 'Bright-eyed and bushy-tailed?'

Teddy glared at him. 'Is there a bathroom?' he asked.

Sam laughed. 'Let's go exploring.'

They had left the door unlocked the night before, so they stepped confidently through it. It was still dim inside because of the shutters, but enough light seeped through the chinks in the wood that they could make sense of the space. Jack immediately swept off to take stock of the adjacent rooms, while Libby and Sam and Teddy tried to take stock of the one they were in. It was a medium-sized space that seemed to be some sort of lounge area, with a gallery overlooking it from above. There was an extremely ancient television on a table on the wall across from them, and Libby peeked under one of the dustcovers on the furnishings to reveal threadbare sofas in a vivid shade of rusty orange.

'What *is* that?' Teddy asked, his nose wrinkled. 'Some sort of weird computer?'

'It's a television,' Sam told him, laughing. 'A very old one.'

'It's so tiny!' Teddy exclaimed. 'And yet also so big.'

'It's a paradox.' Sam looked at Libby. 'How long did you say it's been since Mrs Dash was here? Because this looks like the last time anyone was here was 1952.'

'Televisions weren't that small in 1952,' Libby said. 'It's been here at least since the eighties.'

The next room had a flimsy folding table in it that had definitely seen better days, and a few mismatched chairs. The room after that was a kitchen, as rusty orange as the sofas had been, with vivid marigold-coloured appliances.

'I am getting a distinctly seventies vibe from this room,' said Sam.

'The fridge is yellow,' Teddy said. 'The stove is yellow. The sink is yellow. It's a lot of yellow.'

'I think it used to be the style,' said Sam. 'Or *a* style, at least.' He reached over and turned the tap on, and water came out. It was the same rust-orange colour as the tiles, but at least something in the house was working, because not a single light switch was having any effect. Sam said, 'That's not bad, we'll just let the water run the rust out. Of course, it's decades of accumulated rust in these pipes, so it might take a while.'

'It can't have been decades,' Libby said, 'she made it sound like she'd been here more frequently than that, and look, it has appliances.' Libby opened the fridge.

And then immediately closed it because the stench was too much to bear.

'I don't think I would call that an appliance,' Sam remarked drily.

32

'I think something died in there,' Teddy said, holding his nose.

Jack came barrelling back into the room, apparently attracted by the smell, barking wild alarm.

Sam said, also holding his nose, 'The power's out, so anything in the fridge met a bitter end.'

They kept walking, because there wasn't much else to say about the kitchen, and encountered a tightly wound spiral staircase going up to the first floor. Beside the staircase was a stable door with the top half standing open, which seemed to lead into the next part of the house.

'Up or through?' Sam asked Teddy.

Teddy gave him a look. 'Oh, *now* it matters what decision I want to make?'

'Up,' Sam decided.

So up they went. Jack didn't seem to care much for the staircase but he braved it for Teddy's sake, and when they reached the top they found themselves in a loft space overlooking the lounge they'd entered through. The loft had been subdivided into a couple of bedrooms with nondescript but serviceable furniture and quilts on the beds so filthy with dust that Libby couldn't even imagine what colour they were under the greyness. And in between the two bedrooms was a bathroom. As seventies rust-orange as so much of the house had been (that was probably the underlying colour of the quilts, too, Libby thought), but still a bathroom.

'Does it work?' asked Libby, and Sam flushed the toilet, and it flushed, so they took turns using the bathroom, and

Libby felt a little bit better about everything. She'd wanted an adventure, but she preferred one with indoor plumbing.

'I don't know what we're going to do about the electricity situation,' Sam said as they headed back down the staircase to the stable door. 'We'll have to ring Mrs Dash. I see no other option.' After a little bit of shoving, he persuaded the bottom half of the door to open.

And they stepped into a space that felt like a completely different house. They had been standing on peeling lino in the previous part of the house, but now the floor beneath their feet was some sort of tumbled stone, rough-hewn and terribly impressive. They entered a long, narrow room stretching along the back of the house, and it was scattered with broken plant pots, and there were heaps of dried, dead vegetation on the floor.

Libby decided not to think about how many spiders lurked within.

Sam leaned over and tried a light switch and suddenly the room was flooded with harsh light from a series of elaborate wrought-iron lanterns hung at intervals from the ceiling.

'Light!' Libby exclaimed, relieved beyond words. She'd been worried that she had no idea what they were going to do if the electricity to the house was broken.

'Oh, good,' Sam said wryly. 'The better to see all the debris.'

And with the lights on, the room was filthier than it had seemed in dimness. But Libby didn't mind. It could be swept and cleared out. Things were looking up.

This part of the house was the opposite of the previous side of the house. Where those rooms had been small and merely serviceable, the room they were in now was grand and much bigger than it needed to be. The ceiling was very high overhead, and the light fixtures, while not chandeliers, were still much more elaborate than an ordinary light fixture. And, more importantly, all of them seemed to work. The long room spilled into a central entrance hall, big enough to fit some furnishings comfortably, although it was completely empty, save for a very wide staircase leading upwards. Off the hall were a few large rooms, all of them with enormous fireplaces, big enough for Teddy to step into.

'Don't,' Sam said, grabbing Teddy before he could follow Jack into one. 'You've no idea what's in there. Jack! Get out of there!'

Jack came out absolutely covered in soot, which he shook off himself, so they were also covered in soot.

'Oh, dear,' Libby said.

Teddy glowered as if he hadn't just been about to dirty himself the same way.

One of the rooms connected eventually to what seemed to be a kitchen. Much less modern than the kitchen in the first part of the house, which was saying something, since that kitchen hadn't been updated in at least a generation. The stove here was cast iron, and Libby had no idea how she would even use it. And the sink was enormous, wide and deep and seemingly carved from one huge slab of granite. When Libby turned the tap, rusty water gushed out.

'It could be workable,' Sam said. 'At least the electricity is okay in here.'

'It would be like going back in time,' Libby said. 'I feel like I could only make venison in this kitchen. Which is too bad, because I was going to learn to cook while I was here.'

'What's venison?' asked Teddy.

'Deer,' Libby said.

Teddy wrinkled his nose, considering. 'Ew.'

'You eat chicken and cows and pigs,' Sam pointed out.

'*Ew,*' said Teddy. 'I never really thought about that before.'

'Well, this might at least work until I can get the power fixed in the other part of the house,' Sam said, stepping back and looking around the kitchen.

It was, like every other room in this part of the house, much bigger than it probably needed to be. In the centre of it was a very large rustic table of rough wood that Libby liked the look of. She could imagine kneading dough on the table to make elaborate breads.

She leaned against the table, finding it so heavy that it didn't even budge.

Sam said, 'That table is going to go down with this house. You're never moving it out of here.'

'I love it,' Libby said. 'It's so French-farmhouse.'

'It's in a French farmhouse,' said Sam. 'That's probably the definition.'

'But the stuff in the other part of the house didn't seem like French-farmhouse stuff at all,' said Libby. 'This is much more what I was thinking.'

'I wonder if Mr Hammersley will want to carve it,' said Teddy.

'I don't think we ought to carve the house's antiques,' said Sam.

Teddy gave him a look. 'If it was anything super-valuable, they'd have this house a lot more locked up.'

'He has a point,' Libby said.

'Let's go upstairs,' Sam suggested.

Libby had loved the downstairs of this part of the house but the upstairs was the true *pièce de résistance*. There was a central gallery full of shrouded artwork and pieces of furniture, and off the gallery were four large bedrooms, all with fireplaces and four-poster beds covered with delicate linens and laces and toiles that had definitely seen better days but still seemed so quintessentially *French* to Libby. Each of the bedrooms had an adjoining bathroom that didn't seem quite original to the house and must have been converted at a later date. They were very large bathrooms, with the expected bits and pieces in place.

And one of the bedrooms, at the back of the house, had a series of graceful French doors all along one end. Sam walked over to one of them, unlocked it, and opened it, then leaned forward to unlatch the protective faded blue shutter and threw that open as well.

They found themselves standing on a balcony so large it could have been called a terrace, and beyond them rolled the landscape of Provence, green and purple and gold and silver – just like Max's painting had been. They stood in the warm sun and looked out at the French countryside, even

Jack and Teddy struck silent and still by the beauty of it, Teddy possibly grudgingly impressed.

Sam took a deep breath and said, 'Well. This may have made the whole thing worth it.'

Chapter Five

Holiday lets available in Avignon
Holiday lets available in Marseilles
Holiday lets available in Gordes

It was grey and dreary on Christmas Street and Bill Hammersley, Sam's next-door neighbour and longest veteran resident of Christmas Street, stood beside Sam and waited for the children to arrive home from school. Bill did this every day, in all types of weather. Bill didn't notice weather. In Bill's day, no one worried about a little thing like *weather*.

'I wish we'd get a break from this,' Sam said, turning the collar of his coat up.

'A break from what?' asked Bill.

'The weather,' said Sam.

'Who even notices the weather?' barked Bill. 'What's it got to do with anything?'

Sam laughed. 'Well, I suppose it depends on the person, because I think it's really got Libby down. She's angling for

39

a summer in the French countryside. What do you think about that?'

'Oh, that's lovely,' Bill said. 'France is lovely.'

Sam stared at him, looking amazed.

'What?' Bill asked self-consciously.

'I did not expect you to say that,' Sam said. 'I expected you to say France would be a waste of my time or something.'

'Nonsense,' Bill scoffed, a little embarrassed. 'It's lovely.' And then, because Sam continued to look amazed, and because Bill supposed it wouldn't hurt anyone to admit it, 'My Agatha loved France. We had our honeymoon there. Couldn't go back as often as she'd've liked but she really loved what time she spent there. Some of our happiest days.' Sam continued to just look at Bill, so Bill snapped, 'What?' at him.

'Nothing,' said Sam. 'That's lovely. So you and Agatha had a good time in France and a long, happy marriage. Maybe I should take a page out of your book.'

Bill shrugged, wishing he hadn't said anything at all. 'Do what you like.'

'Did you enjoy Max's art exhibition last night?'

Bill couldn't believe he was relieved to have the conversation shifted to an event that had served tiny, unidentifiable nibbles, but he was. He said, 'Can't say much for the food but the art was good.'

'Well,' remarked Sam, 'I don't think that Max would want you to say much about the food as opposed to the art.'

'He is bloody good with a paintbrush,' Bill said, 'even if

40

I don't understand half of what he's talking about. He kept going on about dreams. In my day, people just painted landscapes and portraits.'

Sam laughed. 'Honestly, Bill, modern art has been around for a while. And Max definitely had some landscapes and portraits in there.'

'If you commissioned a portrait from him and it came back looking like that, you'd think he wasn't really a painter,' Bill remarked. 'But now, he tells you that he's painting you a dream, and I suppose I can see how that makes more sense.'

Sam laughed again.

Sam noticed that Libby did not bring up the house in the French countryside for the entire evening, which he appreciated, because he'd had a busy day at work and hadn't been able to devote as much time to pondering it as he'd wanted to. The next day, though, he sat in on a supremely dull conference call and poked around holiday lets in various points in France. They all looked delightful, drenched in sunlight, some of them with swimming pools glimmering in welcome. They described idyllic villages and charming market towns, a bucolic French lifestyle of food and wine and flowers, of late dinners in twilit gardens and equally late breakfasts of flaky croissants. By the time Sam was done reading the holiday-let propaganda, he was ready to *move* to France, permanently.

41

He rang his sister Ellen, because his impulse when he was trying to make a major decision was always to talk to Ellen. She had guided him through many crises, and Sam thought it was a good job she didn't charge him for therapy sessions, because he would have owed her a small fortune.

'Hello,' Ellen answered cheerfully. 'What's up with you this fine day?'

Sam looked outside at the same grey, dreary view he'd been looking at for a week and said, 'You're in a good mood.'

'And why shouldn't I be?' asked Ellen, sounding a little bewildered.

'No reason,' Sam said, realising he'd confused her. Maybe she was just in an ordinary mood, and maybe everyone around him had been feeling a bit down because of the weather. 'I don't know. The weather?'

'Oh, well, it's March,' said Ellen. 'How are you?'

'I have a question for you.'

'As long as it's not Teddy's homework, then I should hopefully be able to answer it.'

Sam snorted. 'Teddy's homework is, as you know, thoroughly beyond my abilities.'

'My poor little nephew,' said Ellen. 'How will he ever make it to university at this rate?'

'Hopefully by doing his own work. Anyway. Do you think I'm ... ' Sam trailed off, trying to think of how to frame what he wanted to ask.

' ... an extremely annoying brother?' finished Ellen for him. 'Yes. Absolutely.'

'I'm a wonderful brother,' Sam said, 'and you're a liar. No, am I cautious with Teddy?'

'Cautious with him?' echoed Ellen, sounding thoughtful.

'Like, do I . . . ' Sam huffed out a frustrated breath. 'Do I worry too much about how things will affect him? Do I not let him do things that all the other kids get to do? Do I think too hard about too much?'

'You definitely think too hard about too much,' remarked Ellen. 'But, I don't know, I don't think you were always that way. I think you had a lot of stuff happen in your life. A lot of stuff people don't exactly plan for. When Sara died, and Teddy became entirely your responsibility, I think you understandably became a bit more fretful. You didn't want to make the wrong decisions for him. You still don't. No parent does, of course, but I think you feel very keenly this idea that you're flying without a net. Which you really aren't any more, but I think you got used to that idea. So yes, I think you might worry a bit more than other parents do, about ordinary things no one would notice. But I don't think that's irrational of you. I don't think anyone would *blame* you.'

'It's not that I blame me,' Sam said. 'I know that I'm doing the best I can at being a dad, I mean, I'm not angry with myself. But I don't want to stifle Teddy. I don't want to deny him experiences he should be having because I'm scared.'

'I haven't noticed you doing that. Honestly, Sam, the two of you are so brave and strong and I'm so proud of both of you. But it's why I like Libby for the two of you. It's like, when Libby's around, you don't have to be as brave or strong. And I think that's good for you.'

'Yeah,' Sam agreed, thinking hard. 'That's true.'

'Now what's this all about?' Ellen asked. 'This didn't come out of nowhere.'

'Libby's got this opportunity for us to spend the summer taking care of some French farmhouse.'

'Sorry, did you say "French farmhouse"? As in, going to France for the summer?'

'Yeah.'

'The *entire summer*?'

'Yes.'

'Can you afford it?'

'Well, apparently it would be free.'

'Then I think there's only one question left,' said Ellen.

'Okay,' Sam said. 'What's the question?'

'When do you leave?'

Sam, after his conversation with Ellen, was in the mood to procrastinate. Really, he'd procrastinated almost the entire day, but such were the advantages of working from home: no one was policing *when* he got his work done.

So Sam went to visit Max, as he hadn't spoken to him since his art exhibition. He wanted to tell Max how much he'd enjoyed it.

He found Pen also in Max's kitchen, both of them with cups of tea in front of them.

'Come in, come in,' Max beckoned him. 'We're enjoying cuppas whilst Charlie naps. Come and join us.'

'I don't mind if I do,' said Sam. 'I was hoping to be asked to tea as I'm seeking to procrastinate for as long as possible. Much like you, Pen.'

'I'm not procrastinating,' Pen denied. 'I'm doing important research for my next article.'

'Really? What's your next article about?'

'Art. All the different types of art that exist in the world. You know. Like I was discussing at Max's exhibition.'

'Oh, yes,' said Sam. 'Speaking of exhibitions, that was the reason for my visit. I wanted to tell you how very much I enjoyed all of your art.'

Max set a cup of tea in front of Sam and looked tickled pink. 'Thank you! I know all of you are just saying these things to be polite, but I'm going to tell myself that you really mean all of them.'

'We do!' Pen protested.

'We really do,' Sam agreed earnestly. 'Or at least I do. I've never properly stopped to look at someone's art before. Not even yours. I'm glad I got the chance to do it, and your paintings are beautiful, and they *did* make me think about dreams. You're very talented.'

'You're brilliant,' Pen added, because apparently she thought Sam should have been more effusive.

Max said, 'Please. Tell me more,' and winked, and Sam and Pen laughed. Then Max added, 'In all seriousness, this is so lovely to hear. The show went really well, but I felt like that could have been just a fluke. Or one person with truly terrible taste buying up all my paintings. Or something.'

'Hey,' said Sam, 'even if it's one person with terrible taste, it's still one person whose terrible taste is *you*, and that's something.'

Pen gave him a look. 'Is it? Not much of a pep talk, was that? You should have said it's not one person with *terrible* taste, it's one person with *phenomenal* taste.'

'Well, Max knows what I mean!' Sam defended himself.

'I do,' Max assured them, laughing. 'And, really, you sound like Arthur, who says taste is too subjective to matter much and I should just be happy anyone wants to buy my stuff. He makes it sound nicer than that, but he still sounds like an insurance agent, bless him.'

'Well, I liked your paintings, so if I have terrible taste, so be it. Libby liked them, too.'

'Yes, she was especially taken with the landscape one,' remarked Max.

'I think she thought it was a sign,' said Sam.

'A sign of what?' asked Max.

'She wants to go to the French countryside for the summer.'

'What?!' Max and Pen exclaimed in unison.

'How lovely,' Max said.

'That sounds *amazing*,' Pen said.

'When and where and how, tell us the details,' said Max.

Sam wished now that he hadn't brought it up at all. 'I'm not really sure,' he said. 'To be honest, I haven't entirely agreed to it yet.'

'You're not sure if you want to go and spend the summer in the French countryside?' asked Max in disbelief.

'I mean, I'm sure it would be beautiful and all but I'd miss you lot,' joked Sam.

Pen and Max both gave him flat, unamused looks.

'Okay,' Sam said, 'so that wasn't very funny, I suppose.'

'What are you scared of?' asked Pen frankly.

'I'm sorry, I don't remember this being a therapy session.'

'We'll send you the bill later,' Max said dismissively. 'For now it's very important we get to the bottom of your resistance towards the French countryside. I spent time in France when I was studying art and the countryside is gorgeous. So romantic, too, perfect for a honeymoon, and if I recall correctly, you and Libby haven't had yours yet.'

Sam said, 'We'd take Teddy with us, of course, and that's a long time to be away from home, in a foreign country, and as I told Libby, I've only just got *this* country feeling like home. But I think maybe I'm being a little overprotective of Teddy.'

'I am hardly going to criticise you for being overprotective,' said Max, 'because I definitely understand the impulse now that Charlie's in the world. But France is lovely.'

'I think it sounds like an amazing opportunity,' said Pen. 'I *wish* I'd got to spend summer hols in France. What does Teddy think?'

'I've yet to ask him,' Sam admitted, and, off Max and

Pen's shocked looks, 'I wanted to get myself used to the idea first!'

'Well,' said Max, 'you've got a child who actually communicates with you in words you understand. I would take advantage of that and ask Teddy what he thinks.'

Chapter Six

Dear Pari, The house still doesn't really have lights but it does have KITTENS. Jack's scared of them, but I think they're going to make great pets.

Teddy thought that Mrs Dash's house was the stupidest house he had ever seen. First, he had to sleep *outside in their car*. Which turned out to be fine, because inside the house was even worse. There was one part of it that didn't even have *lights*, which meant it could be a hiding place for bandits, it would have made a *perfect* hiding place for them. And then there was the part that had fireplaces so big Teddy could walk into them, and they were filthy with soot that made him violently sneeze, but at least the lights worked there.

And then there was the last part of the house, where the floors were so old they were basically dirt, and the windows were so tiny that even after Sam managed to pull the shutters open there was barely any light. The electricity worked in that side of the house as well, but there weren't many lights in it. Many of the rooms had no lights at all.

Teddy was going to keep a journal of how horrible his time in France was and he couldn't *wait* to put all of this in it.

Libby, as they walked through, said softly, 'This must be the very oldest part of the house.'

There was a sudden commotion from the room ahead of them, with Jack barking wildly and then exploding out of the room and past them, to the front of the house, maybe out of the house entirely.

'Uh-oh,' Teddy said.

'Okay, maybe you should stay back,' Sam said.

'No way!' Teddy protested. 'Finally something interesting has happened!'

'It could be something dangerous,' said Sam.

'Like what?' Teddy sneered. 'A ghost?'

'There's no such thing as ghosts,' said Sam. 'I'm going to go *by myself* into the next room.'

Teddy rolled his eyes and heaved a sigh and said, *'Fine.'*

Sam crept into the next room way more slowly than was necessary. Teddy waited with Libby.

Libby called, 'Everything all right?'

Sam said, 'Oh, God. Yes. Come in.'

Teddy ran into the room, but Sam caught him and pulled him back. 'Shh,' he murmured. 'We don't want to bother them too much.'

The room wasn't much: dark and dirty and almost

empty, like all of the rooms in this side of the house. A few broken-looking wooden chairs and, most importantly, on the floor in the middle of the room, a cat, green cat eyes glowing. And in front of the cat were a bunch of tiny, mewling babies.

'Kittens!' said Libby. 'She must have thought this was a safe place to give birth. And then we bring a dog in here to disturb her. Sorry, Mummy Cat.'

The cat didn't look too happy. The kittens made tiny beeping noises, like a miniature meow.

Sam said, 'Do you think she belongs to one of the neighbours?'

'What neighbours?' asked Libby. 'This isn't Christmas Street.'

'Oh!' exclaimed Teddy. 'This can be a pet for our very own! I mean, it's great we share Jack and all, but this cat and the kittens can be *all ours*. Well, we can give a kitten to Pari, she'll probably want one. And Mrs Pachuta might want one, too, she really likes cats. And maybe Millie will want one, and Pen, and do you think Mr Hammersley likes cats?'

'How many kittens do you think there are?' Libby asked.

Sam said, 'I don't think we're going to be adopting all these cats.'

'Daaaaaaad,' Teddy whined. 'Everything here is *terrible* except for these kittens.'

'The mum is a stray. She's a wild cat, and her kittens are wild kittens.'

'Actually,' Libby remarked, 'I think I read somewhere

that stray cats will sometimes domesticate themselves, seeking a family to live with—'

Sam gave her a look, and Libby stopped talking.

'Anyway, how wild can she be if she's in our house?' Teddy argued.

'This isn't "our" house,' Sam said.

Teddy smiled happily at the cat and the kittens and said, 'It's about to be!'

With the excitement of house exploration over with, more pressing concerns began to raise their heads. Mainly, the fact that they needed to eat something. They had packets of crisps and a few chocolate bars from their trip, but they clearly needed actual food. And they weren't in London, so there was no shop just up the street that they could pop into for some milk.

Sam checked on the state of the fridge in the kitchen in the middle part of the house. It was ancient but the electricity was working, so when Sam stuck his hand into it, it was cold enough that he thought it could manage to keep some food fresh.

'Mrs Dash,' Libby said, reading through the sheaf of papers Mrs Dash had given to her, 'has made a list of nearby villages and what days they have markets. We should go to one and do proper French shopping.'

'I think it will be difficult to do anything but proper French shopping,' said Sam, 'seeing as how we are properly in France.' He looked at Libby, sitting at the enormous table in the kitchen. Sam had coaxed all of the shutters open with plenty of energetic tugging, and had thrown open the tall, gracious windows in this side of the house as well. Sunlight was streaming over Libby, and a light breeze was playing with her red hair, and Sam always thought she looked beautiful, but he thought she had never looked more beautiful than at that moment. That Provençal light that had inspired so many painters was evidently just as inspiring to Sam. He wished that he knew how to paint so he could paint Libby just like that.

Maybe he'd commission a portrait from Max.

Libby looked up and smiled at him, her eyes bright with excitement, and Sam amended his previous thought. No, *now* she looked more beautiful than she had ever looked before.

'We *are* properly in France,' she agreed happily. 'And I know we got off to a rough start but I really think it's going to be smooth sailing from hereon in.'

'Oh, no,' Sam groaned. 'You're going to jinx us. The ghosts of this house are all going to come upon us and wreak havoc.'

'There's no such thing as ghosts.'

'Well, why doesn't the electricity work in the other part of the house?' asked Sam.

'That's not a *ghost*. It's an old house.'

'That is clearly the newest part of it, though. Anyway, why didn't Mrs Dash mention the electrical problems? We shall have to do something to rectify that. And to get Wi-Fi put in. This house has clearly never seen any twenty-first-century indulgence like internet. Honestly, I'm not entirely clear why suddenly Mrs Dash was insistent someone come and check in on this place this summer? It looks as if no one has been here in a good twenty years. It's not as if she keeps the place up.'

'I don't know,' Libby admitted. 'I did think it would be a bit more lived-in. I had the impression she came here more often. I'll have to try to ask her. Although, she's in Brazil backpacking, so she warned me she wouldn't be very accessible.'

Sam arched an eyebrow and said, 'I suppose I'll just send her a bill at the end of the summer for all the work we're going to have to put into this place?'

'We *are* staying here for free,' Libby pointed out. 'She did ask if we could do a bit of upkeep while we were here.'

Sam wanted to point out that this all seemed like much more than 'a bit of upkeep' and that he felt a little taken advantage of, like Mrs Dash had just got herself a load of free labour to make her abandoned country home actually liveable by twenty-first-century human beings. But he didn't want to be too sour at the outset of the experience. So he said, 'We should go find a market and eat.' He walked over to the window and leaned out of it. Teddy was in the back garden with Jack, moping his way up and down a few gravel-strewn paths between overgrown hedges. Only Teddy could have made playing in the back garden look sulky.

But Sam still smiled. Yes, this was a mess, but he was

in France on holiday with the two people he loved most. And Teddy had looked brighter at the prospect of kittens than Sam had seen him in a long time, so maybe they were turning a corner. 'Teddy!' he called. 'Let's go and find a market.'

Chapter Seven

Your Turtledove Year 4 student has been working on hot-air balloons. Would that we could all fly away to sunnier climes! Coo-coo!

'You're really rubbish at homework,' said Teddy.

Rubbish, thought Sam, and smiled at the Britishness of it. Teddy's accent was still American, and he still had an American slant to his vocabulary, but British pieces were creeping in. He said, 'I promise you, I did get through Year 4 when I was your age. I knew this stuff back then. It's just that then you get old and you forget everything. What can I say?'

Teddy sighed heavily and looked over the maths worksheet he was supposed to be doing.

Sam smiled and said, 'How are things going at school?'

'Great,' Teddy said happily, relieved to be getting to talk about something other than his maths homework. 'We made *real* hot-air balloons.'

'Real hot-air balloons?' Sam echoed, surprised. 'For you to ride in?'

Teddy gave him the *must you be so utterly clueless* look. 'No, miniature ones, of course. But they're still real. They work on the same principle as regular-sized hot-air balloons.'

'Wow.' Sam was impressed. 'I don't know if I knew you could do that.'

Teddy continued to regard him dubiously. 'What did you even do when you were in school?'

'It was the Dark Ages,' replied Sam. 'We were busy inventing the wheel.' Teddy snorted.

Sam said, 'I really feel like everything's settled in nicely here, don't you?'

'Mostly,' said Teddy.

'Mostly?'

'I still *hate* having to learn French.'

'What a perfect segue ... ' said Sam.

'What's a segue?' asked Teddy.

'A transition,' said Sam. 'You started talking about exactly the thing I wanted to talk to you about.'

'Learning French?' Teddy looked confused.

'How would you like to spend the entire summer in France?' asked Sam grandly. 'You could practise your French all over the place.'

'That sounds terrible,' said Teddy. 'I just told you I hate learning French.'

'It's more fun when you're actually *in* France,' Sam said.

'Is it?' asked Teddy sceptically.

Sam couldn't help but laugh. He'd expected objections from Teddy to the summer in France but he hadn't expected them to be exactly this. He said, 'Yes, but we wouldn't really be going to France to improve your French skills. That would be an added bonus.'

'Why would we be going to France?'

'On holiday,' Sam said. 'We've got an opportunity to spend the summer at a house in the French countryside. We could go and see a bit of the world, eat a lot of pain au chocolat, spend a lot of lazy days in sunshine.'

'What about Jack?' Teddy asked immediately, and gestured to where the dog was curled up close beside him, snoring.

Jack, hearing his name, lifted his head and thumped his tail against the floor a few times, before deciding that his nap was too important and going back to sleep.

In all of Sam's worried musings about the implications of spending the summer abroad, Jack hadn't entered into them once. Sam said blankly, 'What about Jack?'

'Who will take care of him?'

'The street will take care of him. Jack is hardly dependent upon us. Everyone will happily take care of him for us.'

'But that's not fair!' exclaimed Teddy.

'Not fair?'

'Summertime is the *best* time, I get to just hang out with Jack all day. And Pari. And I thought maybe Abeo could come over more this summer. And it was just going to be a *proper* summer.'

'Yeah,' Sam said. 'I know.' Because he *did*. This was why

he'd been worrying about taking Teddy away from the friends group he'd built up. He'd suspected that Teddy wouldn't be thrilled about the idea.

'You and Libby could go,' Teddy suggested.

Sam blinked. 'Really? And leave you here all alone?'

Teddy shrugged. 'Everyone could check in on me every so often. And I wouldn't be alone. I'd have Jack.'

'Check in on you every so often,' Sam repeated. 'You think you're entirely capable of taking care of yourself most of the time?' Teddy shrugged again.

'And you wouldn't miss me?' Sam asked, slightly hurt by how cavalierly Teddy was proposing spending the summer apart.

'Well, yeah,' Teddy said slowly, suddenly concentrating very hard on petting Jack's fur. 'Of course I would. But I don't want to stop you if you want to go away with Libby and stuff. Like, you don't have to stay for *me*.'

Oh, Sam thought, and crouched down to be closer to Teddy's level. 'Hey,' he said gently, waiting for Teddy to look up and meet his gaze. 'Do you think I wouldn't miss you desperately? Because I would. I don't want to go away for the summer without you. I'm not going to leave you. I would be utterly lost without you. I am not confident of my ability to take care of myself without you around the way you are.'

Teddy's smile was full of relief, and Sam felt sorry for however Teddy had gained the impression that Sam might not want him around for six weeks.

Or Libby, Sam realised.

He said, 'Libby wants you to come, too,' in case that wasn't clear to Teddy.

'Okay,' said Teddy. 'But. It would still be a summer all alone. Again. When I just had a summer all alone. In another new place.'

'Yeah, but it would be fun,' Sam said. 'Hasn't all this turned out to be fun? We'll make more friends. Won't that be fantastic? Not many people get to spend the summer in a genuine French farmhouse.' He tried to make it sound as fantastic as he possibly could.

Teddy did not look convinced.

'Think it over,' Sam suggested, and ruffled Teddy's hair.

Teddy had been invited to dinner with the Basaks. Teddy and Pari already spent so much time together that ordinarily neither family seemed to feel much need for them to spend dinnertime together, too. But apparently Sai, Pari's brother, was spending the night at a friend's and Diya, her mum, had made entirely too much food (as usual) and Sam had kind of wanted some time alone with Libby anyway so it all worked out.

'Should we still talk about our daily adventure?' Libby asked, grinning at him, as they sat down to dinner.

Sam laughed. 'I suppose. What was yours?'

'Did you know Mrs Dash really is getting the kids to make real hot-air balloons now?'

'Yes,' Sam said. 'So I was informed by Teddy.'

'So today they practised getting them to fly. And it was quite something. Some rogue hot-air balloons floating down all the hallways, knocking about against doors and windows, with children chasing after them, and then other children in furious tears because theirs wouldn't fly. I suspect that hot-air balloons might be henceforth prohibited at Turtledove Primary. Coo-coo!'

Sam laughed through the story, envisioning the scene, and saying as Libby reached her conclusion, 'Teddy said nothing about all of that. I'll have to ask him about it at bedtime.'

'What did you do today?' Libby asked him.

Sam took a deep breath and considered. 'It was actually a bad day.'

Libby cocked her head curiously. 'Oh, no . . . '

'The French trip. Teddy was not enthusiastic about the French trip.'

Libby drew her eyebrows together in obvious confusion. 'What's not to be enthusiastic about? It's an entire summer holiday in France. I would have *loved* an opportunity like that as a child.'

'No, I know, but, I think, you know, there's been a lot of transition for Teddy recently, and he's not entirely sure of his place in all of this.'

'You mean his place with *us*?' Libby said. 'Because obviously his place is with us. Does he think . . . Does he not . . . Does he not feel like we're his family?' Libby's teeth worried at her lower lip, her eyes full of obvious distress at the idea that Teddy might not feel sure of

61

his place in that family, might not feel sure that they *were* a family.

Sam understood Teddy's point, understood that Teddy wanted to stay put at the end of this extended time of upheaval. And at the same time he understood Libby's point: maybe they needed to get away from Christmas Street, just for a little while, and learn who they were as a family. Maybe Teddy had grown so used to being out on the street all the time that he'd forgotten to grow comfortable with his new stepmum.

The more Sam thought about it, the more he thought he was right: they needed this holiday, the three of them, to solidify the fact that they were a unit now, a unit who should rely on each other, who should feel sure of their prominent importance in each other's lives.

That's what they needed.

Just like that, Sam decided it: they were going to France.

Teddy, Jack in tow, got back from Pari's to find Sam and Libby both waiting in the lounge, with no telly on, and immediately cast his mind back for what he might possibly be in trouble for. He really couldn't think of anything he'd done recently to make Sam and Libby look so serious.

Which meant maybe something else had happened. Teddy couldn't really remember his mom dying, just vague fleeting impressions of the days afterward, of how tightly Sam had held him and slept in his bed with him and needed Teddy to be really good and be there for Sam because Sam just really needed hugs.

Teddy, trying not to feel nervous, said, 'Hi,' and then because he couldn't help it, 'What's wrong?'

Libby and Sam both smiled, but they were weird smiles. They didn't make Teddy feel better.

'Nothing,' said Sam. 'Everything's good. We just wanted to talk to you.'

'Okay,' Teddy said, and slowly sank onto the sofa. He thought about his dad wanting to go to France for the summer with Libby, and thought, *This is it. This is when they tell me they're going to go.*

Sam said, 'We wanted to talk about France.'

Bingo, thought Teddy, and was happy that Jack was pressed close up against him so he could bury his fingers into his fur for comfort. 'Okay,' he said.

'We're going,' Sam said.

'What?' said Teddy.

'We're going to go,' Sam repeated, like that was going to make this any clearer.

'It's going to be so much fun,' Libby said, and beamed at him like that was *true*. Like there was any fun in the universe to be had without Pari and Jack and Mr Hammersley and the rest of Christmas Street.

'But.' Teddy fixed his dad with a hard look. 'You said I could decide.'

'I said you should think about it,' Sam corrected him.

'Well, that's *insufferable*,' said Teddy.

Sam lifted his eyebrows. 'Insufferable?'

'It's a vocabulary word,' Teddy said. 'And it fits this entire situation. I've thought it over, and I don't *want* to go to France. I don't want to be alone with no one I know.'

'You know us,' Sam said harshly. 'You know Libby and me.'

'That doesn't count,' Teddy said.

'Why doesn't it count?' demanded Sam.

'It just *doesn't*,' Teddy insisted stubbornly, and looked down at his feet. He wanted to stamp them against the floor but he had a feeling that would make this insufferable situation even worse.

'Well,' said Sam, 'we *do* count. In fact, that's the whole point of this holiday: to remember how much we all count to each other.'

Teddy gave his dad his best unimpressed look.

'You know,' suggested Libby slowly, 'maybe we could take Jack along. Would that help?'

'I mean,' said Teddy, 'it wouldn't *hurt*.'

'I didn't even think about bringing a dog with us,' said Sam. 'Can we even do that? What are the regulations on that?'

'We can figure it out,' said Libby, shrugging. 'I mean, he's up to date with all his jabs, so I'm sure it can be done.'

Sam said, 'I don't know about bringing Jack with us.'

Teddy said, 'So you want me to spend the entire summer in a strange place I don't know anything about, when you know I don't want to go and you told me I could decide and then don't care what I want anyway. You don't even care that having Jack along would make me feel better.'

'Plus Jack probably really wants to see France,' added Libby, and Jack wagged his tail in agreement.

Sam sighed. 'Jack's a dog. I don't think he really cares about France.'

Teddy was appalled. 'You don't think Jack wants to see the world?! He's always trying to see the world! He's very curious about things! That's why he's always visiting everybody's houses and stuff. He wants to know what's going on! Now, this way, he can know what's going on in France!'

'He *is* a very inquisitive dog,' said Libby.

'Well, I know when I'm defeated,' said Sam. 'We can look into whether it's possible to take Jack to France with us. Mrs Dash might not want a dog in her great-aunt Clarissa's house.'

'Wait a second,' Teddy said. '*Mrs Dash?* Is Mrs Dash going to France, too?'

'No,' Libby said. 'Mrs Dash is going to Brazil. But we'd be staying in Mrs Dash's house. Well, the house she inherited from her great-aunt Clarissa.'

'What!' exclaimed Teddy. 'We're staying in my *teacher's house*? This is even weirder. You married one of my teachers and now we're going on holiday with the other?'

'Not *with* her,' Sam said.

'This is super weird,' Teddy said. 'We should just have every one of my teachers move in with us.'

'Wait a second,' Pari said. '*That* is entirely not fair.'

They were sitting in the Basak lounge, trying to teach Jack tricks, while Sai and his girlfriend Emilia revised in the kitchen, because all they did these days was revise and revise.

Teddy moved his hand in a circle to try to urge Jack to roll over and said, 'I know, right? It's not going to be any fun *at all.*'

'What do you mean?' said Pari.

'What do you mean, What do I mean?' asked Teddy, confused.

'You get to go to *France* to stay in *Mrs Dash's house*? *With Jack?* It's going to be so cool!'

'Yeah, but, like, *you* won't be there. So how much fun will it really be?'

Pari considered thoughtfully. 'That's true. I am pretty fun.'

'Unless ... ' Teddy looked at Pari. 'Maybe you could come, too!'

'Oh, yes!' Pari exclaimed. 'Of course! I can go, too!'

Well, that idea made everything much better, Teddy thought. He wasn't going to be all alone in France after all! 'We are going to have so many French adventures,' said Teddy happily.

'Probably Mrs Dash's house is going to be full of *frogs,*' said Pari. 'Jack's going to love that.'

'Why would it be full of frogs?' asked Teddy.

'France has a lot of frogs,' Pari told him wisely.

Teddy shrugged and said, 'Okay, Jack, what about shaking hands? Can you do that trick?'

Pari gasped. '*Teddy*,' she said. 'I've had ... An Idea.'

'Oh, no,' said Teddy. 'What is it this time?'

'You know how we've been training Jack to put on a show?'

'Yeah.'

'We could have the show *in France*. Imagine putting on a show at Mrs Dash's house! It would immediately be the best show we could ever put on. Everyone will be so impressed.'

Diya was about to tell Pari to eat a few more pieces of the cauliflower she'd tossed into the curry, because Pari was adept at avoiding cauliflower, when Pari said, 'Oh! I forgot to tell you! I'm going to go to France this summer.'

Pari's dad, Darsh, froze with his fork halfway through the air on its way to his mouth. Sai, who generally wolfed dinner down as quickly as possible so he could get back to his phone or Emilia or everything he did that wasn't revising and taking his future *seriously*, even paused in inhaling the food on his plate. Diya stared at Pari.

Pari happily continued eating, avoiding all cauliflower.

Darsh said, 'What do you mean?'

'Teddy's going to France with Jack, and I'm going with him. We're going to stay in Mrs Dash's house.'

Sai straightened and put down his fork and said, 'This is totally not fair. I wanted to go backpacking through the Alps with Emilia this summer and you wouldn't let me go! But Pari gets to go to France with Jack?'

'No,' Diya said. 'No one's leaving London this summer. What are you talking about, Pari?'

'What!' shrieked Pari. 'But Teddy and I have it all planned! We're going to teach Jack how to be a French dog!'

'A French dog?' Darsh repeated. 'What's a French dog?'

'That is not the most important detail,' Diya told him. 'The most important detail is why your teacher would put these foolish thoughts into your head? Do you think it was proper for Mrs Dash to invite you to her home for the summer?'

'Oh, Mrs Dash didn't invite me. Mrs Dash invited Teddy. Teddy invited me.'

This was even more bewildering. 'Why would Mrs Dash invite Teddy to her house? Don't you think that's odd? Isn't that odd, Darsh?'

'I don't understand what's happening,' Darsh said, 'except that nobody is going to France.'

'If Pari's going to France, I get to go to Italy,' said Sai.

'Everyone's staying here in London. No one's going anywhere,' said Diya.

'Teddy is,' said Pari. 'Teddy's going to France. To stay at Mrs Dash's house.'

'I bet Sam would let me go to Italy,' grumbled Sai.

'Hmm,' said Diya.

The knock on the door was so light Sam almost wasn't sure he'd heard it, except that Jack immediately came trotting down the stairs from where he'd been sleeping with Teddy in his bedroom and stood on alert by the front door.

'I *thought* I heard someone at the door,' remarked Libby, from the couch where she was marking papers.

Sam put aside *Remembrance of Things Past*, which he was pretending he was going to read in preparation for their trip to France. Libby had commented that a guidebook might have been a more helpful thing to read, and after a few pages Sam couldn't argue with that.

Diya was at the door, and Jack wagged his tail and gave a little bark and Sam said, 'Shh.'

Diya said, 'Hello.'

Sam said, 'Hi. You were so quiet we weren't sure we heard the door.'

'I didn't want to wake everyone up,' said Diya. 'It's late.'

'Yes,' Sam agreed. 'Is there something wrong?'

'Are you letting Mrs Dash kidnap your son?' Diya asked.

Sam blinked at her. 'I'm sorry, am I what?'

'Pari says you're letting Teddy go off with Mrs Dash for the entire summer, and I ask you: What do you really know of this woman? Do you think that's entirely safe? Do you know that she only asked Teddy to spend the summer with her? Not any of the other students in the class? Don't you find that concerning? Why should she single Teddy out like that? I would be *extremely concerned* if I were you.'

Sam gaped at Diya, who looked extremely self-righteous in her condemnation of Sam's parenting skills. And then he said, 'Okay, virtually none of this story is true, which I suppose is what can be expected when the story is got through two nine-year-olds. Come inside out of the damp.'

Diya dutifully followed Sam inside. 'Teddy isn't going to France for the summer?'

'Yes,' Sam said. 'But we're going with him.'

'Hello, Libby,' Diya said as they entered the lounge area.

'Hello, Diya,' Libby said pleasantly. 'How are you?'

'Dealing with two children who now *also* want to go to Europe,' Diya said. 'You are putting ideas in everyone's head. I didn't realise you were so friendly with Mrs Dash as to go away with her.'

'We're *not*,' Sam replied. 'Mrs Dash has a house in France and she was looking for someone to look after it over the summer.'

'And we volunteered,' Libby said.

'For the entire summer?'

'Well, Libby has the summer off, and I can work from anywhere,' said Sam.

'And you're taking Jack? Pari seems to be under the impression that you're taking Jack.'

'Oh,' said Sam. 'Yes, I told Teddy he could bring Jack along. Teddy's a little nervous about spending the summer without his friends.'

'Well, Pari is also under the impression that you're bringing *her* along.'

'Ah,' said Sam. 'Well. That hasn't really been discussed but I'm sure she's welcome to visit.' Sam glanced at Libby over Diya's head, and Libby nodded.

'Absolutely,' said Libby. 'All of you are. Sai included. We'll have the house for six weeks, so we may as well have everybody round at some point. Maybe everyone can come out for a few days to finish the summer off.'

Chapter Eight

Patisserie
Ouvert Tous Les Jours
Croissant
Pain au Chocolat
Brioche au Sucre
Tarte au Citron
Macarons

There was a medieval village clinging to a hilltop, not far from the farmhouse in the scheme of things. Sam had the impression these villages were scattered through the near countryside, which was going to be helpful.

The village was like something out of a storybook, with its steep, narrow, rocky streets with ancient houses clinging tightly to them. Not even Teddy could resist racing up the steps with Jack.

Libby paused to look back at the view, and Sam joined her, the countryside spreading out below them, growing fuzzy in the distance. It *was* truly gorgeous. Sam had been to France before and didn't remember it being so beautiful. Maybe you had to get a bit older to appreciate that. Certainly Teddy seemed unimpressed with the view. Although he clearly was grudgingly impressed by the village's nooks and crannies.

Sam strolled hand in hand with Libby, until they came closer to the village's main square. There was a café with Wi-Fi, and they settled in for a quick lunch while Sam checked in with work. Afterward, they picked up croissants at a small patisserie and then ate them by a little stone fountain, watching a group of old men play pétanque on a patch of dry gritty ground adjacent, helped out by a small throng of onlookers who kept explaining what the players could do better.

When they were done with the croissants, they walked along the stalls of the market, buying cheeses and cured meats and bread so fresh that it was so springy to the touch Teddy kept asking what was wrong with it, which made Sam despair.

'It's *supposed* to be like that!' Sam said.

'Like *that*?' said Teddy.

Sam looked forlornly at Libby. 'He has apparently never had good bread.'

'Don't worry,' Libby promised. 'I'll learn to bake bread while I'm here.'

'Where?' asked Sam.

'I feel like probably everyone in France knows how to bake bread, right?' said Libby, shrugging.

They browsed through fresh produce that smelled so delicious that Sam couldn't believe it was the same stuff they bought at the supermarket in London. He held up a bouquet of fresh carrots and presented them to Libby with a flourish, who laughed, because after their meeting in the supermarket Sam had proposed to her using carrots a year later. Carrots were a gesture of great romance in their relationship, Sam thought, smiling.

When they had bought more than enough food, they dealt with the more prosaic shopping. Things like, of course, the kettle, and coffee and tea, because they could possibly survive without Wi-Fi, or electricity, or a proper hot shower, but they could not be expected to survive without a *kettle*. And then it was on to the cleaning supplies. Sam had never purchased so many cleaning supplies at one time. Not to mention the fresh bedding that they simply needed given the state of the bedding at the house. Really, this 'free' holiday was costing an awful lot of money.

They ran all of the taps in the house to clear the rust out, and changed out all of the bedding, and swept and dusted the bedrooms to make them sleepable, and then, thoroughly covered in French dust, they scrubbed the bathroom down and finally showered. It wasn't the hottest shower of Sam's life but it was decent, and the bathroom window was flung open to a view of Provençal countryside and Sam could spot fields of lavender waving in the distance, so that more than made up for the lukewarm water and terrible water pressure.

Sam napped and when he woke Libby and Teddy were

out in the back garden, sitting in the sun. Libby was reading an ancient cookbook she said she'd found in one of the kitchen cupboards, struggling through the fact that it was entirely written in French, and Teddy was managing to play a half-hearted game of fetch with Jack. Libby had apparently mapped out the garden, and she enthusiastically showed him where the overgrown remains of a kitchen garden were, overflowing with rosemary and thyme, tomatoes and beans and peppers and lettuce. There was an orchard with peaches, plums and pears all practically drooping off the trees, and a grove of olive trees, crowned with their distinctive silvery leaves, with hyacinths interspersed between the trees. There was a rose garden, run wild like the rest of it, with abundances of blooms spilling over onto the paths. And off to one side, hidden behind the very oldest part of the house, was a sudden explosion of sunflowers, taller than Teddy, in the most vivid and cheerful shade of yellow imaginable. Sam had never really seen a sunflower grove like that before, and he could see why Libby was *ooh*-ing and *aah*-ing over it. The whole thing *was* like a fairy tale. Including the lack of modern conveniences, Sam thought drily.

'But how is the garden like this?' Sam asked, bewildered.

'Like what?' asked Libby, too enchanted to be suspicious.

'Like *this*. All . . . growing.'

'It's a garden. It grows.' Libby shrugged.

'Not without help,' Sam said. 'Trust me on that one. I have never been able to successfully grow a garden before.'

'Well, don't kill this one!' Libby warned him in alarm. 'It's brilliant!'

'I'm just saying, the house is a complete disaster area but this garden is tip-top.'

'Maybe the unreliable French caretaker is really into gardens,' suggested Libby. 'Anyway, what does it matter, when it looks like *this*.'

It *was* so gorgeous that at the moment all the rest of it seemed very unimportant. There was a fountain out in the back garden, choked with ivy so that Sam doubted it would ever work again, but it was still picturesque, and there was a patch of overgrown grass in front of it that Libby spread a blanket over. They sat outside as the sun grew lower in the sky and the house glowed ochre in front of them. With its shutters and windows mostly flung open, the house looked cheerful and welcoming, like somewhere Sam was excited to spend the next few weeks. He no longer felt like ghosts were hiding behind the chimneys on the roof, and when the various printed curtains flapped in the breeze, they looked like linen and toile and lace, instead of anything other-worldly.

'Teddy!' Sam called. 'Come and sit with us!'

Teddy obediently came over, and they ate the meats and cheeses they'd bought in the market, tearing pieces of bread, and slicing figs and drizzling fresh French honey over them, and not even Teddy could completely pretend it wasn't incredibly delicious. Later, when the sun went down and the impossible stars had broken out overhead, Sam told Teddy to choose a bedroom.

'Because I *do* care what you think,' Sam said.

Teddy looked at him for a long moment, but he didn't

say anything clever in return, and he didn't roll his eyes. He just chose a bedroom, and Jack curled up at the foot of his bed, and Sam and Libby went to the bedroom with the terrace, and they slept with their doors standing open to the French air, and that was their first day.

Chapter Nine

Travel and Reservation
London St Pancras to Paris-Nord
Only valid on date and train below

The news spread along Christmas Street: the Bishops were going to France, they were taking Jack with them, and everyone was invited to visit for a few spectacular days at the end of the summer.

It was one of Jack's nights to stay with Bill, and Bill was grateful for that, even though he would never have admitted that out loud. Out loud he would have said that Teddy could keep Jack every night, it didn't matter to him. But Sam was careful to make sure Jack still stayed with Bill some nights, and even though Bill scoffed and said it wasn't necessary, it *was* nice to have the company during the evening.

Especially in the winter, when nights were long and the damp cold seeped into Bill's bones in a way it never had in his younger days.

'Don't get old,' Bill advised Jack, petting him. 'But then, I suppose the alternative's even less appealing, eh?'

Jack wagged his tail, just a bit, just to acknowledge the solemn wisdom of what Bill was saying.

Bill said, as they settled together in the lounge and Bill flipped through the telly, 'Well. Going to France for the summer. What do you think about that, Jack? Think you'll learn some new tricks over there? Come back wearing a beret and saying "ooh-la-la"?' Jack looked dubious, and Bill laughed and petted him some more.

'I think you'll like France,' Bill said. 'They say it's the French countryside, so you'll like all that open space to run around in. Pretty meadows they've got in France. Lots of pretty flowers. My Agatha used to go wild for the flowers in the meadows in France. I think you'll like them.'

Jack looked unpersuaded by the flowers, so Bill added, 'Plus there'll be lots of squirrels around, I'm sure. French squirrels, so they'll probably be a mite slow on account of all the cheese and croissants they eat over there. You'll probably be able to catch yourself a French squirrel, what do you think about that?'

Jack looked much more excited about the prospect of slow French squirrels than he had about wildflowers.

Bill gave him one last pat and said, 'I suppose I will miss having you around, though. It'll be a bit dull around here. I've got used to you and Teddy running around wreaking havoc. I've even got used to Sam endlessly coming round wanting to chat. What'll I do with all the quiet?'

Ordinarily Sam saw Bill as they waited together with Jack for the children to come home from school. There was really no need for Bill to do this, but he seemed to enjoy it and Sam had to admit he looked forward to the company as they waited. The rest of his Day Gang – Max and Pen and Diya and occasionally Millie, depending on her work schedule – were often finally getting themselves down to work by the time of the afternoon when Sam was awaiting the children. Well, except for Millie, who was much more diligent about getting her baking done than the rest of them were about their obligations, but Millie, while undeniably friendly, still tended to keep to herself, not as naturally gregarious as the other street inhabitants.

On this particular day, with work under control, Sam decided to walk over to Bill's earlier than their usual school pick-up time and talk to him about France.

Bill looked startled when he opened the door. Jack, barking excitedly, came out of Bill's house and bounced around a bit, and then stretched dramatically, the way he did when he was just waking up from a nap.

Sam laughed and scratched behind Jack's ears and said to Bill, 'I hope I didn't wake *both* of you up from a nap.'

'Nonsense,' Bill barked. 'I never sleep during the day.'

'Sleep is for the weak,' Sam guessed.

'Exactly,' said Bill. 'Jack was napping only because Jack sleeps in between excitement.'

'And there's an awful lot of excitement on this street, isn't there, Jack?' said Sam.

Jack wagged his tail in agreement.

Bill said, 'Is there something wrong? You're here early, aren't you?'

'Yes. I wanted to talk to you before the children came home.'

'What's wrong?' Bill demanded immediately.

Sam was amused. Bill was part of the indelible fabric of Christmas Street and was definitely fond of all of his neighbours, and yet he also never altered his gruff, standoffish exterior. 'Nothing. I wanted to talk to you about France.'

'Yes,' said Bill. 'I heard all about how you're going away for the summer and taking Jack. Fine by me. It'll be a good experience for him. Just make sure you keep an eye on him and don't let him get all addle-minded in a foreign country.'

'I'll keep an eye on him,' Sam promised. 'You talk about him like he's your son, going off for a grand tour.'

Bill scoffed but said nothing to deny it.

Sam smiled and said, 'I didn't really want to talk about Jack and France, though. I wanted to talk about *you* and France.'

'Oh, do you want some advice on things to do? It's been years since I've been to France. They've probably gone and made everything *modern* now, same way as this country has.'

'Probably,' Sam agreed affably. 'You ought to come and visit us at the end of the summer and find out.'

Bill stared at him for a long moment of silence, then said, 'Visit you?'

'Yes. We'll have a house. Everyone's coming. You should come along, too. Just for a few days. No harm done, really. If you hate it, I suppose you could go home early. But everyone will be there with us. And wouldn't you like to see Jack?' Sam knew better than to suggest that Bill might miss Jack; Bill, he suspected, would never admit to missing anyone ever. Except for maybe Agatha, if pressed.

Bill shrugged, looking uncertain, as Jack came to nudge up against his hand, looking for a pat.

Sam continued, 'Probably a good idea to make sure I'm taking proper care of him, that he hasn't got addle-minded by being in a foreign country.'

'That's true,' Bill allowed grudgingly, 'but still. I'd be in the way. All of you young people, you'll have things to do. You don't want me tagging along.'

'We all love to have you tag along. Always. And Libby's mum is coming to stay, too.'

'Hmph,' Bill said, patting Jack and not looking at Sam. 'I don't know. It's still a lot of trouble at my age to travel all the way over there, and then all the way back. But I suppose there is Jack to think about.' He paused. 'And Rebecca. She mightn't want to be all alone with all of you young people, either. She struck me as realising how insensible you lot can be.'

Sam smiled.

82

'I talked to Mr Hammersley today,' Sam remarked over dinner. 'I think I've convinced him that he should come to stay with us when everyone else comes up at the end of the summer.'

'Oh, that's lovely,' said Libby, smiling at him. 'I was hoping that you'd work your magic on him.'

Sam looked at Teddy, sulking into his curry. 'Well, Teddy? Doesn't that sound like fun?'

'Whatever,' Teddy said. 'That last weekend is the only time France will be any fun at all.'

'That's not true,' Sam said patiently. 'You're going to have a great time all summer, and then when Pari comes, you can tell her all about all the adventures you've already had.'

'Pari's the one who always comes up with the adventures,' Teddy complained. 'I still don't understand why she can only come for a few days at the end.'

'Because her parents don't want to be without her all summer any more than we would want to be without you all summer,' Sam explained patiently, for possibly the fortieth time since Diya and Darsh had made this decision. 'Besides, don't you think she would miss her mum and dad? Wouldn't you miss Libby and me?'

Teddy looked doubtful.

'I feel terrible about the situation with Teddy,' Libby said fretfully as they got ready for bed.

'Don't,' Sam said. 'He's fine. He'll come around. He's

sulking with special determination but he's going to have a great time in France. *We're* going to have a great time as a family. I can't wait.'

Libby looked at him closely, as if to ascertain he wasn't lying and actually was looking forward to France. 'Really? I know I kind of bossed you into it.'

Sam shook his head. 'You didn't "boss me into it". That's not how this relationship works. You had a great idea, and I realised it was a great idea. We're going to have a spectacular time in France.'

Libby began to look convinced, a smile breaking over her face. 'I think I might take cooking lessons.'

'That sounds *fantastique*,' Sam said, and Libby laughed.

'Since we're checking in with each other to make sure we're all right.' Libby got into bed and snuggled against him. 'Are you all right with my mother coming to stay?'

'Of course,' Sam said, because he *was*, even if he was also experiencing some trepidation over it. 'Your mother can come to stay whenever.'

Libby snorted, both sceptical and amused. 'You're so gallant.'

'I mean it,' Sam insisted. 'We got along perfectly well before. I think the wedding was just a stressful time for all of us. We've made the whole thing up. Your mother and I will be thick as thieves by the time the week in France is over.'

'I hope so,' said Libby.

'Hey.' Sam tugged her closer, squeezed her tighter. 'Don't worry about it, okay?' he said softly. 'It's all going to be brilliant.'

Mrs Dash wasn't terribly forthcoming with information, which was just like Mrs Dash, who thought many of the world's mundane details were overrated. When Libby had asked for photographs of the property, Mrs Dash had said, 'It borders beautiful countryside, and glows with the life foibles of many generations,' which hadn't been helpful. Libby had given Sam that description at dinner one night and Sam had laughed and laughed and Teddy had said, sounding completely resigned, 'Yup. Sounds like Mrs Dash.'

The lack of detail meant Libby was free to make up all the details herself. The house looked like a million different things in her head, had a million different rooms, was a complicated mash-up of styles torn between so rustic that it had dirt floors to something like the Hall of Mirrors at Versailles. The house could be *anything*.

Libby found that thought freeing and exciting – just what she had been looking for.

Of course, it wasn't great for planning purposes.

'How many bedrooms does it have?' Libby asked Mrs Dash.

'It depends,' Mrs Dash answered, in her usual vague and grand style, 'on what you mean by "bedroom".'

'I mean a room where people sleep,' Libby replied.

'It depends,' Mrs Dash answered, 'on what you mean by "sleep".'

And so it went, vague and fuzzy, but Libby chose to interpret it as romantic. They needed, Libby told Sam, to surrender to the romance of the French lifestyle. If that meant not knowing how many bedrooms it had, so be it. They'd cross the bridge of their visitors when they came to it, Libby determined. It would add to the spontaneous fun of the entire endeavour.

Sam asked if the house had Wi-Fi, which Libby termed dangerously unromantic, and then Sam had laughed and kissed her up against the door because he could.

When the holiday was looming, just around the corner, so close Libby could already taste the champagne, she told Mrs Dash how much she was looking forward to the summer.

'It will be a grand adventure for you,' Mrs Dash agreed. 'And the mystery of my dear Great-Aunt Clarissa's house shall be enjoyed by all of you.'

'The mystery of it?' echoed Libby.

'Oh, yes,' said Mrs Dash. 'Haven't I mentioned it yet? It's ever so slightly haunted.'

'What?' said Libby, startled.

'Oh,' said Mrs Dash, and waved her hand around carelessly. This made various bits of silky gauze around her person float about in dramatic reaction. 'Please don't worry yourself about them. As long as you leave them be, they cause no trouble.'

'Leave them be?' echoed Libby.

'The ghosts,' Mrs Dash replied, with an *of course* implied.

'But,' said Libby, 'there's no such thing as ghosts. I mean, this is just a romantic tale.'

Mrs Dash gave Libby an indignant look. 'I assure you, it *is* a romantic tale, but that does not make it any less true. Does it not make perfect sense that the ghosts of all the spirited men and women who have made a house into a home would linger in that place, would keep playing their parlour games and forming their bridge quartets and sharing their gossip and intrigues? Where else, after all, would they go?' she demanded sternly.

And Libby didn't know where else ghosts would go, if they did exist. Her only response would have been to reiterate that ghosts did not exist, which Mrs Dash did not seem to like.

So Libby said uncertainly, 'Oh. So it's haunted by all of its past inhabitants.'

'Mostly,' said Mrs Dash. 'We assume so. They don't exactly sit down to tea.'

'And they're mostly happy inhabitants?'

'The ghosts are not harmful. I am sure the house has seen its share of tragedies but the ghosts seem mostly to be mischievous. They are trickster ghosts. You must beware the pranks they will play. They have cunning senses of humour.'

Chapter Ten

*Sorry I've been out of touch, I'm having internet issues,
I'm going in search of Wi-Fi.*

Promise to be on the conference call later!

On the second day, Sam woke up determined to deal with
the electricity issue and see about getting some Wi-Fi into
the house.

He got out of bed and showered and dressed and then
stood on the terrace for a little bit, holding his mobile up
to see where he could get the best signal. Inside, Libby
stretched on the bed and called, 'What time is it?'

'Almost nine,' he called back, frowning at the phone.

'Mmm, I still feel like I could sleep for ages. I haven't
caught up on the night of sleeping outside yet.'

Sam didn't point out that Libby had slept very well
outside, while he had slept not at all, because he thought
that would be rude. He just said, as he walked back into
the bedroom, 'Well, I'm going to see if I can get someone
to come out and help me with the electricity and getting

some Wi-Fi operational around here. You can stay in bed a bit longer if you want. I'll go check on whatever mischief Teddy and Jack have managed to get up to.' He leaned over Libby in the bed and kissed her cheek.

'I hope Teddy's full of adventure today,' Libby said.

'Don't worry about him,' Sam urged her again. 'He's totally going to come around.' She smiled, and he left her to her late morning. She was, after all, on holiday.

Sam found Teddy and Jack downstairs in the kitchen. Teddy had a bowl of cereal in front of him. Jack was devouring a bowl of dog food.

'Look how self-sufficient you are in France,' Sam remarked.

'Jack and I wanted to check on the kittens,' Teddy said.

'Oh, dear,' said Sam. 'You are going to terrorise those poor kittens. The mummy cat is going to take them away immediately.'

'No, no.' Teddy shook his head. 'I think we're all getting to be friends. She didn't even hiss at us this time.'

Sam sighed and reminded himself that Teddy's fixation on the kittens was definitely better than sulking. He grabbed a handful of cereal that he stuffed dry into his mouth to serve as breakfast and made himself a cup of coffee. Then he said, 'I'm going to go out into the garden and get some stuff done. Why don't you leave the poor cat family alone and come outside with me?'

Teddy consented to spending some time in the fresh air, and he and Jack commenced playing fetch with a stick Teddy had found on the ground in the orchard. Sam sat at the base of the defunct fountain and glanced through Mrs Dash's sheaf of instructions. They were all singularly unhelpful, and Sam, not for the first time, worried about the usefulness of Teddy's education at the hands of Mrs Dash the previous year. But there was a single piece of information that Sam thought he could use: *General questions and assistance: Victor*, with a telephone number written after it.

So Sam dialled Victor.

Victor answered with, *'Allo*?'

'Hi,' Sam said, hoping Victor would speak English, because Sam didn't really want to have to stumble his way through all of his questions in French. Their time in the village yesterday had brought home to Sam how very out-of-practice his French was. 'This is Sam Bishop. I'm staying at Mrs Dash's farmhouse.'

'Which farmhouse?' Victory responded. His English was accented but clear; he was obviously fluent, to Sam's great relief.

'Mrs Dash's?' Sam repeated. When Victor didn't immediately react to that, he added, 'Er, Great-Aunt Clarissa's?'

'Ah yes! The Bernard house!'

Sam had no idea if he was staying in the Bernard house or not. He just said, 'Yes,' to move things along. 'So we just got here the other day and we've got a few questions and Mrs Dash put your name down as—'

'No, no,' Victor interrupted. 'We should not do this over the telephone! Our first meeting! I should have been told you were arriving! I will come to you and you can ask me all in person!'

And then Victor hung up.

'Okay,' Sam said uselessly to the phone, and then tucked it into his pocket.

He supposed there was nothing left to do but wait for Victor.

Sam waited the entire day for Victor.

Libby came downstairs shortly after ten, looking very refreshed, and found him still in the garden with Teddy, aimless and unproductive.

She said, 'I thought you were sorting the electricity and the internet.'

'I am,' Sam said. 'This is me sorting the electricity and the internet. I looked for the fuse board but was unsuccessful, so now I am waiting for Mrs Dash's jack-of-all-trades, who's called Victor. Sorry, Jack,' he said to Jack, who had bounded over at the mention of his name.

'Oh,' said Libby. 'The caretaker? Well, that'll be helpful, then. We can ask him loads of questions about how long the house has been shuttered and what the deal is with the garden. In the meantime, I think we should finish getting the house into shape.'

And so they went back into the house and went through it room by room, uncovering old squashy furniture and landscape paintings that had clearly seen better days. Everything in the house needed a good cleaning, with more professional supplies than they had. They did the best they could cleaning but Sam was convinced that the paintings still had a layer of soot over them, and all of the bronze and silver accents on the furnishings and light fixtures had tarnished and needed to be repolished. But Libby said she liked the shabby feel to the house. It added character, she told him. Sam was reminded of being told the London house had character when he had decided to buy it, and that 'character' mainly turning out to be damp and electrical issues that had cost a small fortune. But at least the small fortune caused by this house's character wasn't his responsibility.

In the upstairs gallery they uncovered a grandfather clock that had stopped telling the time one day long ago at 3:27. Libby and Teddy tried very hard to determine how to wind the clock back up but it required a tiny key to insert in a tiny lock and Sam had no idea where that key might be.

'Can you pick the lock?' Teddy asked him.

'I think you have very interesting ideas about what talents you think I have,' Sam replied.

Teddy sighed and went back to thinking uncharitable thoughts, presumably about France and Sam's talents as a father.

'Maybe we'll find the key,' suggested Libby optimistically. 'It could be in one of the desks or dressers around here. Or maybe one of the kitchen drawers. It'll be a summer project.'

They pulled dustcovers off lots of fragile-looking tables that needed to be polished, and spindly chairs whose various velvety seats were threadbare to the point of near non-existence. At the top of the stairs they uncovered a mirror so old and damaged that it didn't reveal a reflection when they stood in front of it, only a watery suggestion of a world beyond. It was so spooky that Sam shuddered when he looked at it and mouthed *Ghosts* at Libby over Teddy's head. Libby rolled her eyes.

On either side of the spooky mirror were two portraits of women. Under the layers of grime, they seemed to be studying each other warily. Sam was no expert in women's fashion, but these paintings both looked like they dated from the 1920s or maybe 1930s. They certainly weren't dressed in the enormous dresses of the nineteenth century. The woman on the left was a brunette dressed in a black flapper-style dress, with a long strand of pearls around her neck, and the woman on the right was a blonde in tweed, as if she were about to go hunting, her hair caught up under a wide-brimmed hat. The woman in black stood in a room, with a line of windows behind her, while the blonde woman was outside, under a tree, with a spaniel curled up at her feet.

'Who do you think they are?' Libby asked, looking between them.

Sam shrugged.

'Do you think one of them's Great-Aunt Clarissa?' Teddy asked.

'Maybe,' Sam said.

'No,' said Libby. 'I think these portraits are too old for that. Unless Great-Aunt Clarissa is really Great-Great-Aunt Clarissa.'

'Well, we didn't exactly get Mrs Dash's family tree—' Sam began.

And then a gong sounded throughout the house, making all of them jump. Jack went racing down the stairs, barking manically.

Libby said, 'What on earth ... '

Sam, feeling like his teeth were still vibrating inside his head, said, 'Was that the *doorbell*?'

'I think we should make sure people don't use it again,' said Teddy, his hands pressed over his ears.

'Agreed,' said Sam, as he jogged down the stairs. 'A sign on the door would not go amiss.'

He opened the door on a man about twenty years older than he was, who spread his arms open wide and exclaimed, '*Bienvenue*!' Jack went shooting out into the farmyard to investigate the intruder.

'Thank you,' Sam said, and then guessed, 'Victor?'

'That is me. And you must be Sam.' Victor smiled genially and shook Sam's hand. He had a very wide smile. It seemed to take up his entire face.

'Yes,' said Sam. 'And that's Jack.' Sam nodded towards Jack.

'*Bonjour*, Jack,' Victor said, patting Jack's head.

Jack looked like he hadn't quite made his mind up about Victor yet.

'So how are you liking the place, eh?' Victor said. 'Settling in? It's a beautiful piece of land, yes? Just a beautiful piece of land.' He spread his arms wide again, encompassing the entire countryside around them.

'It is very beautiful,' Sam agreed. 'A little run-down.'

Victor hmph'd like he disagreed with Sam's assessment of 'run-down'.

'How long has it been abandoned?' Sam asked.

Victor looked affronted. 'You would call this abandoned? Have you seen the beauty of the garden?'

'The garden is beautiful, yes, but the house is a bit . . .' Sam trailed off politely.

'Oh, the house.' Victor waved his hand around negligently. 'The house takes care of itself.'

'Does it?' said Sam dubiously.

'The ghosts help out.'

'Uh-huh,' said Sam. 'When's the last time Mrs Dash was here?'

'Not long.' Victor gave Sam a Gallic shrug. 'A summer or two?'

'Just a summer or two and the house looks like *this*?'

'Charming, yes?'

'Yes,' Sam agreed, because clearly this conversation was pointless. 'We just need some electricity.'

'Is the electricity not working?' Victor asked, sounding unconcerned.

'Not quite,' said Sam.

'Oh, well.' Victor shrugged. 'The sun is out during the day, and the stars are out at night, and what more do you need, hmm?'

'Wi-Fi,' Sam answered.

'Wi-Fi?' Victor echoed, as if this were a strange foreign language Sam was speaking.

Sam's stomach sank to his feet in seemingly agonising slow motion. This, he thought, did not bode well. 'Internet?' he suggested as a clarification.

Victor shrugged, unimpressed by Sam's need for internet.

Sam wondered how he was going to go about acquiring internet, then decided to tackle one thing at a time. 'Let's start with the electricity,' he said.

Victor shrugged again and stepped inside the house, and caught sight of Libby and Teddy, hovering halfway down the stairs.

'Oh!' he said. 'Hello! More guests! Good, because it isn't good people should be alone in this house.'

'It *is* rather big for one person,' Libby said, smiling at him. 'Are you the one who's been tending to the garden here? It's gorgeous. Is it all right if we use some of it?'

'Oh, please, please do so!' Victor exclaimed. 'I have been tending the garden for it to be used! It is good that people are here now using it! And not just the ghosts, eh? Ghosts haven't much use for a garden, you know. Too busy being naughty.'

Teddy looked wide-eyed and alarmed. 'Naughty how?'

'I'm sure Victor doesn't actually mean that they would harm us,' Sam said.

'Oh, no, of course not. Just make your life a living hell,' explained Victor cheerfully. 'For instance. Say you want electricity. Eh? Hmm? You want electricity? The ghosts decide, no, you don't get electricity.' He shrugged. 'No electricity for you.'

Sam tilted his head. 'But ... what if we want electricity?'

'You have to bargain with the ghosts.' Victor floated his hands around in the air, his fingers trembling, clearly intending to encompass all of the 'ghosts' that might be hovering around them.

'Who are the ghosts?' Teddy asked, doing a poor job of covering up his fear. He had been so dismissive of the ghosts before but Sam could see that he was changing his mind about them in the face of Victor's calm conviction that the ghosts were hanging about mucking things up for them.

'There's no such thing as ghosts,' Libby stated firmly.

'Oh, look!' said Victor, and pointed.

Sam couldn't help the fact that he looked up the stairs, in the direction Victor indicated, fully expecting to see a ghost at the top of it.

But there was nothing there.

'What?' Libby asked.

'You've uncovered the ghosts,' said Victor.

Everyone looked back up at the top of the stairs.

'I don't see anything,' said Sam.

'Do you have special ghost-hunting equipment?' asked Teddy uncertainly.

'The portraits!' Victor exclaimed. 'You've uncovered the portraits!'

'Those two women?' said Libby quizzically.

'Those are the ghosts?' said Sam.

'Well, this house is full of ghosts. This house is ancient, yes? This house is as old as the hills. There have been people living on this ground for so much longer than any of us can remember. Who are we to say how many ghosts there are, and who they might be, and where they might dwell? All I know is this house is full of ghosts who love a good laugh, and I hear tell those two were like that.' Victor nodded at the portraits.

Sam looked back at the paintings, dim and grimy at the top of the stairs. The women in them didn't exactly look fun-loving.

Libby said, 'Who are the women in the portraits? Do you know?'

'No idea,' said Victor cheerfully.

Sam blinked at him. 'But you just said—'

'Come, let's have a look at your electrics,' said Victor.

Teddy looked at Sam and accused flatly, 'You have us staying the summer in a *haunted house*. Who knows what might happen?'

'There's no such thing as ghosts,' Libby insisted.

Victor walked through the newest portion of the house, the part without power, and flipped the switches as uselessly as Sam had. He muttered to himself as he poked into wardrobes and under sinks and into a crawlspace at the edge of the loft. He was more successful than Sam at locating the fuse board, although he seemed to just stare at it uselessly, which Sam felt he also could have done. Jack followed Victor around, keeping a wary distance, evidently suspicious of Victor's intentions.

Then Victor said, 'You know what your problem is?'

'No,' said Sam. 'What's the problem?'

'Ghosts,' said Victor, and tapped his nose as if that was the universal signal for *ghosts*.

'But there's no such thing as ghosts,' said Libby in

exasperation. She didn't mind the *story* of ghosts – in fact, she thought it added to the atmosphere of the place – but she didn't like the idea that all these people seemed to be *seriously believing* in it. She had wanted a French adventure, but she hadn't wanted *ghosts*. She'd just wanted cheese and champagne and croissants.

'And with that attitude,' remarked Victor, 'you'll never get your electricity back.'

'What do you mean?' asked Sam.

'Well,' said Victor, with another of his ever-present shrugs, 'you'll need to make an offering to the ghosts. So they know you deserve electricity.'

'What do you have to do to deserve electricity?' said Sam.

Victor shrugged again.

'Okay,' Sam said, his voice that desert-dry tone that was so very Sam and that Libby loved so much, the way she loved all things Sam. 'Well, you've been very helpful.'

'I do what I can,' said Victor, with his typical good cheer. 'Have a good time! Let me know if you need any other help!'

They stood in the farmyard to see Victor off. It was now late enough that, although the sun hadn't fully set, it was low in the sky, tinting the farmhouse's stone a lurid shade of red, and beyond the farmhouse, night was approaching, velvet blackness creeping over the sky.

Sam said, after they were done waving after Victor, 'We're never going to get internet out here. I'm going to have to depend on mobile coverage to get my work done. And the village café.'

'I'm sorry,' Libby said sincerely.

'Well, there are worse things than having to work at a little café in a charming French town,' Sam pointed out.

'Dad,' said Teddy, 'what about the ghosts? Can we talk about them, please?'

'Well,' said Sam, 'Victor said they were fun-loving ghosts, and we're fun-loving people, so I shouldn't think they'd really want to harm us.'

'Should we put an offering out?' Teddy asked.

'I don't really know what that would be,' Sam said.

'There's no such thing as ghosts,' Libby insisted. She felt a little unmoored by Sam's willingness to indulge this nonsense. She would have thought he'd be dismissing it out of hand. That seemed more in keeping with Sam's rock-steady world-view, which she was coming to realise she depended on.

'But if there are,' said Teddy, 'we should probably put an offering out.'

'Tell you what,' Sam said, slinging an arm over Teddy's shoulders, 'I'll look up what a good ghost offering might be.'

'Good idea,' said Teddy. 'And make sure you point out that it's for French ghosts. That might make a difference.'

'Good point,' said Sam.

'Pari would know what to do about French ghosts,' grumbled Teddy.

100

When they headed up to bed that night, Libby paused at the top of the staircase and looked at the portraits of the two women. She wanted to know who they were, not because they might be ghosts but because they had been *people*. Thinking about them as some kind of supernatural pranksters ignored the fact that they had lived and laughed and loved, probably in that very house.

The women seemed to glare stonily at each other across the foxed mirror, as they must have done for decades. The portraits looked gloomy and unhappy, and Libby wondered if they would prefer to be moved to a different wall, to get a different view. Surely they were tired of staring at each other. And then she realised that she had fallen into the same trap of fanciful thinking that contained the ghost theory of electrical failure, so she gave herself a mental shake and walked into the bedroom.

Sam was out on the terrace. Libby could already tell that he adored the terrace. She'd found him on it several times already in their brief time in the house. The night was dark all around them, with stars twinkling above and a few lights glimmering from various points in the valley, where there was another farmhouse and maybe a village. The hills in the far distance were punctuated with hazy brushstrokes of light as evidence of people.

'Look at all the people with electricity,' Sam said wryly, gesturing to the vista.

Libby said, walking over to him, 'We have electricity, just not *all* the electricity.'

'Yes,' Sam agreed, and tucked her against him, kissing the top of her head.

Libby sighed. 'It's so beautiful here. Everything looks like a painting. Max is going to love it.'

'He will. I can't wait for him to see it. For all of them to see it.'

'Let's not wish the summer already over,' said Libby.

Sam laughed. 'No. Of course not. Sorry.' He slid his hands up and down Libby's arms, in a soothing gesture. 'Are you feeling all right?'

'What?' said Libby, surprised. 'Yes.'

'You didn't eat much tonight.'

'I know. I didn't feel like eating.' Libby shrugged, feeling like Victor. 'No big deal.'

'Hmm,' murmured Sam, and kissed the top of her head again.

'I think,' Libby said suddenly, 'that I'm thrown by all this ghost talk.'

'Look,' Sam said reasonably, 'we're nice people. The ghosts aren't actually going to do anything to us—'

Libby turned in his arms. 'No, see, that's what I find so odd about this. *There's no such thing as ghosts.* Why is everyone acting as if it makes any sense at all for us to be talking about ghosts, putting out offerings for ghosts, hoping the ghosts will give us our electricity back?'

Sam tilted his head, looking surprised by her outburst. 'I didn't realise this was bothering you so much. I thought it would be just the sort of odd French charm that would appeal to you.'

Libby was upset with herself. 'I know. It should. It just seemed out of character for you. I expected ghosts to come up and you would be the practical one, telling everyone not to get carried away with supernatural explanations and just fix the wiring, and instead you're going along with it. It makes me feel all . . . ' She frowned, searching for the word. 'Unsettled.'

Sam, after a moment, said softly, 'You're not wrong. I see why you say that. I would never have said I was inclined to believe in ghosts. And then . . . Sara died, and I kind of . . . I don't know . . . the idea that maybe she wasn't entirely gone was . . . seductive, I suppose.' He made a frustrated sound. 'I hate this, I don't want to make you feel like I'm comparing you to Sara, or wish you were Sara, or that the fact that I still miss Sara means I don't love you, or—'

'Hush,' Libby said, pressing her fingers softly to his lips. 'I get it.' Because she did. She never felt like Sara was somebody to compete with; Sam never made her feel that way. And she completely understood that it was natural that Sam would always miss her, especially everything she wasn't getting to see with Teddy. If he wasn't averse to the idea of ghosts because he liked the idea that Teddy's mum wasn't entirely missing out, Libby totally understood that.

Sam looked at her, wide-eyed, and spoke against her fingers. 'Do you?'

She nodded. 'It's okay. Let's put out some kind of offering to the ghosts.'

Sam smiled.

Chapter Eleven

Don't worry about the ghosts! Turns out they're merry
pranksters! ☺

Libby's phone rang as she was walking home to Christmas
Street, texting Sam not to worry about the house ghosts.
Her phone flashed *Isla*, so she quickly answered, because
it wasn't often she heard from Isla, an old uni friend with
a glamorous globetrotting lifestyle.

Libby answered with, 'Hello? Have you managed to
squeeze in time to catch up with an old friend between
running with the bulls in Pamplona and climbing Mount
Kilimanjaro?'

Isla laughed and said, 'I have done neither of those
things. As well you know. I just do boring backpacking,
volunteering here and there—'

'Bringing good to the entire world,' Libby finished.

'Hey, you're a teacher, you're doing good, too. It's just
that I'm doing good without settling down.'

'You're bad at roots,' Libby said, because it was

104

practically Isla's motto. She had said it frequently at uni. In fact, Isla had often been so jittery at uni that she would talk Libby into last-minute weekend trips where they would pile into Isla's old car and drive it basically as far as it would go before breaking down. They were madcap schemes that Libby remembered with great fondness, but she had been very happy to settle down, taking root on Christmas Street, while Isla had taken her degree and then flown away, happily circling the globe again and again, with never a home address.

'I'm bad at roots,' Isla agreed cheerfully. 'But I'm on an overnight train between Berlin and Malmö and I am bored out of my skull.'

Libby laughed. 'So bored that even a conversation with me looked better?'

'Oh, damn,' said Isla, also laughing, 'I didn't even realise how that sounded.'

'I'll forgive you,' said Libby. 'So, Berlin to Malmö. What do you have planned in Malmö?'

'No idea,' said Isla.

'And what did you do in Berlin?'

'This and that,' said Isla.

Libby chuckled and shook her head. Isla wasn't there to see it but Libby was fairly sure she would be able to sense it. 'Your life, Isla, I swear.'

'Yeah,' said Isla. 'It can sometimes be a bit much.'

It was the first time Libby had ever heard Isla say anything like that, and it made her pay closer attention to the conversation. Now that she was thinking about it, Isla *did* sound tired, in a way she usually didn't. Libby said, a little concerned, 'You okay?'

'Yeah,' Isla said, with a sigh. 'I am. Truly. I'm just feeling tired tonight. I don't know why. I missed talking to someone who knew my name, you know? I don't often get like that but tonight I wanted to talk to someone who knows who I am.'

'I know who you are,' Libby promised.

'Tell me about married bliss,' Isla said. 'And your fascinatingly normal life in London.'

'It's lovely,' Libby said. 'But very dull. We stay in the same place all the time. You'd be so bored.' She gasped suddenly. 'Except! We're going to France this summer!'

'Ooh, lovely,' said Isla. 'France is lovely.'

'A colleague of mine owns an old, rambling farmhouse, we have the run of it, and you should come to stay.'

'What?' said Isla, sounding caught off-guard.

'You know you can come to stay whenever you like, but I know if you come back to London, you've got to see your whole family and it's a whole production. But if you visit us in France, you'll still be indulging your wanderlust ways, only with someone around who knows your name and who you are.'

Isla was silent for a long moment, which Libby knew meant the idea appealed to her, because Isla was really so seldom silent.

Libby eventually prompted, 'Isla?'

'I'm still here,' Isla said. 'I was just thinking. It does sound like it might be nice.'

'You can come whenever you like,' Libby said. 'We'll have plenty of room. And you can stay as long as you like. At least say you'll consider it. We don't have to pin you down with plans, you can be free-spirited and come and go whenever you feel like it.'

'Well,' said Isla after another moment of silence. 'I admit it does sound tempting. If only so I can meet this husband of yours and make sure he's good enough for you.'

'He is,' said Libby. 'And please don't terrify him.' Isla laughed.

'I'll text you all the details,' said Libby. 'You can just show up at our door.'

'You're a really good friend, Libby. I'm not sure I say that enough.'

'I'm not sure you say that ever,' teased Libby lightly.

'Okay, I deserved that,' said Isla ruefully.

'Let's talk again soon,' Libby said. 'Let's not go so long exchanging hurried emails that don't say much.'

'Yeah,' Isla agreed, and she sounded fervent about it. 'It was good to hear your voice.'

'Have fun in Malmö,' Libby said.

'Have fun in France if I don't see you there,' said Isla.

'You'll see me there,' said Libby confidently.

They ended the call, and Libby texted Isla the details, as she'd promised. And then she texted Sam: *Btw, there's no such thing as ghosts, so it doesn't matter what sort of ghosts they are, as there AREN'T ANY.*

Sam texted back: *DO NOT TEMPT THE GHOSTS.*

Chapter Twelve

Potage Julienne: Carrots, turnips, leeks, celery, chopped cabbage, tapioca

The next day, Libby decided, was as good a day as any to start cooking, considering they had cleaned the kitchen while waiting for Victor the day before. It was ready in all its intimidating rustic splendour. Armed with her ancient French cookbook, she prowled through the gardens, picking any produce that looked edible. Then she went back into the kitchen and spread all of it out on the counter: a few lumpy tomatoes, dark green courgettes and bright green asparagus, long slender leeks, a smattering of peppers of all shapes and sizes, carrots so orange they seemed like they ought to be fake, celery so crisp Libby could smell its fresh scent, clouds of spinach and lettuce leaves, small cabbages and cauliflowers, a few ill-shaped onions and potatoes. It was an embarrassingly abundant harvest of foods, especially combined with what they'd bought at the market, but Libby had no idea what to *do* with it.

Teddy watched her with interest, which was more than he had shown towards Libby in a while, so she was relieved. 'Is that stuff safe to eat?' he asked dubiously.

'Why wouldn't it be?' Libby asked. 'It's been grown in our very own garden, warmed by the sun and fed by the rain. It's probably safer to eat than the stuff we buy in supermarkets at home.'

'Yeah, but who knows how many animals have stepped on it and sniffed at it and who knows what else,' pointed out Teddy.

Libby hadn't really thought about that. 'I'll just . . . wash it all really well.'

Teddy looked as if he thought they might all die during their summer in France at the hands of Libby's terrible cooking.

And then a voice called, '*Allo*? Where is everyone?'

'Oh!' exclaimed Libby. 'We're in the kitchen, Victor!'

Victor entered the kitchen and kissed Libby's cheeks and eyed the produce lined up on the counters. 'And what are we doing here? Cooking a grand feast? Using my garden for exactly what it is intended for?'

'Is any of this stuff poisonous?' Teddy asked Victor.

Victor laughed and tweaked at Teddy's nose, and Teddy looked first taken aback and then murderous.

'Did you know I'm almost ten?' Teddy demanded.

Victor laughed like that was a funny joke.

Teddy frowned.

Libby, to try to save the conversation, said, 'We've got all this beautiful produce out in the garden, I thought I'd try to make something out of it. Of course, I'm not the world's best cook. I'm merely passable. I can keep us fed but I'm no French chef.'

'Fancy training is not required,' Victor said graciously. 'Only a love of food and a desire to feed your soul and the souls of others, eh?'

That made cooking sound so beautiful that Libby couldn't believe she'd wasted so much of her life not knowing how to do it. 'That's what I want to do,' she said.

'Ah,' said Victor. 'My daughter, Pauline – she owns a small café in one of the villages. She would be very pleased to teach you.'

'Really?' said Libby, thinking that she hadn't expected such good luck.

'*Oui*,' said Victor, nodding, just as Sam came into the kitchen.

'Hello, Victor,' said Sam. 'What are we up to?'

'Victor has a daughter in one of the villages who can give me cooking lessons,' said Libby enthusiastically.

'Oh, that's wonderful,' Sam said. 'And what about our electricity?'

'I have come to see what progress you have made. Your electricity has come back, eh?'

'No,' Sam said. 'It has not come back.'

Victor gestured to the house. 'I see lights.'

Lights were glowing through the windows of the middle part of the house.

'Right,' said Sam. 'We always had electricity there. It was in the *new* part of the house that we needed the electricity.'

'Oh, right, right, yes, of course,' said Victor, sounding as if he was not at all interested in the correction. 'You have left an offering to the ghosts, yes?'

'Yes,' said Teddy. 'Sunflowers, lavender, and some stones we found in the garden. It's not working. Probably because Google says ghosts like food but Dad won't let us put food out because he's scared of mice.' Teddy fixed Sam with an accusatory look.

'Well, sometimes it takes some time. You cannot expect everything by the end of the day, eh? You must give all of nature time and room to breathe.' Victor gestured with his arms, in and out, as if the world around them was breathing. 'You cannot grow a sunflower in one day. Neither can you please ghosts in one day.'

'How long does it usually take?' asked Sam, sounding politely restrained.

Victor shrugged.

Chapter Thirteen

Libby! I've been trying to get in touch with you! When
you get this text, ring me back!

Libby woke one morning feeling as perpetually exhausted
as she had for a while now. It had been over a week now,
and she kept waiting for the adrenalin crash of the travel
to wear off and to regain her usual energy. But she refused
to let the lingering weariness get her down. Victor had
spoken to Pauline and Libby was going to spend the morning with her, learning how to 'feed her soul', as Victor kept
putting it. Libby couldn't wait.

They went into the village and Sam settled into the café
to work while Teddy sulked around the central village
square with Jack. Libby found Pauline's café as Victor had
directed her to: by just asking for Pauline.

Pauline was a cheerful, gamine Audrey-Hepburn look-
alike, dressed in an apron, with her hair caught back in a
messy bun from which tendrils were escaping. She looked
like she'd been working hard but it made her glow instead

of sweat. It was so very *French*, Libby thought. For a moment, she thought she might look like an idiot in front of Pauline.

Then Pauline said, 'Look. I want you to know. At first I learned how to cook because my father had an extremely sexist idea of the life skills his daughter might need.'

Her English was flawless, conversational, comfortable with idioms in a way Victor's wasn't. It caught Libby by surprise, as did the elegant eye-roll that accompanied her speech.

'Oh,' said Libby, not knowing what else to say.

'My father would say that cooking is all about feeding your soul or whatever. But I wanted to be a lawyer.'

'Oh,' said Libby again. 'What happened?'

'I became a lawyer, and then I said, "Oh, no way," and went back to cooking and feeding souls. I say all this because I don't want you to think that I think all women have to cook or something. I just think that cooking can be very fulfilling to some people, and maybe you're one of them, and that's cool.' Pauline shrugged, and the resemblance to her father became stronger.

Libby said, 'Well, I have no idea how to cook anything, really, so I'm hoping you can give me some basics. I've got this whole garden full of fresh vegetables and I don't know what to do with any of it.'

'Hmm,' said Pauline consideringly. And then she said, 'Well. A garden full of fresh produce. Maybe a *pistou* soup? It's a traditional Provençal vegetable soup. What do you say?' Libby was ready for anything. She said brightly, 'Let's give it a try.'

Pauline cooked with a smooth familiarity Libby envied and wished she could aspire to. She chopped vegetables with clean, sharp purpose, creating tiny, uniform chunks of carrots and courgettes and leeks. Libby tried to keep up but it was hopeless.

Pauline also talked as she cooked, an endless stream of gossip about the town, tossing her vegetables into her soup pot, tearing up fresh basil with her hands and showering it over the vegetables like confetti. Sometimes a worker came in from the front of the café and they would have an abrupt conversation in French.

'Customers,' Pauline huffed at one point, as if they were a grave inconvenience.

Libby said, as they waited for the flavours of the soup to blend and develop, 'I'm staying in Mrs Dash's farmhouse.'

'The old Bernard place,' Pauline said. 'Yes, my father said.'

'Do you know anything about it? Like, who owned it before Mrs Dash? Well, her Great-Aunt Clarissa, I know, but I guess what I'm asking is if you know about the ghosts.'

Pauline, tasting the soup, looked over at Libby with amusement. 'Well, I know *about* the ghosts, because my father never shuts up about ghosts. He's got a ghost story for every location in the countryside. He is the keeper of vague tales of mischievous spirits. But, as for any further details, he is useless.'

'Well.' Libby didn't *want* to agree, but ... 'Yes. Kind of. We're just so interested in the history of the house.'

Pauline tossed some more seasoning into the pot, stirred, tasted, then nodded briskly. 'You should go to Château Laurent.'

'What's that?'

'Local chateau. It's a vineyard. Kind of a tourist attraction. But Raphael, who helps run the place, keeps archives. History has always been his hobby. He and my father have a regular poker game where they accuse each other of cheating. I grew up with him around, and his stories have *much* more detail. If you want to know about the ghosts of the Bernard farmhouse, you should ask Raphael. Also, the chateau is charming, you should see it anyway.

'Here. Taste the soup.' Pauline held out a spoon.

'It's delicious,' Libby said, because it was, with impossible layers of flavours spreading out over her tongue. Libby hadn't known vegetables could taste like this.

'Not bad for your first try, right?' said Pauline, and began scooping some into a takeaway container.

'But you did all the work!' Libby protested.

'You watched, though,' Pauline said. 'Don't worry. You can learn cooking by osmosis. Trust me.'

Isla Hughes was thinking one majorly important overriding thought, and it was an unusual one for her: she was thinking that she should have planned ahead.

Isla wasn't a planner. Libby had always laughed at her in uni. *You knew you had that project due,* Libby would chide her. *Why didn't you start it sooner?* But that just wasn't the way Isla worked.

But, in a strange town in the middle of Provence, at a random train station, Isla was thinking that she should have planned ahead. Libby wasn't answering her mobile, and Isla had no idea where Libby's house might be, and Isla had no idea where she was going to spend the night, and, really, why hadn't she rung Libby to tell her she was coming? Why was she always so terrible at making life choices that made *sense*?

Isla sat on a bench outside the train station and glanced up at the midday sun and tried not to feel too sorry for herself. She was in France in the middle of a glorious summer day. Things could be much, much, much worse. But she couldn't help the wave of self-pity that washed over her. She had fled to France because she had been beset by an unaccustomed loneliness that had crept up and felt suffocating. And now here she was in France feeling lonelier. What if this had been a huge mistake? What if all she ever did in her life was make huge mistakes?

Isla rubbed at her temples, at the headache starting there, and said fiercely to herself, 'Stop it, you're fine, you make great life choices.'

'Does your therapist make you say that out loud periodically, too?'

Isla jumped, startled, and looked up.

There was a woman by the bike stand a few feet away,

cheerfully unlocking her bike. She had a mop of dark hair peeking out from underneath her hat, and was wearing skinny jeans, a blue-and-white-striped shirt, sunglasses and a wide-brimmed floppy straw hat. The outfit looked a little over the top to Isla. Sunglasses *and* a hat seemed like overkill.

The woman smiled at her and said, 'You okay? Generally speaking, that kind of behaviour is the sort that worries me.'

She was American, Isla catalogued vaguely, trying not to feel thrown. She was in France, somewhat lost, randomly talking to a strange American.

Isla said, 'I'm okay, just . . . ' She held up her mobile and smiled brightly. 'My friend's not picking up her phone.'

'Got your lines of communication crossed?' said the American sympathetically.

Or I didn't ring her to tell her I was coming because that would have been the responsible thing to do and I'm committed to mucking up everything in my life, thought Isla.

The American was smiling at her like some sort of response was required, and it wasn't as though Isla could say what she'd just thought, so instead she said, 'Yeah. A bit.'

'I'd offer you a ride, but I don't think I'd be very good at balancing you on my handlebars.' The American smiled widely, gleefully, like she was hilarious and this was hilarious and the sort of charming, madcap thing that happened in France.

Isla smiled back, less widely and less gleefully but with a twinge of her old sense of adventure. Yes. Charming and madcap. She used to live life that way.

The American said, 'I can wait with you. Until your friend shows up.'

Which was mortifying, since Isla had no idea if Libby was ever going to show up. Isla might end up getting on the next train back to Paris. She said, 'No, that's okay. I mean, I'm sure I'll be fine.'

'Beware the roving gangs of werewolves,' said the American, winking.

Isla tried for a laugh, which she knew was the proper response, and it didn't even feel as rusty as she'd thought it might.

The American said, 'Actually, wolves used to be extinct in France. They're making a comeback. Slowly. So. You know.'

'Beware the roving gangs of werewolves,' Isla said gravely.

The American grinned. 'Exactly.'

'I'll look out for them.' Isla glanced around her.

The place where she was looked like the sleepiest, dullest town in history. No one looked anything like a werewolf.

'Well,' remarked the American, 'they'd be really bad predators unless they were good at sneaking up on you, so, you know, keep an eye out.'

'Will do,' Isla said, and then made a ridiculous little salute for some reason.

The American lingered for a second, staring at Isla, probably because she'd bloody *saluted* her, and then she said, 'Okay. Well. Good luck with your friend.'

'Thanks,' Isla said.

The American took off on her bicycle, ringing her bell once, a happy chime of farewell.

Isla muttered under her breath, 'You just *saluted* her, what were you even thinking?'

And then her mobile rang in her hand and Isla jumped a mile. She realised at that moment she'd genuinely never expected Libby to ring her back. She'd just assumed this trip would turn out as pointlessly as all the rest of her trips had.

Isla answered immediately. 'Libby!' She thought her voice sounded swamped with relief, panic barely kept at bay.

Libby, sounding concerned, said, 'Are you all right? Is there something wrong?'

'No.' Isla forced herself to sound the way she always had for Libby, the Isla of old, bright and playful and spontaneous. She could do that. She plastered a smile onto her face. 'Actually, I've got a marvellous surprise for you.'

Libby gasped. 'Oh, are you coming for a visit?'

She sounded . . . more than happy. She sounded like she genuinely couldn't wait to see Isla. And Isla immediately felt better about everything. It was nice to remember what it was like to be *loved*, and *wanted*. For so long she had been surrounded by strangers who didn't care who she was or where she was going. Isla could have cried right there on the bench. She was glad the cute American woman had left, so that she wouldn't witness Isla's weird breakdown.

Isla hoped she was keeping the tremor of emotion out of her voice when she said, 'I've got even better news.'

'Better news?' Libby sounded quizzical, bewildered.

'I'm already here.'

'Already here?'

'In France.'

Libby gasped again. '*What?* In France? Where?'

'In Provence, actually. I took a train to where you told me, and I'm hoping it's close enough to your house that I can find my way there. Where's your house?'

'Near a tree that looks like Winston Churchill,' said Libby.

'What?' said Isla, sure she'd heard incorrectly.

'Stay put,' Libby said. 'We're coming to you.'

Libby wasn't sure she entirely believed Pauline's proclamation that she was going to be able to learn cooking by osmosis but she met back up with Teddy and Sam with enough *pistou* soup tucked under her arm to feed all of them for dinner, and with a vague idea that she might be able to make it again given all the produce she'd laid out on the countertop in the kitchen at the farmhouse.

'Success?' Sam asked, looking pleased by her expression, so Libby hoped she looked triumphant.

'Do I look successful?' she asked.

'You're glowing,' said Sam.

'Oh, good,' said Libby. 'I must be getting more French. Pauline glowed the whole time she was cooking.'

'We're speaking metaphorically, right? Because if it's literal, I'm alarmed.'

Libby laughed. 'Oh, also, I got a recommendation from

her for a local tourist attraction that might be able to tell us more about our household ghosts.'

'Really?'

'Château Laurent, it's called. Some local chateau, I guess. It's got a vineyard, too, so I guess it sells wine and stuff.'

'I don't know how much that will interest Teddy,' remarked Sam.

'He might be interested in the ghost story,' said Libby.

'I feel like Teddy hasn't made up his mind if he thinks the ghost story is rubbish or he's scared to death of the ghost story.'

'Like father, like son,' Libby teased.

Sam grumbled good-naturedly, calling Teddy over from where he was being taught pétanque by a local. Libby thought Teddy looked better, more engaged. Maybe he was just the sort who needed to have other people around him.

Sam was chatting with the men who had been teaching Teddy, and she was wondering idly if his French was improving as she pulled out her phone and glanced at it, and saw the missed call from Isla.

Libby had been having a good day, she really had been, and yet still seeing the missed call came with a vivid sense of relief. Maybe this time in France was *too much* adventure. Maybe she just needed an old uni friend to show up and ground her. That probably explained why she felt so weepy and emotional over the very idea of Isla being around.

When Libby found out Isla was already in France, her joy was absolute. She ended the call with Isla just as Sam and

Teddy came up to her. Sam had his hand ruffling through Teddy's hair, and Teddy was ducking away from him but just with the usual amount of embarrassment, not with the added sullenness he'd had lately.

'Exciting news!' she exclaimed.

They looked at her expectantly.

'My old uni friend Isla is coming to visit!'

Sam looked pleased. 'Oh, lovely. I'm looking forward to meeting her.'

Libby said, 'She's here *now*.'

Sam blinked. 'What do you mean?'

'She's in France. She just rang me from a train station. I told her we'd go and pick her up.'

'Oh,' said Sam. 'She just showed up in France?'

'It's such an Isla thing to do. Just show up and trust it'll all work out. Seriously, you're going to *love* her. She's so much fun. Isla's the best.' Libby was aware she was gushing, but she couldn't believe how excited she was about Isla's visit.

Teddy said, 'Does she like dogs?'

'Absolutely,' Libby assured him and Jack.

'Does she like cats?' Teddy asked. 'Because we have those, too.'

'Sure,' Libby decided, because she couldn't remember one way or the other.

'How does she feel about ghosts?' asked Teddy.

Libby's friend Isla had long, pin-straight, dark brown hair that went halfway down her back, with a choppy, chunky fringe that only certain people could pull off. Isla was one of those people. She was so striking standing by the train station with a knapsack slung over her shoulder, her jeans ripped and her T-shirt so worn and faded that there was only the hint of the design that had once graced it, that Sam thought she looked like someone you'd pluck out of a crowd and ask for their life story. She just looked like she had a good one.

Libby leaped out of the car and she and Isla embraced tightly, in that way of old friends who hadn't seen each other in a while.

Sam remarked to Teddy, as they sat in the car and watched the reunion, 'I am vaguely nervous.'

'Why?' Teddy asked, sounding bored by his father's internal drama.

'Because meeting one of your wife's best friends is an important moment. And I didn't have to do it with your mum because all of her best friends were also my best friends.'

Teddy said, 'You went to uni with Mom the way Libby went to uni with Isla.'

'Yes,' Sam confirmed.

'So, in a way, you're meeting the person who met Libby because Libby wasn't meeting you,' said Teddy.

There was a moment of silence in the car.

Sam said, 'That's complicated logic, and I'm not sure it made me feel any better.'

Teddy shrugged.

Libby was leading Isla towards them now, so Sam took a deep breath and stepped out of the car.

Libby was introducing happily, 'This is my husband Sam—'

'Sam!' Isla exclaimed, and gave him a tight hug. It caught Sam by surprise but he was pleased by it. 'Look at you.' She released him and took a step back and made a big show of examining him critically, before nodding. 'Yes. You look like the sort of man Libby should have married. Perfect.'

'Oh,' said Sam, smiling. 'Well, that's good.'

'And that's Teddy,' Libby said. 'And Jack the dog.'

The house was a bit absurd, meandering, and silly, with its electrical challenges and its stray cat family and the utter impracticality of the enormous rooms in the section of the house they were living in. And Isla loved it. It somehow felt like exactly what she had been looking for, without knowing it.

Then again, maybe that had just been having Libby around. Having *people* around.

She didn't know Sam and Teddy but they seemed nice and, because she was Libby's friend, Sam at least was invested in being nice to her (Teddy seemed a little more . . . mercurial), and Isla soaked it up. God, she really had been *so* lonely, and she'd known that she was but the full extent of it was breaking over her now that she was remembering what it was like *not* to feel that way.

Libby suggested that perhaps Isla might be feeling tired after her journey, and maybe they should all enjoy a siesta. Isla was grateful for the break. Libby scurried into a bedroom and briskly changed the bedding, Isla protesting that she could take care of that, and then Libby, with a shaken head and a smile, left her to her nap.

Isla woke feeling refreshed, excited to be in a house with a dear friend who she could catch up with. She headed downstairs to find the household preparing for dinner.

In the long Provençal twilight they sat in the back garden and lit candles and had crusty fresh bread and a delicious vegetable soup that Isla could not get over and Sam kept raving about, with '*You* actually made this? *You?*' while Libby blushed and Isla deduced that Libby had not learned much more about cooking than she had known in uni. They watched fireflies dance through the olive grove and Isla could not believe how lovely everything was. She was *so* glad she'd come. A spontaneous decision that had actually worked out for a change!

Teddy drooped to sleep on a blanket on the grass, Jack curled up next to him, and Sam poured out wine.

Libby said, 'I've been fighting a headache all day,' shaking her head at it.

Sam said, 'Have you? I'm sorry. You should have said.'

'It's fine,' Libby said.

'I don't want to keep you up,' Isla said. 'If you'd rather go lie down.'

'Are you kidding me? I am *so* excited that you're here, I'm definitely pushing through the headache.'

'It might be an adrenalin crash,' Sam said, studying Libby. 'That would make sense. You ran yourself ragged before we left, with all of the planning and anticipating. No wonder you're exhausted now.'

'Well, solidarity, Lib,' Isla said, lifting her wine glass in a brief toast. 'Let's let the French air revive all of us. And the croissants.'

'I'm fine,' Libby told Sam. 'Stop fussing.'

'We're sorry we missed you at the wedding,' said Sam.

'Me, too,' said Isla ruefully.

'She was off in Morocco,' Libby said. 'Or, wait, was it Thailand then?'

Libby's voice was teasing but Isla looked uncomfortable, rounding her shoulders a little bit and saying, 'I don't remember. But I should have made it home for your wedding. I'm sorry I skipped it.'

'Oh, no,' Libby said, hurriedly. 'Don't apologise. I didn't mind. You were off having an adventure.'

'We support adventures,' said Sam. 'Did you wonder about the pile of detritus at the top of the staircase?'

'Now that you mention it,' said Isla, but when they'd reached the top of the staircase there had been a minor commotion because Jack had taken off after something that Libby had shrieked might have been a mouse and by the time everything got settled Isla had forgotten about the strange pile of flowers.

'It's a ghost offering,' Sam said.

126

'Does the house have ghosts?' asked Isla, sounding intrigued.

'It depends on who you talk to,' said Libby.

'Everyone who believes in ghosts says yes,' said Sam. 'Including our ... what would you call him? Caretaker? Advice-giver? French guardian?'

'I rather like that idea,' mused Isla. 'I wonder if we all receive French guardians when we get here. I've certainly encountered some helpful people in my brief time here.'

'Well,' said Sam, 'if he's our French guardian, he's not terribly helpful. His name is Victor, and he periodically comes by to remind us that there is nothing he can do about the electricity but continue to suggest that we persuade the ghosts to cooperate.'

'Also, his daughter is giving me cooking lessons in the village,' said Libby.

'Oh, so *that's* the deal with the soup,' said Isla. 'It was *magnifique*. This woman must be an excellent teacher.'

'Okay,' said Libby. 'To be perfectly honest, Pauline made the soup. I just watched her. But she says that's how you learn to cook: by osmosis.'

'Huh,' said Isla.

'Hmm,' said Sam, sounding suspicious.

Libby laughed. 'No, really, I don't know, there *was* something about the way she cooked, so comfortably, so automatically – watching her, I felt like maybe it was just a rhythm I needed to learn, and that watching her, learning to move in that rhythm, would help me feel the food the way she could. Or hear it, I guess, because it was almost like she could hear music I couldn't hear, the way she was arranging the herbs and chopping the vegetables. It's all just a matter of . . . learning the dance.' Libby made a dramatic gesture, like she was preparing for the tango.

'You're sounding very French,' remarked Sam.

'So, the ghosts are the reason the electricity is broken?' asked Isla.

'According to Victor,' said Sam.

'It's a little ridiculous,' said Libby, 'but at least we have electricity in part of the house.'

'The ghosts are indeed benevolent,' said Sam.

Isla laughed, then said, 'It's an old house. It's bound to have a few ghosts in its past. Who among us doesn't?'

Sam eventually went up to bed, probably sensing that Libby wanted some alone time with Isla. Sam was usually good about sensing when Libby wanted a bit of space, and she felt like she needed some at the moment. Sam was lovely, always very lovely, Libby was just . . . overwhelmed at the moment. She watched Sam shake Teddy to something resembling wakefulness, enough to get him out of the garden and up the stairs, and Jack followed behind, stretching and yawning.

Isla said, 'Really, Lib, this is lovely. This is exactly what I needed, and I didn't even know. Exactly what I was hoping for.'

Libby managed a smile, glancing out over the gardens, up towards the house. The light went on in the bedroom she was sharing with Sam.

Isla said, 'Do you like it here? You seem quiet. I imagine you're homesick. I would love to see Christmas Street, too.'

Isla sounded wistful, and tired, and Libby thought of what a long journey she'd had, and how ridiculous Libby was being, she didn't need to burden Isla with everything whirring through her head right now. It was such a silly thing to even burden her with, that she was tired and head-achey and out of sorts and maybe not cut out for travelling after all. She'd let Isla enjoy her holiday. It wasn't like Isla had come here to be her *therapist*.

Libby said lightly, 'Yeah. I might be a little homesick. Things have been . . . a bit up in the air here.'

'Up in the air?' Isla sent her a slight frown.

'Unexpected,' Libby said. 'Uncertain.'

'It's an adventure,' Isla said wryly. 'That's how they are.'

Libby looked at her. 'And how do they turn out?'

Isla considered, then said slowly, 'Some are better than others. This will be a good one.'

'I hope so,' Libby said, and glanced back up at the house.

Isla studied her. 'I know the house is maybe not quite what you expected, it's odd and unusual, but everyone seems to be handling it well. No one seems upset about it. Has it been tense?'

Libby shook her head. 'No. The opposite of that, really. Sorry, I'm just . . . I'm just off.' She wrapped her arms around herself and rubbed them against a sudden chill.

Isla grinned widely suddenly and said, 'Maybe it's the ghosts,' and fluttered her fingers playfully.

Libby said, 'Oh, God, you're right, according to everyone, they love to play practical jokes, and everyone *did* tell me not to upset them. You're probably right, it probably *is* the ghosts, playing this enormous practical joke on me. But, I mean, it's serious, but it probably seems like a cosmic practical joke to them.'

Isla was staring at her. 'What?' she said.

Libby shook her head. 'No. Nothing. Never mind. I'm babbling. It's been a long day.'

'And I've made it even longer,' said Isla.

'Do *not* apologise,' Libby said. 'Let's make a rule not to apologise to each other for the rest of this holiday.'

'Deal,' Isla laughed.

'So,' said Libby, and shook herself out of her self-centred introspection. 'Enough about me. What about you?'

'Oh.' Isla shrugged and drew her finger along the table in restless circles, watching it closely. 'You know. Same old, same old.'

'Same old, same old?' Libby echoed, raising her eyebrows. 'How is there any same old, same old in *your* life? It's all . . . I mean, it's all adventures like this, isn't it? Weird houses and good food and ghosts?'

'Yeah, and weren't you just pointing out how overwhelming that is?' Isla fixed her with a look.

'Yeah, for *me*,' said Libby. 'Because I'm, you know, a boring primary school teacher with a boring, old married life. You're . . . You're *you*. Even in uni, you were always . . .

anxious to fly. I wanted to stay home and study and you wanted to get on a train and see where it might take us.'

'Yeah,' sighed Isla. And then again, 'Yeah.'

Libby looked at Isla and thought that she was a terrible friend. There was clearly something going on with her, and here Libby had just taken her at face value, the cheerful perpetual wanderer who never suffered the fits of self-doubt that Libby had always been prone to. Maybe Libby had just never seen past Isla's whirligig surface. 'Hey.' She leaned forward and placed her hand over Isla's, stilling it on the table and squeezing it lightly. 'What's up?'

Isla gave her a blinding smile Libby didn't buy for one second. 'Nothing.'

Libby gave her her most unimpressed look. 'Whatever it is, it's okay.'

'It's . . . nothing. It's like you say. It's been a long day, and I'm tired. And I've been travelling a long time, and I'm tired. That's all. I promise.' Isla turned her hand over to thread her fingers through Libby's and squeeze back. 'Thank you so much for letting me recuperate here at this beautiful house with your beautiful family.'

Libby studied her face, and then decided to let it drop. 'Even if there are ghosts?'

'Look,' said Isla, laughing, 'no French farmhouse worth its salt doesn't have ghosts.'

Sam tucked Teddy into bed. Teddy immediately rolled over, muttering into his pillow, and fell back to sleep, and Sam smiled down at him and smoothed his hair down and thought of how he used to be able to carry him up to bed when he fell asleep, and how that seemed like just yesterday.

'You moved pretty fast,' Sam whispered into Teddy's hair, leaving a kiss there, and thought of ghosts, and Sara, and whether she could see how fast it had all happened. Watching Teddy play pétanque on the square had been wonderful, Teddy had been laughing and happy and full of life, and Sam had felt anticipation for the summer ahead of them, joy for the child he had and the wife he had and everything that was yet to happen to them.

Jack leaped up onto the bed with Teddy and curled there, tail thumping a bit as he settled.

Sam smiled at him and scratched behind his ears. 'Good night, Jack,' he whispered.

Then he walked to the room he was sharing with Libby.

The doors stood open to the terrace to catch the night air, and Sam could hear the murmur of Libby and Isla conversing in the garden down below. He couldn't make out words – which was good, because he didn't want to eavesdrop – but he could pick out Libby's laugh, and it was familiar and lovely and comforting. He stretched out in bed and listened to that laugh ringing out again and again, and thought that things kept moving fast but they were all *good* things.

He was still awake when Libby came to bed, not

intentionally but he'd only been dozing, so when she crawled in next to him, he woke fully and turned to gather her against him.

'I didn't mean to wake you,' Libby whispered.

Sam shook his head a little. 'You didn't. I was awake.'

'You were snoring,' said Libby, amused.

'Lies,' said Sam softly, and found her hand and squeezed it. 'Hey, I'm sorry.'

'For what?' Libby asked, sounding surprised.

'I don't know, I feel like I was caught up in things today and didn't notice you weren't feeling well. Things at work ... '

'Working is stressful under these conditions,' said Libby. 'I totally get it.'

'I'm right about the adrenalin crash, I think. You've seemed tired recently. And off.'

'I *feel* tired,' Libby admitted.

'It's okay to feel tired,' Sam said. 'We're on holiday. For a while. You can just relax and catnap all day if you want to.'

Libby kissed the tip of his nose. 'You're sweet, and I wish. But I'm not going to waste this amazing holiday! Tomorrow I'm going to Château Laurent.'

Chapter Fourteen

Welcome to
Château Laurent!

We're so happy you've decided to visit
our beautiful grounds!

Buy some wine to take home to enjoy!

The next morning, Libby went downstairs and regarded her produce and decided to give an omelette a try. How hard could it be? It was just an omelette.

Except that she vastly underestimated how long the first omelette should cook and vastly overestimated how long the second omelette should cook. This odd ancient kitchen was very different from Pauline's cosy, lived-in space, where it seemed like Pauline cooked entirely by practised intuition, the stove sensing when she wanted the heat turned up or down, like a horse that knew its rider. Libby's antique stove did not have the same relationship with her. The temperature seemed to career wildly, and Libby found herself almost in tears as she fought with it. Pauline made it look so easy, everyone made everything look so *easy*, and instead Libby was struggling so hard to stay afloat, and she was terrible at all of it, terrible at handling this family she suddenly had, how was she ever going to cope, what had she been thinking, getting involved in all of this so quickly?

Sam came downstairs just as she was waving the smoke away.

'Looks like the dance needs a little more practice,' Sam remarked.

'I'm going to figure it out,' Libby promised desperately.

'Hey,' Sam said, sounding surprised. 'No pressure here. It's fine if you don't. Are you okay? You seem—'

'I'm fine,' Libby insisted, trying to regain calm as she started another omelette from scratch. Pauline made cooking look meditative, soothing, Zen. Libby at the moment strenuously disagreed with that impression.

'Are you . . . crying?' Sam asked hesitantly.

'It's the smoke,' said Libby, swiping furiously at her eyes.

Teddy came into the kitchen, yawning and rubbing his eyes, Jack trotting behind him, and Libby seized upon the distraction, 'Good morning, Teddy! You are just in time for the perfect omelette!'

Teddy looked suspicious. 'With the poisonous vegetables?'

'Poisonous?' Sam echoed.

'Teddy is sceptical of our amazing vegetables grown in our very own garden,' Libby said.

'And he thought fresh bread had something wrong with it,' remarked Sam. 'I fear I am raising a very citified child.'

'Nothing wrong with that,' said Teddy.

'Aha!' said Libby, succeeding in flipping an omelette that was neither runny nor burnt. A miracle. Maybe this was all going to be doable after all. Maybe the ghosts would work with her instead of against her. 'This one is going to be perfect! Perfect breakfast before going to hunt up some ghost stories, how about it, Teddy?'

Teddy looked displeased. 'Do I have to go to the boring wine place?'

'It's not going to be boring,' Libby said, sliding the omelette in front of him. She wished Teddy seemed more excited. She had really thought he would start to thaw once they got to France. 'It's going to be an adventure for us! Don't you want to know more about the history of this lovely place where we get to stay?'

Teddy shrugged.

'You should go,' Sam told him. 'What are you going to do here all day? It'll be deadly dull. Plus, this will be a lovely outing for you and Libby.'

Teddy sighed and poked at his omelette. 'Do you think you're going to learn to make, say, chocolate croissants?'

'Pain au chocolat, they say here,' said Libby. 'And I think I need to work my way up to that, if I can't even make an omelette. But I mean, I guess if it will make you happy,

I will give pain au chocolat a try.' She said it with grim determination.

Sam laughed, like this was all a lark. 'Don't sound so excited about it.'

Libby tried to laugh as well. She was, after all, supposed to be having *fun*.

'You and Teddy are quite the pair,' Sam continued. 'Pain au chocolat sounds like fun and so does Château Laurent.' Isla came into the kitchen, yawning. 'Isla, don't you think Château Laurent sounds like fun?'

Isla blinked. 'I . . . don't know what that is, but absolutely! Sounds like fun!'

'Oh, Isla thinks everything is fun, she's always been like that,' said Libby.

She only realised how harsh that sounded when everyone looked at her.

'I mean,' Libby stammered, 'but she's right this time, of course! Château Laurent is going to be brilliant!'

'Absolutely!' Isla agreed enthusiastically again, and then, 'What is it?'

'Some place where we're going to learn about ghosts,' Teddy explained, managing to sound very dejected about it.

'Well, that sounds kind of amazing,' Isla remarked.

'It *is* going to be amazing,' Libby said. 'Sam has to work again today, so we're going to drop him off at the café to borrow some Wi-Fi, and then drive up to Château Laurent.'

'And the people at the chateau will know about the ghosts?' asked Isla.

'Apparently Raphael will,' answered Libby.

'I'm guessing you don't mean the Renaissance painter?' said Isla.

'No,' said Libby, 'some sort of Provençal historian, or something. It is, like many things in France, unclear.'

That was probably the wrong thing to say again, as it made Sam look at her in bemusement. 'Not all things,' he said jovially, and pulled her in to plant a kiss on top of her head.

Libby managed a smile.

Château Laurent was apparently a tourist attraction. It showed up on Isla's GPS. 'Look!' Libby exclaimed. 'We can just follow a map!'

'Will the map be right?' Teddy asked dubiously.

'It should be,' said Isla.

'It seems almost too easy,' said Libby. 'Will the ghosts really let us discover their secrets this easily?'

Teddy rolled his eyes.

'Hey,' Isla reminded them reasonably, 'you don't know what you're going to find with this Raphael bloke. He may turn out to be the least helpful individual ever.'

'Good point,' said Libby.

'Turn left,' said Isla's GPS.

The drive wasn't especially long but it was complicated, full of turns and twisting roads, and Isla remarked, 'It's rather isolated, isn't it? Are chateaus always out in the middle of nowhere like this?'

'No idea,' said Libby. 'I've never been to one before.'

'Our house is out in the middle of nowhere,' said Teddy. 'It's got, like, a scary number of stars in the sky.'

Isla laughed. 'I think it's the usual number of stars, I think it's London that's got the scary low number and makes the universe look lonelier than it actually is.'

'Aw,' said Libby, 'that's a nice way of thinking about it.'

Isla said, 'It's a bit melodramatic.'

'I like it,' said Libby. 'It's nice to feel like you're not alone in the universe.'

'But I don't want to meet aliens *at all*,' said Teddy fervently. 'That would be worse even than ghosts.'

And then they found themselves driving through an open set of curlicue iron gates, and then along a gracious drive lined with poplar trees, perfectly cultivated in a well-manicured row. And then the poplar trees gave way to a little bridge over a stretch of water, and the chateau, set in the middle of its own island, enormous and covered in turrets.

Libby parked the car in the gravel courtyard and they stared up at the magnificence of the house all around them. Their farmhouse was big enough, but it might have filled half of a single wing of the chateau they were looking at now. And it was as well maintained as the poplars along the drive had been. The stone gleamed white in the bright sunshine, and the quoins shone as if they were gilded, and the windows winked at them, clean and sparkling.

Teddy said, sounding awestruck, 'It's a castle.'

'Basically,' Libby agreed.

'What are we supposed to do here?' asked Isla. 'Are you sure a village historian lives *here*?'

Libby shrugged and got out of the car with Isla.

'*Bonjour!*' called a voice off to their left, and then a woman came striding along the courtyard towards them. She had three beautiful greyhounds trotting next to her, so sleek that Isla felt they could have been introduced as the masters of the house and she would have believed it, they suited the house so well. The woman was older and dressed casually, and looked pleasant and welcoming.

'Hello,' Libby said to her, pulling Teddy out of the car. '*Parlez-vous anglais?*'

'Yes,' the woman said, smiling at all of them. 'Are you here for a vineyard tour?'

'Not really,' she said. 'We're here for Raphael.'

'That means you're here for a vineyard tour,' said the woman, and turned on her heel, marching across the courtyard with the dogs in tow and throwing over her shoulder in a sing-song voice, 'This way, *s'il vous plaît!*'

Isla found herself walking along a fairly steep hillside, hands out for balance, following the older woman who was scrambling through the vineyards like a mountain goat, calling shrilly, 'Raphael! Raphael!' The greyhounds bounded in the woman's wake, barking for Raphael as well.

Teddy grumbled, 'See, we could have brought Jack! They have dogs all over the place here!'

140

'You don't know that Jack would have got along with these dogs,' said Libby reasonably.

'Jack gets along with everyone!' Teddy protested. 'Jack even gets along with cats! Jack just doesn't get along with squirrels, and I don't see any squirrels here.'

'I don't think vineyards want to have squirrels,' mused Libby.

Isla found herself grinning. This was not at all what she had been expecting to be doing just a few weeks earlier, and it was reminding her of how adventures really could be good things every once in a while, and right now she wouldn't change a single second of her life because it had led up to this moment.

And right then, when she was grinning at Libby and not really paying attention to where she was going, she basically fell over a body sprawled on the ground in the vineyard.

At first Isla thought her adventure was going to turn into some kind of grisly murder mystery, but then the body moved, and crawled out from underneath the vines, and it was the cute dark-haired American from outside the train station.

Isla gaped at her in shock for a long moment, and then suddenly launched into action.

'Oh, my God, I am *so* sorry!'

'No, no.' She waved her away, tilting her head and looking quizzical but smiling. 'How did you come to be wandering around the vineyard?'

'Well,' Isla began, and then realised that she was going

to have to talk about ghosts and village historians and finished with, 'It's a long story.' She held out a hand to help the woman up from the ground.

The woman dusted herself off and said, 'Well, I'm looking forward to hearing it,' retrieving the straw hat tucked under one of the vines and plopping it on her head. Then she grinned at Isla like she really was looking forward to hearing it.

Isla didn't know what to say.

Libby saved her by saying, 'Hello?' in a questioning tone of voice. 'Everything good?'

'Yeah,' said the American, and shifted her attention to Libby.

'I tripped over her,' Isla said.

'I saw,' said Libby.

'No lasting damage,' said the American. 'I think I'll survive.' She looked back at Isla. 'You've got quite a little party of intrepid travellers along these vineyards.' She gestured to Teddy and the woman with the greyhounds, now a short distance away. A man with a straw hat of his own on his head had popped up in between vines a few rows away, and they were heading steadily towards him. 'I guess you found your friend,' the American continued.

'Oh,' said Isla. 'Yes.' She indicated Libby. 'This is her.'

Libby looked confused but fluttered a little wave. 'Hi.'

'We met outside the train station,' Isla explained. 'When I was waiting for you.'

'Oh,' said Libby. 'Right. Well, I'm Libby.'

'Brooke,' said the woman, and they shook hands.

Libby looked between them and then said, 'Well. I think

I should check in on Teddy and see what he's up to,' and then ran off up the vineyard.

Subtle, thought Isla, and looked back at the American. *Brooke*, she thought. It seemed like a name that suited her, brief and no-nonsense.

Brooke smiled at her and said, 'Well, at least I know your *friend's* name.'

'Oh,' Isla realised. 'Right. It's Isla. I'm Isla.'

'Isla. Nice to meet you.' They shook hands, solemn and formal, in the middle of the vineyard.

'We've already met,' Isla pointed out.

'Yeah, but this is the formal meeting,' said Brooke. 'Plus it gave me the excuse for this.'

'For what?' asked Isla.

Brooke held up their still-joined hands.

Isla, vaguely embarrassed, jerked out of the hold, and then wondered why she'd done that. Brooke clearly had been okay with it.

'Sorry,' Isla said, flustered. 'Sorry. I'm ... I didn't mean to ... Wow, I'm making a mess of everything.'

'No,' Brooke said slowly, but her head was tipped again, as if she was trying to make Isla make sense.

Let me know when you figure me out, Isla thought, and said, 'I've made a habit recently of mucking everything up. Am I mucking this up?'

'I don't think so,' said Brooke consideringly. 'I guess it depends on what you think is happening to muck up.'

Which gave Isla pause.

'Was that too forward?' Brooke asked hastily. 'Sorry, I'm

143

told I have a habit of being too forward. I mean, I'm usually told that by obnoxious men who don't like to have a woman in charge, but, like, *anyway*, maybe *I'm* the one mucking things up.'

Isla found herself smiling widely. Something about Brooke charmed her deeply, and she didn't even know what it was. Brooke wasn't a person who knew her and loved her, but it was like the possibility existed that she might be. Which was absurd, they'd just met, and Isla didn't believe in soulmates or love at first sight or fate, she never really had, and the pointlessness of her world ramblings seemed to have confirmed that for her, but still, as with before, she found herself thinking that every silly life choice had led up to this moment and that was a good thing. Maybe a very good thing.

Isla said, 'I don't think you are.'

'The way you're looking at me,' remarked Brooke, 'I agree.' Then she paused. 'That was too forward again, wasn't it?'

'I think I like it,' Isla admitted.

'I *hope* you like it,' Brooke said.

'Forward again,' said Isla, and Brooke laughed.

'So are you in charge of the vineyard?' Isla asked.

'I don't know if I would say "in charge of",' Brooke replied, with a little thoughtful frown.

'Oh,' said Isla. 'I just meant – because you referenced men having issues with a woman in charge—'

'Oh!' said Brooke. 'Right. Yes. Of course. I mean ... former lives. My former corporate life.'

'It's a former life?'

'I'm trying a bit of an adventure. Roaming around Provençal vineyards.'

Isla smiled wryly. 'Ironic.'

'Why is that ironic?'

'Because I was trying to do the *opposite* of an adventure.'

'Lingering around a train station in a foreign country hoping a friend picks you up isn't an adventure?'

'Not for me,' Isla said ruefully.

'Wow,' said Brooke. 'I can't wait to hear all about what an adventure is usually like for you.'

Isla smiled at her for a second, and then decided to try her hand at being as forward as Brooke. 'So far, I'm really pleased with how this non-adventure is turning out.'

'What a coincidence,' said Brooke, grinning broadly. 'So far *I'm* really pleased with how my *adventure* is turning out!'

Libby called, 'Isla!' and waved her down.

'Let me just ... ' said Isla apologetically, and met her halfway along the vineyard.

'I don't want to interrupt,' Libby said, 'but Raphael apparently has *clippings*.'

'Clippings?' Isla echoed blankly. 'I've missed a lot, haven't I?'

'Oh, a whole thing,' said Libby breezily, 'but *I've* missed even more, I suspect.' She gave her a look.

'Stop it,' Isla told her, caught between embarrassed and smug.

'Uh-huh,' said Libby. 'You can stay here and flirt whilst we go along with Raphael to see his clippings.'

'I ... ' Isla glanced over her shoulder at Brooke, and suddenly felt seized with panic. She had just met this woman, and sure, they were flirting nicely in a vineyard, but what were they going to do when everyone *left*? What if they ran out of things to talk about? What if everything went to hell with a startling quickness that left Isla breathless?

Libby said, 'Really. Stay for a bit. We'll be fine.'

Isla looked at Libby. 'I hope you trust this Raphael. "Clippings" isn't a euphemism, is it?'

Libby laughed. 'Go off to your vineyard worker, we'll catch up later.' She gave her a warm hug and then turned to rejoin the rest of the party.

Isla paused for a moment looking after her, and then turned back to Brooke.

Brooke said, sounding amused, 'Is she leaving you here in the vineyard?'

Isla said, 'What would you say if she did?'

'I'd say that the chateau has lots of rooms,' Brooke replied.

'Oh, that was good,' said Isla. 'Very smooth.'

'I'm very smooth,' responded Brooke. 'Did you see how I smoothly sprawled out on the ground so you would trip over me?'

'I'd totally believe you did that on purpose,' said Isla.

'And it totally worked,' said Brooke.

They smiled at each other for a moment, and then Isla said, 'She's not leaving me. She's going to look at Raphael's clippings. Which I'm hoping is not a euphemism.'

Brooke laughed. 'Not at all. Raphael is an amateur

146

historian. He told me so much about the area when I first moved here.'

'You mean you're not from here?' said Isla, innocently wide-eyed.

Brooke laughed again. 'So what's your friend researching?'

'Ghosts,' said Isla.

'Oh, wow.' Brooke smiled wryly. 'That's a weighty topic.'

'Do you know any ghost stories?' asked Isla.

'Probably too many,' said Brooke, and Isla understood the sentiment. Brooke glanced out over the grapevines, then said, 'So have you spent much time in a vineyard before?'

'One of the glaring gaps in my misspent youth,' said Isla.

'Well, let me show you around,' offered Brooke with a grin.

Raphael took them into the cellar of the chateau, which was so sprawling, with so many twisting dusty corridors coiling off into different directions, that Libby thought you could get lost there for decades.

She said to Teddy, 'Keep close,' physically hauling him in against her.

Raphael said briskly, 'This way, please,' setting off at a quick pace down one of the corridors.

The woman, whose name they still didn't know, said, 'Don't worry, it's safe down here.' The greyhounds raced to lope ahead of Raphael, clearly knowing the way.

Teddy said, 'Are there dungeons down here?'

'For naughty little boys,' Raphael barked.

Teddy sent Libby an alarmed and accusatory look.

Libby said, 'He's joking.'

'Am I?' said Raphael, but then he sent a wink over his shoulder.

The corridor eventually widened into a large storage area, filled with casks on either side that Libby assumed held wine. Down the centre of the long, low-ceilinged room were small, tall tables, stretching in a line. Wine glasses stood ready on the tables, as if this room were always ready to host a tasting party.

'This is the tasting room,' the woman said, which made sense.

Raphael slipped between two of the casks and opened a small door tucked into the stone wall. Beyond the door was a round chamber, lit by narrow windows up by its ceiling, where daylight crept in. The room had a desk covered with papers, and bookshelves overflowing with what looked like photo albums, but they were crowded with bits of yellowed newsprint sticking out of them.

'This,' said Raphael, making an expansive gesture, 'is my history room. Please admire appropriately.'

Libby wasn't sure if this was a sign of Raphael's inexpert English or if Raphael meant to command them to admire it.

She said, 'It's lovely. So they're your archives?'

'If you insist,' said Raphael, humming to himself now as he scurried along the bookshelves, pulling out and then discarding albums.

Teddy said, 'So do you have anything about spies? Or maybe pirates?'

Raphael said, 'Pirates? Bah! But yes, of course, plenty about spies.'

'*Really?*' said Teddy, eyes shining. He looked happier again, the way he had with the pétanque in the village the day before. Libby was happy to see that light back in his eyes.

Raphael placed an open photo album on the desk. 'Adélaïde Faure.'

It was the brunette woman from the portrait in the house, wearing a floppy-brimmed hat and a high fur-collared coat, her hair crimped against her head. She was smiling what seemed like a secretly self-satisfied smile out at the camera, a Mona Lisa sort of smile, that made Libby want to know more about her, more about what she knew to make her smile like that. There was a brief article accompanying the photograph, in French of course, within which Libby could make out the name *Adélaïde Faure*.

'What does it say?' Libby asked of the article, because not only was it in French but the newsprint was so faded she could barely make it out.

'It is a piece about her newest car,' said Raphael. 'Adélaïde was known for her love of cars and horses. Anything that went fast.'

'So I take it she had a fast reputation?' Libby guessed.

'For liking things that went fast,' said Raphael blankly.

'She means *scandalous*,' the woman with the grey-hounds said.

'Oh,' said Raphael. 'Well. Not in France. Why should she cause scandal in France? She spent a great deal of money, of course, but who can blame her? When you have money, you must spend it.'

'So Adélaïde was rich?' Libby said.

'Adélaïde's husband was rich,' Raphael corrected her. 'Marcel Faure. He was older than her, and died shortly after their marriage, and left her with a sizable fortune.'

'And *that* wasn't scandalous?' said Libby.

Raphael shrugged.

'Adélaïde lived in the house I'm renting?' Libby asked.

'Yes. She was fond of the house. It was where she grew up. Although technically when she lived in it as an adult it belonged to her brother. Arnaud Bernard. And that is where *she* comes in.' Raphael put another book on the desk, open now to a photograph of the blonde woman, her hair tucked back into a pretty chignon, with a jaunty cap tipped low over her forehead. Her smile was wide and welcoming and sweet. 'Meet Mary Bernard. The British wife of Arnaud Bernard. They met,' said Raphael, 'during a romantic French summer. Such as you British have been seeking for ever. They married, and Mary moved into the house.'

Libby thought of the romantic French summer she was theoretically currently having. With a few spanners thrown into the works. 'I'm guessing it didn't quite work out the way Mary thought?' she guessed wryly.

'Adélaïde was abroad the summer her brother met Mary. She returned home in the autumn to her house having a new mistress. I am told that they fought like . . . ' Raphael's brow furrowed in the direction of the greyhounds, and then cleared as he remembered the idiom. 'Like cats and dogs.'

They mounted worn, uneven stone steps up to the ground floor of the chateau, to a room that had been remade to sell wine. The ceiling still had an impressive mural of cherubs up above, where it vaulted over their heads, and the fireplaces at either end of the room were elaborately carved, and the long, tall windows were edged in gilding, but the entire space of the room was devoted to sturdy shelves holding bottles of wine, with tasting tables scattered about, in between other bits of bric-a-brac and merchandise.

Libby's head was still deep in the story of the two women who had fought over the house she was living in, these prankster ghosts still fighting for control to this day. A new wife, struggling to find her place in the life of the man she married. At this moment, Libby strongly identified with Mary Bernard.

So when the woman with the greyhounds said, 'Oh, you simply must taste some of the wines,' it took Libby entirely by surprise. It shouldn't have, of course – she was at a vineyard – but still.

'Oh,' said Libby, unsure what to say. 'I ... I'm fighting a headache. I think it's dehydration. The very thought of wine makes my head pound. Besides, I've got to drive us home, and I'm sure Teddy would be bored to death by a

151

whole wine-tasting anyway. We'll just find Isla and see what she's up to.'

Maybe Isla would be done flirting now.

Libby felt selfish for wanting to interrupt Isla's flirtation but she was in a selfish mood at the moment. She really wanted her friend right now, she thought.

'So do you think we learned anything important in there?' Teddy asked as he and Libby stepped out into the courtyard.

'Well, I thought it was interesting,' said Libby. 'Let's go back out to the vineyard and see if we can spot Isla.'

But they met Isla coming back into the courtyard from the vineyard, still with the American, Brooke. They were still talking animatedly to each other, and Libby, despite all of her inner turmoil, smiled. She really was glad that everyone else's holidays seemed to be going well.

'Hello there,' Brooke said pleasantly.

'Hi,' said Teddy.

'You must be Teddy,' Brooke said. 'Isla was telling me all about you, and about your brand new kittens.'

Teddy perked up the way he always did when talk was of the kittens. 'Yes.'

'We've got a stray kitten litter of our own around here,' said Brooke.

'Can I see?' asked Teddy eagerly.

'I'm sure she has better things to do than—' Libby began.

'No, no, not at all,' Brooke said. 'I was hoping to find some-one else to be as excited about the kittens as I am. Everyone else here just keeps complaining about the situation.'

'Can I go?' Teddy asked Libby.

'Sure,' said Libby, because who was she to deny Teddy something so simple when he looked so delighted by it, and Teddy and Brooke immediately took off.

Libby looked at Isla, who was watching Brooke leave, and forced herself not to be so caught up in her own problems. 'So,' she said, as playfully as she could manage, 'how's that going?' She nodded in the direction of Brooke.

Isla looked a little abashed. 'Okay, I think.'

'Better than okay, I think!' Libby protested, grinning.

'Okay, maybe,' Isla admitted. 'She seems really nice.'

'She seems really into you,' said Libby.

'Do you think so? It can be hard to tell.'

'I think so. With my objective viewpoint.'

Isla gave her an arch look. 'You are hardly "objective" about me. But it's okay. How was Raphael and the ghost story?'

'Interesting,' Libby said. 'We learned a lot.'

'Did you want to try any of the wine?' asked Isla.

'No,' said Libby, as casually as she could. 'I'm good.'

Isla just shrugged and glanced off in the opposite direction. Probably still thinking about Brooke.

Chapter Fifteen

Soupe au Pistou: oignons, courgettes, haricots blancs frais, haricots rouges frais, haricots verts, plats frais, pommes de terre, poignée de coquillettes, tomates, gousses d'ail frais, basilic.

'So,' said Sam, as they settled down for their usual dinner in the back garden, under the lingering dusky sky. 'Tell me all about what we have learned of ghosts.'

'So much,' Libby said. 'Raphael was *very* helpful.'

'And their house has kittens, too,' said Teddy. 'And dogs. Jack would be right at home there. Isla's friend Brooke is going to come by and look at our kittens.'

'Isla's friend Brooke?' Sam echoed.

Isla looked up sharply. 'She's coming here?'

'I invited her,' said Libby innocently.

'When?'

'When we were at Château Laurent. Before we left.'

'I don't remember this,' said Isla.

'Well, I was sneaky about it.' Libby winked.

Sam looked between the two of them and grinned. 'Oh, *I* see,' he said.

Isla looked mortified.

So he backed off. 'About the ghosts.'

'Yes. Adélaïde and Mary. Those are their names. They had a rivalry over this house.'

'Over the house?' said Sam.

'Adélaïde grew up here,' Libby explained. 'She married rich and he died and she inherited a lot of money but she loved this house, so she came back here to live as a young widow. Unfortunately, her brother Arnaud was living here, and he married a British woman named Mary who he met one summer when Adélaïde was away. So Adélaïde came home from travelling and there was a new, strange woman living in her house. So they fought over who got to be mistress of it.'

'Why didn't Adélaïde just move out?' Sam asked. 'You say she was rich.'

'This was her childhood home,' said Libby.

Sam, who hadn't seen his childhood home in decades, shrugged. 'Okay. Well, then, why didn't Mary leave? You said she was from England, she could have moved home.'

'She did move home eventually. Although she left Arnaud behind her here. This was Arnaud's house.'

'He couldn't reconcile his sister and his wife?' said Sam.

'Apparently not,' said Libby. 'And eventually Mary left to go home to England. She spent the war years in the English countryside. Arnaud stayed here with Adélaïde. When the war was over, Mary would send her and Arnaud's daughter here to spend summers with Arnaud. Adélaïde wouldn't even stay while the daughter was in residence. She would always leave.'

'Wow,' said Sam. 'That was her niece.' Sophie and Evie had been born when Sam had still been young, and he remembered how taken with them he had been. He couldn't imagine being harsh to one's niece.

'It was also,' said Libby, 'Mrs Dash's Great-Aunt Clarissa.'

'*Oh*,' said Sam. 'So that's how Mrs Dash enters the saga.'

'Anyway,' continued Libby, 'Adélaïde and Mary continue to play pranks on the inhabitants of the house, hoping to get them to leave so one of them can be the dominant spirit.'

Sam frowned thoughtfully. 'But that doesn't make much sense.'

'Why doesn't it make sense?' asked Libby.

'Because they could very effectively make us leave the house by being terrifying,' said Sam.

'They've shut off the electricity and taken away our Wi-Fi,' said Libby. 'Isn't that terrifying enough?'

'They've only shut off the electricity in half the house. That's hardly affecting our ability to stay in the main part. Which is arguably the nicer part. At any rate, you would tell me it's just a story anyway, so it doesn't have to make much sense.'

'I don't know,' said Libby. 'Maybe I'm starting to believe in ghosts, after all.'

Libby had tried her hand at cooking again. She had tried the vegetable soup Pauline made. The vegetable soup Pauline made look so easy, so elemental, so *instinctive*.

Libby had no such instinct, apparently. The vegetable soup was somehow both too salty and entirely devoid of taste. Sam and Isla, being polite, struggled through some empty platitudes about it. Teddy scrunched up his face as dramatically as possible and made the most intense proclamations of disgust.

'That's enough,' Sam told him mildly, which did stop the audible complaining, although it didn't stop his faces.

When Sam took Teddy up to bed, Isla helped Libby clean up.

'I might be defective,' Libby announced abruptly.

'Really?' said Isla. 'That sounds not good.'

'I am devoid of instincts,' Libby explained.

'No, you're not,' Isla denied. 'What instincts?'

Libby sighed, handing Isla the plates to wash. 'I don't know. All of them?'

Isla gave her a look. 'Lib.'

'Cooking instincts, for instance.'

'I don't think there's any such thing,' Isla replied. 'And if there is such a thing, then I don't have them, either.'

'I don't know, you think, like, cooking should be straightforward, put the pieces together, do exactly what you're told, and: success. Except it's not like that. It's tricky.

157

Things go wrong, things surprise you, salt is saltier than you expect.'

Isla laughed, like this was a joke.

'This isn't a joke!' Libby protested.

'Look, I think cooking is trickier than you think. If it were easy, everyone would do it. And restaurants wouldn't be, you know, a huge business.' Isla gave her a sideways look. 'What's this really about?'

'I don't know.' Libby leaned against the kitchen counter, worrying at her thumbnail. Beyond the windows, Provence was pitch black, the impossible stars pressing through it. 'Do you ever get the feeling that . . . that everyone else knows what they're doing with life and just when you think you have it figured out, too, you realise that you . . . don't?'

Isla wiped her hands on a dishtowel, looking thoughtful. 'I . . . I mean. All the time. *All* the time. Why do you think I'm standing in someone else's house in France at the last minute? With no future plans, no goal, no ambition, like . . . If everyone else knows what they're doing and you're the defective one . . . ' Isla looked at Libby helplessly. 'Well, I'm right there with you, Lib.'

When Libby dragged herself up to bed, she stood at the top of the staircase and looked at the two portraits, Adélaïde and Mary, the two women fighting for control of the house, the two women who loved to play pranks.

And the child who had eventually been caught in between them.

Libby pressed her hand to her abdomen and thought at the portrait ghosts, *Well, it's a good joke, I'll give you that.*

Then she walked into the bedroom she was sharing with Sam.

Sam was still awake. Libby wasn't sure if she'd expected that, but suddenly she was so glad that it was true. Even in the midst of all the confusion she was feeling, she was very clear that she wanted Sam. Sam always made everything better.

'You're still awake,' she said, and she could hear the gratefulness in her voice.

Sam put aside whatever he'd been working on and smiled at her. 'I am. Is that a good thing?'

'A *great* thing,' said Libby, crawling into bed beside him. She just wanted to press herself against him and forget about all the worrying she was doing about the future. In the present Sam was here and loved her and she could just let him.

'Good,' he said, sounding pleased, and pulled her in and kissed her head. 'I'm sorry Teddy's been . . . Teddy.'

'It's fine,' Libby said, hoping she sounded convincing in shrugging it off.

'No, it's not fine, and I know it's been rough on you, but . . . he'll come round. I'm actually thinking maybe he needs a little me time. He used to have me all to himself.'

'I know,' said Libby.

'I don't say that to imply that I – that *we're* – not so much happier now. With you. You know that, right?'

'Uh-huh,' said Libby, nodding.

'No. Listen.' Sam adjusted so he could see Libby's face, make her look into his. 'I mean it. You believe me, right? Teddy just is a boy going through a moment. You know how it is.'

Since Libby felt like she was also going through a moment, she kind of understood exactly. 'I do know how it is,' she said. 'And it's fine. I get it, Sam. Please don't worry about it.' She smiled at him, hoping it looked convincing. She really did get this. They all needed processing time, and everything was happening so quickly.

Sam smiled back at her, kissed the tip of her nose. 'Anyway. Have you been having fun catching up with Isla?'

Libby wasn't sure she would call their conversations 'fun'. But she just nodded against Sam's chest.

'Good. She's nice. I like her. Not that you need me to approve your friends, but, you know, I like her.'

'Yeah,' said Libby. 'Good. I'm glad. I like her, too.'

'Your vineyard trip sounded like a good time. What an amazing, wonderful, dramatic ghost story you've uncovered.'

Libby choked a laugh. 'It could be spookier.'

'I'm rather relieved not to have it be a ghost story with a lot of guts and gore. Teddy would attempt otherwise but I'm not sure we would ever get him to sleep in this house again.'

'And would that make you sad?' asked Libby.

'I want to spend the rest of the summer in this house.' Sam sounded surprised. 'Don't you?'

'Yes. I was just checking.'

Sam chuckled. 'It's grown on me. All of its idiosyncrasies. Also growing on me are all of the pastries I keep eating at cafés while I work, but hey, it's a holiday, right? If you can't gain weight on a holiday, when can you gain weight?'

Libby made a noncommittal noise.

'So tell me about Isla's friend Brooke,' suggested Sam.

'Oh,' said Libby, seizing happily on this distraction. 'Yes. Isla's friend *Brooke*.' If someone was going to get their life together during this French countryside summer instead of have it fall apart, it should be Isla.

'Who is she?' asked Sam.

'I have no idea. Some woman Isla met at the vineyard. But apparently they'd met earlier? By the train station? It's unclear. But they were *very* taken with each other. They went for a whole romantic walk through the vineyard.'

'Well, someone should have a French romance,' remarked Sam. 'Not that we aren't having a French romance, but it's a rather different sort of romance.'

Libby settled back against Sam with a little sigh. 'Honestly? Seeing Isla with Brooke today made me happy I'm married. I don't want to have to go back to that again, to meeting new people and feeling them out and gauging their interest and wondering if that person's right for you, if the future you could have together would be the right future for you. I'm happy to . . . to know that now.' Things might be a mess but, thinking about it, there wasn't much she would really change. The thought of going back to life without Sam was impossible. It really put things in perspective.

She looked thoughtfully up at the ceiling as Sam stroked his hand down her arm and pressed a kiss into her hair.

Chapter Sixteen

Dear Pari, It's not much fun here, Dad always has to work 😒. I'm trying to sort out some surprises for you with Jack, though!

Libby forced herself to go back into the village for another cooking lesson with Pauline. She didn't feel like it, but she thought that was exactly why she ought to do it. She needed to get herself out of the house. She needed to face her fears. She needed to conquer cooking.

'You're looking grim,' Pauline remarked. 'That is the wrong attitude with which to approach cooking.'

'I need to conquer cooking,' Libby said staunchly. 'I need to find my proper instincts.'

Pauline lifted her eyebrows. 'Your proper instincts?' she echoed sceptically.

Really, Libby thought, there was a special scepticism only the French could achieve. 'Yes. You know. The proper instinct that allows you to make an omelette.'

163

'An omelette?' said Pauline, looking more and more confused.

'I tried to make an omelette the other day and I was a misery at it. It was raw and then it burned and there was smoke all over the place and, I mean, I swear it doesn't help that the stove I'm using is from the fourteenth century, but I bet *you* would have been able to make an omelette because you would have done it by *instinct* and I just don't have that instinct.'

'The omelette instinct?' Pauline clarified.

'Any instinct!' Libby cried. 'I'm worried I don't have any instinct!'

Pauline employed a perfectly Gallic shrug. 'Cooking can be taught. That's why we're having lessons.'

'I don't mean cooking!' Libby exclaimed. 'I mean—' She cut herself off and looked at Pauline.

Pauline just looked back at her with mild interest. Pauline, who didn't know her at all, really. It suddenly seemed much easier to tell Pauline than any other person.

Libby blurted out, 'I think I'm pregnant.'

'Well, then,' remarked Pauline thoughtfully. 'Are congratulations in order?'

'Yes. I mean, I think so. I don't know. I . . . No one knows. Not even my husband. I haven't told anyone. You're the first person I . . . I didn't realise it until . . . I think maybe the ghosts cursed me.'

'The ghosts?' Pauline echoed.

'There are ghosts. The house is haunted. And I said I didn't believe in the ghosts and the next thing I knew they played this prank on me! And now I'm pregnant! I wasn't supposed to be pregnant on my French holiday! I wasn't supposed to be pregnant at all!'

'Ah. I see.' Pauline was still talking in that even, thoughtful tone, like Libby wasn't saying anything very remarkable. She turned away from Libby to start sprinkling flour along the work surface. 'So the ghosts made you pregnant. I'm sure you and your husband had very little to do with it. That's how it works on French soil: the ghosts do all of it.'

Okay, well, when it was said in such a pragmatic way, it did sound rather silly. 'I mean . . . ' said Libby, and paused to take stock.

'I'm *panicked*,' she said finally, and it felt marvellous to admit it, to let it out.

'Do you not like children?' asked Pauline frankly, slicing up thick pats of bright yellow butter.

'No, I . . . I love children. I'm a teacher. Kids are great.'

'Okay.' Pauline shrugged again, measuring out bright white sugar.

'But, I mean, those kids go home at the end of the day. I don't know if *I* can take care of a kid . . . all the time.'

'No one knows until they do it, I suppose.' Pauline switched on her mixer, turned to retrieve milk from the refrigerator.

'Do you have children?' Libby asked.

'I do not,' Pauline replied. 'But that doesn't mean you should not. Especially if you like them. As you seem to. Have you ever had a pet? That's like having a kid, I hear.'

165

'We already have a dog,' Libby replied distractedly, watching as Pauline splashed milk into the mixing dough. It was mesmerising. 'Well, I don't know, a street dog. But we also already have a kid.'

'Oh, I see.' Pauline left the mixer running, turned to face Libby, crossing her arms and cocking her hip against the counter. 'So you don't wish to have another?'

'No, I mean ... He's not mine. Not that I don't love him!' Libby corrected hastily, hearing how that sounded. 'I love him so much, I love him exactly like he's mine, it's not that I don't love having him, it's that I'm not sure I'm very good at taking care of him. Like, he and my husband, they're such a ... They're such a solid unit. My husband is such a great dad, he's ... He's amazing, and all I've done is ... drag everyone into the French countryside so we can live in a haunted house without electricity.'

'You have no electricity?' said Pauline.

'We have *some* electricity,' Libby allowed.

'Ah. Having some electricity means that it could be worse: You could have none at all.' Pauline shut the mixer off, pulled the dough out.

'It's not that I don't want kids,' Libby continued, because now that she'd started talking about this she felt like she couldn't stop. 'That's not it at all. It's that ... We've never discussed it.'

'You and your husband?' said Pauline.

Pauline really did have a way of making everything Libby said sound silly. She married the man. It seems like they should have had this discussion before getting married. 'I mean, sure, we discussed it in the abstract. "If we have kids someday." We didn't, like, sit down and have a plan for it. I like kids, I said. He also likes kids. He has one already. He likes being a dad. He said he was open to having more.'

'Well,' Pauline remarked, kneading the dough. 'That sounds like a beginning, then.'

'But that's what I mean!' Libby said. 'That's just a beginning! There's a world of difference between this abstract discussion about "oh, yeah, I'm up for kids again someday" and there . . . *being a kid*.'

'Do you think your husband would be very unhappy, then?' asked Pauline simply.

Libby pressed her hand against her abdomen and considered. Maybe . . . Maybe this wasn't about Sam at all. 'No,' she admitted softly. 'I don't know. Maybe I haven't told Sam yet because *I'm* the one freaking out.'

Pauline let there be a moment of silence, and Libby appreciated that. 'How long have you known?' she asked eventually, rolling the dough out now.

'A few days,' Libby said. 'I just found out. You have to understand . . . we weren't planning for this . . . so it's not like I had my eyes peeled for symptoms or something. This has taken me utterly by surprise. I'm freaking out because I thought there would be *preparation*. Like, before the abstract became concrete I thought I'd make a *decision*, that I *wanted* this, *consciously*. And instead it's just a thing that went and happened to me and suddenly there's a whole other person inside me and my life literally has changed in the span of a heartbeat. This summer . . . wasn't supposed to be about *this*.'

'Okay,' Pauline said slowly. 'Okay. I absolutely see where you're coming from. If I suddenly found out I was pregnant, I would definitely freak out. But you have a husband. It seems to me, what is the point of a husband if not to keep you company during your freak-outs?'

'That's . . . a good definition of marriage,' Libby admitted.

'So don't you think you'd feel better if you told him?' Pauline continued. 'You'd feel less like your life has changed in the span of a heartbeat and more like you and he *together* have a life that's changed, and that you'll deal with.'

'That's . . . That's very wise,' Libby replied. 'It just feels like there's a huge gulf between knowing that I should tell Sam about the baby and actually telling him. And I mean . . . Okay, he did make this comment. I don't even know if he would remember it if I brought it up now. But when we were telling everyone on Christmas Street about taking this house for the summer, at first someone thought I might be announcing I was having a baby, and Sam laughed and said, "Oh, God, no" like . . . I don't know, not like a person who was hoping I'd tell him I was having a baby soon.'

'But he didn't know,' Pauline pointed out, as sage as ever. 'He probably meant it as something of a joke.' She was now doing something with butter on the dough that Libby was trying to follow without much success.

'No. I know. Of course he did,' said Libby. 'But then he was talking about . . . about the difficulties of dealing with new things, how he really has to adjust to them, how it takes him time to—'

'That doesn't sound unreasonable,' Pauline said. 'Most people are like that.'

'Right. Right. Yes. Of course.' Libby watched Pauline fold the dough over. It was soothing.

'I really feel like you ought to tell him,' Pauline said. 'I don't think you should be trying to adjust to all of this alone. Cooking can only keep you so much company. I don't think it would be much help in the delivery room.'

'Well, my husband will probably be an expert,' Libby said wryly, 'having gone through all this before. And don't think that *that's* not intimidating, too.'

'You shouldn't let it intimidate you,' Pauline said. 'You're lucky to have such amazing expert help around you. Usually young parents have to fumble through it alone.'

'What if he compares me to Sara?'

'Who's Sara?'

'His late wife.' Libby didn't even realise until she blurted it out that she had been worrying about this all along, a simmer in the back of her mind. She *never* thought of being compared to Sara, but now, with a baby inside her, it seemed likely Sam would inevitably compare everything to his first time around.

'Oh.' Pauline hmm'd thoughtfully, then said, 'He wouldn't. I'm sure he wouldn't. Do you feel like he does that?'

'No. Never. But what if Sara did all of this better?'

'Growing a baby? It's not like there's anything you can do about *that*, that's just a thing bodies do. Sam knows that.'

'Yeah. Yeah.'

Pauline put the dough in the refrigerator, then came back and said, 'You should tell him.'

'You're right. I will. Of course I will. I mean, I have to. I just ... I need some time first, I think. I want to be ... composed when I tell him. I want to be unabashedly happy. I want to be happy, and I want him to be happy, and don't you think my baby deserves that?'

Pauline smiled. 'Every baby deserves the world. And your baby seems like an especially lucky one to me.'

'You're very sweet,' Libby said, 'especially considering you're only supposed to be giving me cooking lessons, not therapy, goodness, I'm so sorry I've been rambling at you.'

'No, no,' Pauline said. 'This is part of what cooking helps with. It isn't instinct. It's an opportunity to work at something that's more achievable. You cook and cook and your mind solves all your problems without your noticing, while you're focused on the spices and herbs, the bubbling and the sizzling and all the lovely smells.

'Now. I'm about to teach you how to make pain au chocolat. What do you think about that?'

'I think if you could pull it off then you would be very popular in my French farmhouse,' Libby said.

Pauline laughed.

Sam found Teddy with Jack in the back garden, trying to teach him to walk on his hind legs.

'What's this we're working on?' Sam asked.

'I want him to be able to walk like a circus dog,' Teddy replied. 'I think Pari would be so impressed.'

Sam smiled. 'No doubt. So. I thought maybe we could go exploring.'

'Exploring?' Teddy echoed, sounding surprised.

'Here we are in France, and we've barely seen any of the countryside. Shouldn't we see what there is to discover?'

Teddy was still looking at him in evident surprise. 'Don't you have to work?'

Sam thought of how Teddy must feel so unimportant in his life at the moment, that this wasn't just about Libby but also about work. When Sam wasn't at work, he was with Libby; when Sam wasn't with Libby, he was at work. No wonder Teddy was feeling dejected and out of sorts.

'I've been working a lot, haven't I?' said Sam.

Teddy looked down at Jack, who'd got the treat Teddy had been bribing him with and was munching on it enthusiastically. He shrugged. 'I mean, I get it. You've got weird hours because of the States and everything.'

'Just because you get it doesn't mean you have to like it,' noted Sam. 'I'm sorry about that. I don't like it, either. Maybe, here in France, I'm going to turn over a new leaf and be better about taking some time off. Some time off for you. Time to go exploring, what do you say?'

Teddy looked at him, and Sam thought he would deem that expression a 'tentative beam'.

'Could be fun,' said Teddy.

Libby went home with pain au chocolat, no closer to feeling ready to tell Sam about the baby, never mind feeling able to be a mother, but feeling slightly more able to make dough than she would ever have supposed.

Teddy was marvellously enthusiastic, in raptures.

Sam said, 'This pain au chocolat is miraculous.'

Libby thought of how she could definitely use a few more miracles.

Isla was not nervous about Brooke's impending visit *at all*.

'What time did you say she was coming?' she asked Libby, and pretended that wasn't the fiftieth time she had asked that question.

'She didn't say,' Libby answered, incredibly patient. 'She just said that today was a much better day for her to drop by than yesterday would have been. I'm telling you,' she went on, 'Brooke likes you, you just have to keep being your charming self. And, in the meantime, I'm going to make the two of you a very romantic dinner.'

'Oh, is that what you're doing?' asked Isla dubiously, because whatever Libby was doing could only generously be described as 'cooking'.

Libby laughed again. 'Well, it's what I'm *trying* to do. This is my particular brand of "cooking". I'm practising what I've learnt. You shall get the benefit of my newfound knowledge. Hopefully. Of course, you'll have to eat with the rest of us, so I don't know how romantic it'll be.'

Isla looked at Libby a little helplessly.

'Honestly,' Libby said, 'you're going to be fine.'

'All of my previous relationships would tell you I am *not* going to be fine,' Isla pointed out.

'It only takes one,' said Libby.

'And don't pretend that you weren't terribly nervous when you first started dating Sam, either,' said Isla. 'I seem to remember some fairly rambling voicemails being left for me in those early days.'

At least Libby looked abashed. 'Okay, *maybe*—'

The house's imposing doorbell gonged through the rooms, bouncing off all the hard surfaces and vibrating inside their heads.

'We really *must* do something about that,' mused Libby.

'Do you think that's Brooke?' asked Isla anxiously.

'Probably. Shall I get it or would you—'

'I'll get it,' Isla decided, and went running into the front hall.

And then stopped right before the front door to smooth her hair down and tuck her clothes into place. She hoped she looked as fetching as possible, considering that she hadn't made any effort to look fetching at all in her previous two meetings with Brooke.

Brooke was indeed at the door, wearing her ever-present floppy straw hat to shield her from the sun. Behind her, in the farmyard, Isla could see her bike propped up against the cistern.

'Hi there,' Brooke said. 'I was hoping you'd be here.'

'Did you think I'd run away?' asked Isla and then realised how in-character that would have been for her. She'd spent a lot of time running away lately.

'Maybe,' said Brooke, grinning. 'I didn't want to come on too strong. I didn't know if you'd approve of your friend's just . . . inviting me here.'

'Well,' said Isla, 'I am officially appalled.'

'And unofficially?'

'Happy you're here,' said Isla, and grinned.

They stood there grinning at each other like idiots for a few moments, and then Brooke cleared her throat and said, 'I am ostensibly here to see the kittens.'

'Ah, yes,' said Isla. 'And it would never do to see the kittens without Teddy. Come in, come in, Teddy's in the back garden.'

Brooke stepped into the front hall and gazed about it with interest. 'It's a lovely old house. It's been locked up for a while. It's nice to see some life in it. I don't like to see old houses lonely.'

'Have you lived here long?' asked Isla.

'Oh,' said Brooke. 'No. Not really. Not long at all. But you know how quickly you can get used to particular landmarks in a new place. This was my abandoned farmhouse landmark.'

Isla considered whether or not to pin Brooke down further on exactly how long she'd been in the area. Then again, Isla wasn't exactly volunteering all sorts of information about her life, so she decided to just let it be.

They had time to decide to share these things with each other. An entire summer, in fact.

Isla led Brooke through to the kitchen, Brooke saying, 'I have to say, it's not really what I thought a haunted house would look like.'

'What did you think a haunted house would look like?' asked Isla.

'Darker, I suppose. Dustier. With blood dripping from the ceilings.'

'Well, that's graphic,' remarked Isla. 'You remember Libby, of course.' She gestured to Libby as they entered the kitchen.

'Hello,' said Libby, wiping her hands on her apron and coming forward to give Brooke a kiss. 'It's so good to see you again.'

'Oh,' said Brooke, and reached into the satchel she was wearing to pull out a bottle of wine. 'This is for you.'

'You didn't have to,' said Libby.

'It's a thank-you. For inviting me to dinner. And maybe a bribe to invite me again,' said Brooke.

'That depends entirely on Isla,' Libby grinned.

'Okay,' Isla decided, 'before this goes any further, I am going to duck out in the back garden to fetch Teddy.'

The kittens got bigger every day. They mewled louder and louder by their mum, who daily continued to look very unimpressed by all the humans who visited her. Although she at least seemed to tolerate their presence better. She hissed energetically at Jack, though, who was clearly intimidated enough not to go near her.

'He respects the power of a mama cat,' said Brooke. 'He's a very smart dog.'

Teddy nodded sagely. 'Jack is the best. He knows everything. He's changed all of our *entire lives.*'

Brooke smiled at Teddy. 'All dogs save lives.'

'Yeah, but Jack is special,' said Teddy.

Brooke's smile widened into a grin, and Isla felt curiously like maybe her entire heart was melting inside her chest. Brooke said, 'I believe you.' Then she looked at Isla, and Isla could just imagine what the expression on her face looked like, but Brooke just winked at her.

Libby said, 'Let's leave the kittens be. Isla, I'm sure Brooke would love to see the grounds while I finish the dinner.'

'Would she?' asked Isla drily, because Libby could not be more obvious.

'She can tell us if it would make a good vineyard,' explained Libby innocently.

'Okay,' said Isla, and tried to make it seem like she was only doing this because Libby was being ridiculous, when in fact her heart had decided to stop melting and start trying to run away, racing inside her, at the prospect of a private walk with Brooke. 'I'll try to pretend I know anything about the grounds.'

'I'm looking forward to this,' said Brooke, and she genuinely looked as if she was.

Isla, distracted by Brooke beside her, set off in a random direction, hoping something pretty might be in front of them. Then again, everything in France was pretty. Including Brooke.

Brooke said, 'I don't know if I can tell you if you should plant vines. My knowledge of vineyards doesn't extend to starting new ones.'

'That's okay,' Isla said. 'We are not at all interested in planting vines. We couldn't, it's not like we own this place. Libby's taken it for the summer from a friend of hers who owns it. She only said that thing about the grapevines as a transparent reason for getting us alone together. So,' she added hesitantly, 'if you don't want to be alone together, I completely understand, and you can just, like, take off now.'

'Isla,' Brooke said gently, and Isla couldn't resist looking over at her, meeting her eyes, and then she felt caught enough that she stopped walking, and they just stood, still, on the hillside behind the farmhouse, as the French sun set and turned the air golden all around them. 'I'm very happy to be alone together,' said Brooke, and smiled.

Isla whispered, 'If this is a dream, I don't want to wake up.'

'Agreed,' said Brooke, and kissed her.

Chapter Seventeen

Artichauts à la barigoule: artichauts violets, gousses d'ail, carottes, oignons, citron, thym, feuille de laurier, vin blanc sec ...

With a lot of concerted effort, the kitchen table had been dragged out into the garden, and someone had lit candles all up and down it. Libby had given up on cooking. She didn't want to ruin the evening. She'd begged Pauline to make *pistou* soup and artichokes *barigoule* and tried to pretend she believed Pauline when she assured her she could have made it all herself (she did not believe her at all). But with Pauline's *pistou* soup and artichokes *barigoule*, the evening felt unabashedly romantic, as twilight descended and fireflies lit up down in the olive grove. Isla felt pink and well-kissed and wasn't even embarrassed about how over the top the dinner was. She did notice that Libby avoided the wine but Libby was doing it so smoothly that Isla wasn't sure anybody else had noticed.

She was unexpectedly relieved to not have to carry the

dinner conversation alone, though. She wasn't sure she was up to any level of conversation, so it was nice to have everyone else around.

'So the wine comes from your vineyard?' Sam asked, sniffing at his glass and swirling it around. 'Well, the vineyard where you work?'

'Yes. Grabbed a bottle on my way out the door,' said Brooke. 'It's always easy to grab a bottle when you've got a vineyard right outside.'

'It's good,' said Sam.

'I'll tell the owner,' grinned Brooke.

'So how did you two meet?' Brooke asked Sam and Libby.

'It's all because of Jack,' said Sam. 'Because Jack is *magic*.'

'Oh, right,' said Brooke. 'He changed all of your lives.'

'He really did,' said Sam. 'Were it not for Jack ...' He smiled at Libby. 'Would we be married?'

Libby smiled back. 'I don't know. You probably would have had to work a lot harder instead of relying on canine charm.'

Sam laughed.

Libby said, leaning down to scratch behind Jack's ears, 'It's just nice to have a connection with people. And Jack provides that connection between all of us on Christmas Street.'

Isla was struck by the words, by having that sense of connection.

Brooke said, sounding as reflective as Isla felt, 'Yeah. I get that. It can be easy in modern life, with everything going on, to just ... not make those connections.' She glanced at Isla, sent her a quick smile.

'Exactly,' said Libby. 'So Jack binds us all together.'

'And,' said Sam, 'he helped a very lonely little boy and his equally lonely father be much less lonely. An achievement I can never thank him for enough.'

'Hence why he gets special treatment like holidays in France,' teased Brooke.

Sam tipped his glass in a little toast. 'Yes.'

'Lucky dog,' said Brooke.

'Lucky people,' said Sam into his wine glass. 'And how did you come to end up in France, working at a vineyard? That must have been a stroke of luck in itself.'

'It was ... ' Brooke paused, then said, 'It seemed like a good place to make an escape. Start over. I felt like I needed that, you know?'

'I know,' Isla said. 'Sometimes you just feel like you need that.'

Brooke gave her a smile.

After dinner, Isla walked Brooke out, into the farmyard lit by the bright moon.

'I think ...' said Brooke thoughtfully, like she was pondering a great puzzle in her head.

Isla watched her, curious as to what the conclusion might be.

Then Brooke leaned forward and cupped a hand against

Isla's cheek. Isla couldn't help that her eyes fluttered closed and she leaned into Brooke's touch.

Brooke said, still in that same considering tone, 'Yes. I thought so.'

Isla managed to open her eyes to look at her, limned in moonlight, painfully gorgeous. She looked ethereal, like one of the ghosts the house was known for, like if Isla moved or even breathed too hard, she might disappear altogether. Isla whispered, 'Think what?'

Brooke whispered back, as if she completely under-stood Isla's unwillingness to break the spell around them, 'That it might be a good idea to ask you out on a proper date.'

'We haven't had any proper dates yet?' Isla murmured. 'I don't know what I will do with a proper date. I might be too addled to survive.'

'Too addled,' Brooke echoed, a smile in her voice. 'I hope you keep saying things like that to me. I love them.'

'You're absurd,' Isla chided, meaning the exact opposite, that Brooke was lovely and charming and perfect.

Brooke smiled like she knew exactly what Isla meant and said, 'Let's go on a proper date. What do you think?'

Isla had to agree.

Libby woke long before Sam and Teddy left to go explor-ing, but she pretended that she didn't because she woke up queasy and that was something that definitely needed

181

to be hidden from Sam for the time being. She had clearly tempted fate being grateful for her lack of morning sickness the day before. Once they had left, she went downstairs and tore into a piece of bread, because she'd read in a surreptitious online search that putting something in your stomach was supposed to help, no matter how much you didn't want to do it.

Feeling marginally more like herself, Libby wondered vaguely where Isla was. She decided to shower and get dressed and then she wandered through the house looking for her.

She found her in the oldest part of the house, looking at the tiny kittens. 'Hey,' she said in greeting, and then collapsed down next to her.

'Hey,' Isla said, glancing at her. 'Well, you look kind of terrible.'

Libby groaned and tipped her head back against the wall. 'Do I? Well, it hasn't exactly been a good morning.'

'Oh, no.' Isla looked appropriately concerned. 'What happened?'

'No, it's . . .' Libby looked at Isla and suddenly what she wanted more than anything else in the world was to tell her. To tell *someone*. 'I'm pregnant.' And there, as soon as it was said, it was an enormous relief, a weight lifted. And then Isla yelped, '*What*?' and that shocked reaction made Libby feel less relieved, thinking of how much more shocked Sam was going to be.

'Shh,' Libby said reflexively, even though they were the only ones around. 'Nobody knows yet.'

'Sorry,' Isla whispered, 'that was the wrong response. Congratulations!'

Libby smiled wanly and tried to feel like she deserved the congratulations.

Then Isla narrowed her eyes. 'Hang on, no one knows. Not even Sam?'

Libby shook her head.

'Lib. Why not?'

'It's a bit unexpected,' Libby confessed. 'I don't know what he's going to say.'

'He'll probably be delighted!'

'You just shrieked at me,' Libby pointed out.

'Well, I mean, once he gets past the shock, I'm sure it'll be fine.'

'Let's not talk about me,' Libby decided, because this wasn't helping matters. 'Let's talk about you.'

'Oh, dear,' said Isla, but she couldn't hide the smile that crossed her face.

Libby grinned, delighted to see Isla so happy. 'Things seemed like they went well with Brooke last night?'

'They went really well,' Isla admitted. 'Which is *not* me expressing support for your deviousness in manipulating Brooke into dinner here.'

'I was neither devious nor manipulative!' protested Libby. 'I merely invited her to look at some . . . kittens.' She gestured towards the kittens, grinning.

Isla shook her head and rolled her eyes but the same goofy smile stayed on her face, so Libby knew that was all just for show.

Libby said, 'So what's the next move?'

'A date,' Isla admitted, with that smile widening.

'I knew it!' crowed Libby triumphantly.

'Which direction shall we go in this time?' Sam asked Teddy, and Teddy closed his eyes and turned in a circle and pointed.

And they set off, Jack trotting happily next to them.

This was what they'd been doing, he and Teddy: exploring, just as he'd promised. And the world hadn't ended. He still had time to do his work. He was managing it all. He was, actually, really enjoying their French summer. He felt like he'd settled into it. As he watched Teddy walk beside him, cast in that golden Provençal light, going on about the kittens, he thought that it seemed like a moment he wanted to freeze, keep for ever, this brief shining moment with his son who had once been a little boy who had once been a baby and who now was his own person and would keep becoming more of his own person.

'I'm hoping to find the key,' Teddy said, as they walked up and down rows of lavender, drunk on the scent.

'The key to what?' Sam asked.

'The clock. Remember the grandfather clock was missing a key? Maybe we'll find it.'

Sam looked around them with raised eyebrows. 'In lavender fields?'

Teddy shrugged. 'You never know.'

Sam looked at his American-born son in the middle of these lavender fields and had to admit, 'I guess you don't.'

184

Chapter Eighteen

You should treat a sprained ankle with ice and
elevation and plenty of rest!

Brooke arrived being driven by Raphael, in a raggedy pick-up truck that jolted its way over the rutted drive leading up to the farmhouse. Isla looked at the truck's approach and frowned, then retreated into the house, calling for Teddy.

Naturally Jack answered first, because Jack was usually the most reliable member of the household. He came barking joyfully at her call.

'If only you had the ability to tell me if I'm overdressed for our date,' Isla remarked.

Jack barked and wagged his tail and looked generally offended that Isla didn't think he knew everything there was to know about fashion.

Isla said, 'Okay, I take it back, you're right, you are definitely a clever enough dog to determine if I'm overdressed, but you may not be able to tell me properly, as I fail to speak Dog.'

Jack looked more willing to accept that characterisation of the situation, although still sad.

And then Teddy came into the room.

'What's up?' he asked, not sullen like he was with his parents but not exactly enthusiastic, either. And he looked windblown and raggedy, gone to basics on the French land. Isla thought of the Lost Boys but thought that was too depressing a comparison. He merely looked like a child in the most idealised guise. And troubled in the way that children were, about the most elemental of things. Isla, looking at him, could remember being that way herself. Now she was all caught up in panicking that her red-and-white polka-dot sundress might be too much.

'Brooke's here,' Isla told them.

Teddy looked at the window. 'Yup,' he confirmed happily.

'I need you to tell me what she's wearing,' said Isla.

Teddy gave her a quizzical look. 'Why can't you just—'

'Because then she'll see me!' Isla exclaimed. 'I mean, she could see me. She might. If she looks up. And sees me at the window. And I don't want her to know I'm looking out the window.'

Teddy shrugged. 'We could tell her she must have seen one of the ghosts.'

'Can you please just tell me what she's wearing?' Isla begged.

Teddy looked long-suffering at the absurd foibles of adults but consented to finally look out the window. 'She's wearing jeans. And a white T-shirt. And a silly hat.'

'Oh, dear,' Isla fretted, looking down at the skirt gently

pleated all around her. 'I'm overdressed. I knew it! I was worried! I mean, it's the middle of the afternoon, why would I dress like I'm going to a fancy dinner party?'

'I'm sure it's fine,' Teddy said with a shrug, completely unconcerned, as untroubled as only a child could be, Isla thought.

Isla made a frustrated sound.

'You look really pretty,' Teddy said, unexpectedly kind. 'I'm sure Brooke will think you look really pretty.'

'Yeah, but the thing is,' Isla explained, 'when you're going on a date, you have to look the *same amount* of pretty.'

'This sounds complicated,' said Teddy.

'You have no idea,' Isla replied.

'Dating seems like a lot of work,' Teddy assessed frankly.

'Truer words were never spoken,' Isla informed him briskly. The doorbell blared out over the house, setting Jack to enthusiastic barking. 'Look,' Isla said, 'can you distract Brooke for me while I run and change quickly?'

'You look perfectly nice!' Teddy protested.

'Please?' Isla begged.

Teddy took pity on her. 'Okay. Don't worry. I'm on the job.' He stood a little straighter, like a military general getting ready to salute, and Isla did indeed feel reassured that her date was in decent hands.

She dashed up the stairs and tore apart her wardrobe until she could find her best pair of jeans, the pair that was comfortable enough for her to move around in but still made her look pretty magical, and a soft blue shirt with flowy sleeves that was a little dressier than a T-shirt. She wanted Brooke to know she'd put in effort. Not that she thought Brooke hadn't put in effort in her T-shirt. But still. She was stumbling out the door and into her espadrilles at the same time, overhearing Teddy saying to Brooke, 'No, I'm sure Isla's around here somewhere, this place just has a lot of rooms.'

Isla supposed this was Teddy's way of distracting Brooke. 'I'm here!' Isla shouted, dashing past the ghost shrine into the front hall, where Brooke was standing, looking knowing and possibly also fond, although probably Isla was just imagining that.

'You were lost,' Brooke remarked.

Isla knew she blushed. 'Well. Not really. I mean. It's a big house.'

Teddy looked very bored and completely disinterested in the mechanics of dating.

'Can I go now?' Teddy asked, fidgeting. 'Is everything set now?'

'Yup,' Isla said brightly. 'Totally fine. You can both run along now.' Teddy gave her an unimpressed look and ran off with Jack.

Brooke said, 'I imagine that adults are very exhausting to them.'

'Yeah,' Isla replied, 'when you think about it, it's the adults around them who give children all their cares.'

'We ruin everything,' Brooke agreed, and then, 'You look stunning.'

'Oh.' Isla fiddled with her sleeves, hoping she looked nonchalant and casual. 'It's nothing. But thank you.'

Brooke looked amused, like Isla wasn't fooling her for a second. There was something unnerving about Brooke, like she could really *see* Isla, like she had a way of looking Isla had never encountered in anyone else. But Isla felt like it was unnerving only because it was unusual and unknown. She had the definite feeling that she could get very used to feeling *seen*.

Brooke said, 'I've got a surprise for you,' and took her hand to lead her outside.

Isla felt like she would have followed Brooke anywhere but she stopped right in the front courtyard to say, 'Ta-da!' and point dramatically at two bicycles propped up beside each other. One of them was Brooke's usual bicycle, with a picnic basket strapped to it.

'What do you say?' Brooke asked. 'Up for a ride through the Provençal countryside?'

It was not at all what Isla had been expecting but it was a beautiful day, warm without being unbearable, with a light delicious breeze that smelled like the perpetual lavender on the air in Provence, and Isla could think of nothing more perfect.

'Yes,' she beamed. 'Let's go.'

Isla was regretting her agreement twenty minutes later, when she was beginning to realise that maybe she didn't know how to ride a bike well enough to negotiate the hair-pin bends and narrow roads of the French countryside. It wasn't that Isla didn't know how to ride a bike – because she did – but more like she had never trained for the Tour de France. Brooke, meanwhile, rode a bike like they were competing in the Tour de France at that very moment, zipping along the roads, negotiating around the occasional lumbering car like they were mild obstacles. Meanwhile Isla's hands were tight around the handlebars and she felt like it was taking all of her energy and attention to keep the bike upright and keep herself not-run-over-by-a-car. Every once in a while Brooke glanced over her shoulder at her, and she looked lit up from within, delighted, and Isla managed a smile back and hoped she looked half as interesting to capture Brooke's attention for a little while.

They paused on the shoulder of the road, where some straggling pieces of grass tried to assert themselves against the dry dirt and the encroaching asphalt. The hills of Provence rolled out below them, stretching into infinity, hugging the planet until it curved off into space. Isla, trying to catch her breath, focused on the vista and did seem to feel a growing awareness of a world so much larger than her that surely she would be able to survive something as simple as a bicycle ride, given how complex the world could get, given how *vast* it was.

Brooke said, 'I thought we could find a good spot and settle in for a picnic.'

Leaving the bikes behind sounded like an ace idea to Isla. 'Sounds lovely,' she enthused.

Unfortunately, they clearly should never have paused their forward momentum, because, asked to start back up again, Isla found her bike feeling shaky, her grip on it wobbly, and she tried to ride it, tried to correct an off-balance list to the left by leaning to the right, and suddenly a lorry came careering its way too fast around the curve up ahead, blaring its horn at Isla. Isla was probably not in any very real danger, but she panicked and swerved too sharply and she couldn't have told you exactly how it happened but she found herself on the dusty ground of the shoulder and the bike skidded away from her into the middle of the road.

'Isla!' Brooke cried, and turned her bike around to come pedalling furiously back to her.

Isla was so mortified that she wanted the ground to swallow her whole. It didn't, so she supposed she had to come up with some way to make it through the next few minutes. Her plan was vaguely to pretend that no major thing had happened, so she went to get herself up to cheerily proclaim that she was absolutely fine and how odd it was that she had found herself in this unusual predicament . . .

. . . except that when she went to stand her ankle refused to accept weight and she promptly tumbled back down again. That actually hurt more than the original crash had, or maybe the adrenalin was just wearing off, because she found herself on her back with the wind knocked out of her, staring up at the compelling bright blue of the sky overhead. The same sky everywhere, she thought vaguely, and yet the sky seemed different everywhere.

This blue seemed so *French*.

'Isla,' said Brooke urgently, as she hurried over and dropped to her knees beside her.

Isla squinted up at her. 'I was hoping the ground would swallow me up. No such luck, I guess.'

'If you were hoping the ground was going to swallow you up, well, I guess flinging yourself violently against it is one technique,' remarked Brooke. 'What happened? Did you hit your head?'

'No,' said Isla, wincing as she sat up. 'Mostly what's wounded is my pride. And my ankle.'

'I'm much more worried about your ankle than your pride,' said Brooke. 'I mean, not that I'm not worried about your pride. But your pride shouldn't be hurt at all. That truck was going a million miles an hour.'

'Not quite. I think I'm just a terrible cyclist.' Isla drew in a breath as, with Brooke's help, she carefully got to her feet. 'I should have said something.'

'You're not a terrible cyclist,' Brooke said. 'I was being ridiculous thinking that you would—'

'Oh, God, please don't blame yourself,' Isla said, limping along with Brooke. 'I feel terrible now. It was such a lovely idea for a date. So romantic.'

'It was ridiculous,' grumbled Brooke, her floppy hat shading her face so Isla couldn't see her expression.

'It was lovely,' Isla said again softly. 'It was so lovely.'

Brooke looked up at her, and whatever she saw on Isla's face made her slow, her own expression growing softer. They stood there for a moment on the side of the road, Isla leaning heavily on Brooke to save the weight on her ankle, and just looked at each other, and even with her ankle throbbing and her clothes dusty and twisted and probably the beginning of sunburn across the bridge of her nose, she still thought that this might be the most romantic moment of her entire life.

She couldn't tell if that said more about her previous relationships, or about this burgeoning one with Isla. Either way, she wanted to bottle this moment for ever, to open up and pour herself a glass of it in the dead darkness of winter, when she needed a dose of summer, and heat, and light, and maybe Brooke.

Another car whipped its way past, kicking up enough dust in its wake that they were both set to coughing, and the moment was broken.

Brooke said, 'There's no way you can pedal your way back to the farmhouse. I'll have to call for some help.'

'God,' Isla grimaced. 'This is *so* embarrassing.'

Brooke grinned at her. 'It's a thing to tell the grand-kids about.'

Isla blushed a little at the mention of grandkids but said firmly, 'This is *not* a story that's being passed on.'

Brooke laughed.

They smiled at each other soppily.

Brooke didn't make a move to call for help.

Isla said, 'You know. While we wait for help to come. I bet we could still have our picnic.'

Brooke's lips curved in delight. 'Excellent idea.'

'Should we get you a doctor?' Libby fussed worriedly, as Brooke helped Isla up the stairs.

'No,' Isla denied. 'It's stupid. I'm embarrassed. Don't call anybody.'

'Isla . . . ' sighed Libby.

'Brooke, tell her it's fine,' Isla commanded.

'It's probably not fine,' Brooke said.

'Brooke! And to think I was actually starting to feel warmly towards you.'

Brooke grinned, unrepentant.

'It's not even much of a sprain,' Isla said. 'I think if I just put some ice on it, it'll be good as new tomorrow.'

They made it to Isla's room, and she reclined on the bed gratefully. Brooke stuck a folded-up blanket underneath her ankle to elevate it, and took off Isla's shoes. Isla tried not to focus too much on Brooke's hands on her legs as she gingerly felt the swelling of her ankle, but probably Isla being more worried about Brooke touching her than any pain she might be in indicated that Isla was right and this was nothing to call a doctor over.

'Well,' Brooke announced. 'It doesn't seem too swollen.'

'Do you have medical training?' Libby asked sceptically.

'It's fine,' Isla said firmly. 'I'm fine. I have had much worse injuries. I've broken lots of bones in my time.'

'That doesn't exactly make me feel better,' said Libby, alarmed.

Isla gave Libby a look that she hoped communicated, *Please don't add to my Brooke-induced humiliation.*

Apparently the look was effective, because Libby said, 'Fine. I'll go and get you some ice,' and left them alone.

They looked at each other, both started talking at the same time, laughed, and then Isla said, 'You should go first.'

'You're the injured one,' Brooke said graciously, gesturing to her. 'You should go first.'

Isla said, 'Please don't call any more attention to my injury, I'm embarrassed enough.'

'You shouldn't be,' Brooke said, her voice a low murmur. 'You've looked adorable this whole time.'

Isla blushed again. Brooke made her blush *so much*. She managed to say, 'Despite all of this,' and pointed to her ankle, 'I've had a great time today.'

'So have I. All of that included. Because every moment with you is perfect,' said Brooke earnestly. 'It doesn't need to be qualified.'

Isla thought if she blushed any harder she would spontaneously combust. She said, 'You're too good to be true, and I'm worried that I'm much too boring for you. You love grand adventures.'

'How do you know that?' Brooke asked.

'You moved here, to a place you didn't know and where you didn't know anyone. And you've made a real go of it. You clearly love it here, have a whole sense of community around you.'

'You are just as adventurous as me. Here you are in the same foreign country, with a community around you. You just seem to classify your adventurous streak as a fault in yourself, something to be resisted, that you want to take chances and go places and see and do things you're not expected to. All of that is adventure, and you think it's a character flaw, and I think it's spectacular.'

Isla stared at her.

Brooke leaned forward and whispered, 'Sometimes I worry I've done adventures the wrong way, that I had a lot of them but none of them made me feel *alive*. None of them made me feel like it was worth it. And I felt so ungrateful, I've had the sort of things happen so many people would be jealous of, and instead . . . I've always been looking for something more. Maybe I . . . Maybe I need to find the right mix. Maybe I've just never gotten it right.'

Isla kept staring at Brooke for a long moment, and when she finally managed to speak, it was just to say, 'Me, too.'

Pauline gave Libby another one of her assessing 'hmm's when she saw her.

'It's fine,' Libby said. 'I'm fine.'

'You still have not told your husband?'

'No,' Libby said. 'My brain did not magically solve my problem while I was cooking.'

'I think,' remarked Pauline, 'that my recommendation is that you cease thinking of it as a problem. You must live with this for a very long time, you must learn to make it into something bearable. Desirable even.'

That should be easy, Libby thought. It was a baby. A tiny human inside her. That was terrifying but it was also something that Libby had always vaguely wanted. She hadn't wanted it to be made concrete so soon, so abruptly, but ... this was definitely *desirable*. Maybe all her brain needed was to get used to it, humming away in the background while she cooked, until it became such a prosaic thing that her panic faded and all that was left was the desire. 'Do you think that's possible? To just switch off your thinking like that?'

Pauline gave another of those shrugs that so resembled her father and said, 'No. Not really. It's not a switch. It's more gradual. It's like a sunset. It happens gradually, and then suddenly all at once. It's like that. You cease thinking of this as a problem, and eventually you'll be surprised to wake up one morning and find the solution to it there, all along.'

'That sounds like magic,' said Libby dubiously.

'And you live in a haunted house,' Pauline pointed out. 'Maybe it's time to start believing in magic.' She gave her a knowing look. 'In the meantime, shall we try cooking? How do you feel about that?'

'Like maybe I'll learn cooking through magic, too,' said Libby drily.

'You will,' Pauline agreed confidently. 'You'll see. Now. My plan for today is for us to try some meat.' She gestured to the counter, where Libby noticed the butcher cuts for the first time.

'Is that leg of lamb?' Libby asked.

'Yes,' said Pauline. 'Do you like it?'

'Love it,' Libby said. 'I don't make it much, though. I don't really know what to do with it.'

'Well. We are going to serve it with a green olive tapenade crust. It's going to change your life,' said Pauline confidently.

The lamb with green olive tapenade crust didn't change her life as much as the baby growing inside her was going to, but even Teddy said it was the most delicious meat he'd ever had, and he didn't even mind that it was *lamb*.

'Your cooking is getting to be pretty good,' he said assessingly. He even smiled at her.

Libby felt like that was a huge triumph. *It happens gradually, and then suddenly all at once,* she thought.

Brooke arrived for their second date in a car. She was still dressed casually, but not as casually as she had been for their last date, and Isla, who had carefully chosen navy blue capri trousers and a white blouse with a bow-tie detail, was relieved when Libby, poised as lookout, said, 'She's wearing chic black cigarette trousers. I covet them actually.'

Isla breathed out a sigh of relief. 'Good. Maybe it will be a less athletic date.'

Libby gave her a grin. 'Who doesn't want athletic dates, hmm?'

'Look,' said Isla, 'I just started getting my ankle back

to regular. We can do all manner of athletic things above the ankle.'

'Usually the more important place for athletic things,' Libby remarked.

'Goodbye now,' announced Isla primly.

'Have fun!' Libby called after her.

Isla went out to meet Brooke, who smiled at her and said, 'We're going to take a car this time. Lower risk. I mean, maybe. Considering the high incidence of car accidents, maybe not lower risk. Hmm. This is probably not good date conversation, is it?'

Isla smiled at her. 'I'm okay with it.' Then again, Isla was probably going to be okay with whatever Brooke did. Isla was really easy when it came to Brooke, was what she was learning.

Brooke said, 'How's your ankle? It looks good from here.'

Isla stuck it out and did a full rotation playfully. 'Good as new, see? Fully recovered. No lasting damage.'

'No impact made on you, hmm?' said Brooke.

'Well, I wouldn't go that far,' said Isla.

Brooke smiled and opened the door for her and bowed lavishly.

'Wow,' Isla said.

'I decided to go very traditional on this date.' Brooke closed the door and went around to slide into the driver's side.

Isla said, 'No adventure?'

Brooke cast her a sideways glance. 'What do you mean? A different sort of adventure entirely.' And winked.

She drove them through the countryside as the long, lingering dusk fell over the landscape, suffusing the sky with what Isla thought of as special Provençal light. She said suddenly, 'It's so inspiring.'

'What is?' said Brooke, and Isla realised that she'd been completely silent, lost in her own thoughts, but it hadn't been a bad silence, and Brooke had seemed comfortable with it. In fact, the car felt so cosy, like it was more than a car, like it was an entire bubble wrapped around them.

'The light in Provence,' said Isla. 'Artists have been drawn here for centuries because of that very special light, but I think it's not just artists. I think it's inspiring to everyone.'

'It is,' said Brooke. 'I fell for it the first time I saw it.'

'When was that?' asked Isla, curious.

'I was a kid,' said Brooke. 'When my parents got divorced, my dad, as some kind of apology gift, took my sister and me to France for a couple of weeks. I think in his head it was totally going to make up for our entire lives being in upheaval.' She shrugged.

'Sometimes,' Isla remarked, 'I think parents wish their children could be less complicated little human beings.'

'Yeah,' said Brooke. 'Well, I think sometimes it can be hard to fully grasp the complexity of what you've created. The very idea of it makes my head whirl.'

'Agreed,' said Isla, thinking of Libby panicking over her pregnancy.

'So, anyway,' continued Brooke, 'he took us here. My sister's a couple of years older than me, and she was just on the verge of teenagerhood during the trip, and she was so over everything, like, she moped around the entire two weeks. I remember her in the Louvre just sulking her way through it, which is hilarious, because she went on to become an art history major. So mostly what I remember was that I didn't want my sister to think I was having a good time, so I tried really hard not to have one. And I didn't, not really, but I did remember thinking that maybe I could have had a better time if it had been a different time in my life. I remembered thinking maybe everything would be in a different light. A French light.' Brooke smiled a little. 'It seems silly now, but when you're a kid, you think . . . maybe you just need a new light.'

'I don't know,' Isla said. 'I think that a lot. A different light. The light is different everywhere you go. The sky is different everywhere you go. It's one planet, but there's so much to see.' Isla had felt that way her entire life, restless, wanting to make the world smaller, more manageable, so she could deal with it.

Brooke said, 'Exactly. So many different lights to see things in. And some things stay the same, but some things you just see . . . so differently. And when that happens, it's such an incredible revelation, sometimes I think you get addicted to that and you keep searching for it again and again.'

'Do you think you ever reach a point when you want to just let things be the same for a long time?' Isla asked.

'Hmm,' said Brooke consideringly. They were in one of the little towns now, and Brooke had to concentrate on manoeuvring the car through the tiny car-hostile streets. 'I think maybe what you really do is reach a happy balance, eventually. But there's no rush. Here we are.' She nudged her car into a parking space near the town's main square.

Twilight had fully fallen now, that glorious half-light that made the entire town seem to glow around them, reflecting back the day's light somehow. The fountain splashed merrily in the middle of the square and people conversed animatedly in French in the cafés that spilled outside onto the cobblestones, and Isla followed Brooke into one of those cafés, bright and loud against the night threatening outside.

They were led to a table in a courtyard in the back, completely empty except for them and a violinist, who began playing as soon as they were seated.

Isla looked at Brooke over the top of her menu. 'Really? Did you plan this?'

'Of course I planned this. What do you take me for? I mean, last date I sprained your ankle. I had to work very hard to make this date absolutely stunning.'

'Well.' Isla looked from the violinist to the stars winking overhead to the bright red bougainvillaea spilling around the courtyard. 'You've definitely succeeded.'

'Wait before you deliver any verdict,' Brooke said. 'The food might be terrible.'

The food wasn't terrible. They spread fresh tapenade over crusty bread still warm from the oven and then split a bouillabaisse. Isla felt her overall impression of the evening was sparkling, between the skies overhead and the conversation within and the champagne between. When they walked back to the car, hand in hand, Isla sighed in utter contentment.

'Better date?' Brooke asked.

'Best date,' Isla said. Then, 'But the bar was very low, I just had to not destroy an ankle.'

Brooke laughed.

'Still mulling things over, I see,' Pauline said when Libby arrived for another lesson.

'Getting there,' Libby told Pauline, determined to will it into being. 'I swear. I am. I know you must think I'm dreadfully . . . indecisive.'

'I don't think that at all,' Pauline denied. 'I think you're dealing with an event in your life I have avoided because it terrifies me. You do it in your own time. Like . . . the ripening of a tomato.' She lifted up one of the glossy red tomatoes in front of her.

'Yes,' Libby agreed, wondering how big the baby ripening in her belly was at that moment.

'We're going to try a tomato tarte tatin today,' said Pauline. 'With a little bit of honey and balsamic vinegar to help them caramelise, and some of this lovely fresh thyme from the garden to bring out all the flavours – smell.' She held the thyme out in her hand.

It did smell delicious, but also strong, and it made Libby feel a little queasy.

That must have been evident on her face, because Pauline said, 'Oh, no, do you not like thyme?'

'No, no, I enjoy it, sorry, I just had a moment.' Libby was determined to push through it.

Pauline gave her a close look. 'We don't have to cook today if you're—'

'No, no,' Libby said firmly. 'We're cooking. I want to make this tomato tarte tatin.'

After a moment, Pauline said, 'Well, good, because it would frankly be a tragedy for me not to give you my puff pastry secrets.'

The tomato tarte tatin went over as well as every other previous dish had, except that Teddy requested chocolate next time.

'I want a proper dessert,' he complained. 'You called that a tart and then it wasn't at all sweet. You should make the pain au chocolat again.'

'Well, it was kind of like an apple pie,' Sam said loyally. 'Tomatoes are fruits, after all.'

Teddy was dubious. 'Not real fruits. That had *vinegar* in it.'

'I loved it,' Sam insisted. 'I vote for more of that.'

Libby looked at him and was suddenly teary-eyed. All these bloody pregnancy emotions. This tomato baby inside her was a roller coaster.

'Hey,' Sam said softly, surprised. 'What's up?'

'Nothing, you're just . . . a really great husband. I barely deserve you.'

'You deserve me,' Sam assured her, quizzical. 'Where is this coming from?'

Libby shook her head. 'Nothing. Don't mind me. Cooking makes me emotional.'

Isla gave her a curious look across the table, and Libby shook her head again.

'I'm loving the cooking,' Sam said, and kissed her hand. 'But you know I loved you without the cooking, too.'

'I know,' Libby said, and swiped at her eyes. 'I'm sorry, I have no idea why I'm so all over the place.'

Isla gave her another look.

Sam said, 'It's okay, this tomato tart thing has been so good, it's made me emotional, too.'

Libby managed a watery laugh.

'But just so you know, I'd accept more pain au chocolat as well.'

'Excellent,' said Teddy approvingly.

Isla went to Brooke for the third date, upon Brooke's request. Isla was a little intimidated, driving up to the imposing chateau as if this was a place she belonged. But it was just where Brooke worked, she reassured herself. It wasn't like Brooke was secret royalty.

Brooke met her at the front door, in jeans, T-shirt, and apron. The apron was already spattered over with the detritus of energetic cooking, and Brooke's hair was wilting into curls around her forehead, like she'd been leaning over a hot stove.

Isla said, 'Oh, my goodness, are you cooking?'

'Of course,' Brooke said. 'Well, attempting it. I know how to make one thing, but I know how to make it pretty well.'

'Better than I can say for myself,' Isla said. 'But Libby's taking cooking lessons and she's been using us for her homework, and we have definitely benefitted from that.'

'That's right,' Brooke said, 'she made the dinner the night I was there.'

'Yeah. She makes cooking seem like something even I could do. It's been a revelation.'

'Aww,' said Brooke, as she led Isla back through the chateau. Isla had a dim impression of muted crystal and heavy velvet and lots of height and width to the rooms, but everything seemed closed-up, cast aside. 'I wouldn't try to cook French food. I think Libby's very brave.'

They had entered a kitchen, enormous, high-ceilinged and gleamingly modern. Isla looked from the Aga range to the wine refrigerator and said, 'Not original to the house, I'm guessing.'

Brooke laughed and went to a bottle of wine already breathing on the sideboard. 'Late addition.'

'I was going to bring you wine,' Isla said, 'but it seemed ridiculous to bring wine to a vineyard.'

'You brought yourself,' said Brooke graciously. 'That was all I required.'

'Wow,' Isla said, 'have you been planning for that line all night?'

'I had a whole bunch that I prepared for when you arrived, depending on the different greetings you might give me,' Brooke grinned, and leaned over the pot bubbling on the stove.

'So,' Isla said, 'what are we having?'

'Hopefully, eggplant Parmesan.'

'Yum,' said Isla. 'Well, it smells delicious. What can I do to help?'

'Oh, there's no need,' said Brooke, stirring the pot. 'I've got things covered.'

'I can't just sit here and not do anything while you do all the work,' Isla said, restless. 'I didn't even bring anything.'

'Again, you brought yourself.' Brooke leaned down to pull something out of the oven that she set on the warm, wide, wooden table in the middle of the kitchen. 'You can eat the Brie.'

The Brie did look delicious, the cheese oozing delightfully as Brooke sliced into it and scooped some onto a piece of bread for Isla.

Isla closed her eyes in pleasure. 'What's on this Brie?' she asked, as she reached for more.

'Oh,' said Brooke. 'A bit of this, a bit of that.'

She said it with such off-handed casualness, as she drained some pasta, that Isla said, 'You're lying, you're actually really good at cooking, you do it a lot. Only people who know how to cook are so casual about throwing things together.'

Brooke shrugged over by the sink. 'I don't know. I mean. I guess I've lived on my own enough that I figured out how to feed myself.'

'That is not something that naturally follows from living alone,' Isla said. 'Trust me. I definitely never learned it. I only learned how to get speedier at ringing for takeaway.'

Brooke laughed. 'Well, I guess it was stress relief. I had a stressful job for a while in my twenties, and I came home a lot of days feeling incompetent, then I felt even more incompetent if I didn't know how to feed myself. So I made myself figure out how to feed myself.'

'Weren't you worried you would fail at that, too?' Isla asked, a little amazed, because whenever she felt incompetent, she resorted to doing as little as possible for fear she would keep being incompetent.

'Yes. Terrified. So I started small.' Brooke spooned some sauce from the pot into the bowl of pasta. 'I make a mean grilled cheese.'

'Hey,' Isla said, as Brooke tossed the pasta, 'grilled cheese is one of my favourites.' She wandered over to where Brooke was, just as Brooke left to carry the bowl of pasta over to that table. There was a pile of fresh romaine lettuce leaves heaped up on a cutting board, looking lush and inviting. Isla had never thought lettuce looked inviting until she had seen the fresh cuts of it at the various town markets, and then she'd realised that lettuce all bundled up together in frilly bouquets could basically be considered a flower. She said to Brooke, 'Is this for a salad?'

'Oh, yeah,' Brooke said, 'I totally forgot.'

'Well, that I am capable of doing,' said Isla, and rinsed and chopped the lettuce while Brooke fussed over the eggplant in the oven. Isla found fresh tomatoes ripened in a bowl and chopped them up as well and tossed it all with a silky vinaigrette she made of vinegar and gleaming gold olive oil that she whisked together with a bunch of seasonings she found in the cupboards. She was surprised how at home she felt, cooking there in Brooke's kitchen, considering that she'd never cooked before. 'So, what was this stressful job you had?'

'Oh,' said Brooke. 'No big deal, just, you know, the usual corporate gig. Look at you, throwing in spices like you're a pro.'

Isla blushed, not realising Brooke was watching her, and said, 'Who knows how it'll taste?'

Brooke dipped a spoon in and let the vinaigrette coat it before sticking her tongue out for a delicate taste. 'It's delicious,' she said.

Isla blinked and cleared her throat and said, 'So is the food ready?'

Brooke smiled and said, 'Yes.'

The meal was delicious. Even the salad. Brooke kept praising the vinaigrette and Isla kept saying, 'Stop, stop, it's just a salad, you made an entire meal here.'

'But the meal wouldn't be complete without its salad!' Brooke proclaimed gallantly.

Isla shook her head in mock exasperation and scraped her chair back to clear the dishes but Brooke leaned over and laid a hand over hers.

'Don't,' she said. 'Let's not be ... prosaic, and practical. Let's not *clean*.'

'Well, someone's going to have to clean sooner or later,' Isla said, mouth dry. She felt like she was going through the motions for some unknown reason, clinging to etiquette her mother had drummed into her with such devotion that it was what she was falling back on now. But really what she wanted was whatever Brooke had up her sleeve now.

'Come with me,' Brooke said, her eyes shining with mischief, and took Isla's hand, as if Isla would need extra convincing, when she definitely did not. She was ready to follow Brooke virtually anywhere at any time, but especially when she looked like that.

Brooke led her outside, where the sound of the cicadas buzzed pleasantly all around them. They wandered out into the vineyard and then Brooke tugged her down among the vines. The ground was still warm from the day and above their heads stars scattered like an impossible spray of glitters across the sky.

'Isn't it beautiful?' Brooke asked, voice low and reverent. 'The first time I saw this view, I ... I spent a lot of time in cities, before coming out here. The skies never look like this in a city.'

'That's because the city is its own sky,' Isla said. 'Its own constellation of stars.'

'You make me appreciate cities,' Brooke said wryly.

'I mean,' said Isla. 'Everything has its charm. Right now, of course, I can think of nothing better than this.'

Brooke said, 'I like to imagine I can see the constellations, but honestly, I am terrible at stargazing.'

Isla laughed. 'You can't be terrible at stargazing. It's just . . . gazing up at stars. Aren't you the one who's always telling me not to think so hard about failure?'

'Okay,' Brooke allowed. 'True.'

Isla turned her head to look at Brooke, sprawled on the ground next to her, and said, 'You know, sometimes I think you could be a ghost.'

Brooke turned her head away from the sky to meet her gaze. 'A ghost?'

'Like . . . you're too much to be real. Like *this* can't be real. Like it must all be part of the ghost stories the kids keep telling themselves, about people kidnapped in the secret dungeons or whatever. Real life isn't like this.'

Brooke smiled at her and said gently, 'Yes. Sometimes it is.'

Chapter Nineteen

Bottles
Nappies
Selected toys (PICK A <u>FEW</u>, MAX)
Snacks
Clean blankets

Arthur hadn't given any thought to what to expect from France. The days leading up to the holiday had been filled with stress for him, as he'd tried to organise everything at his desk and make sure things would go smoothly without him there for several days. Not that Arthur fancied himself the most important person at work, but, well, Max was right that he didn't take many holidays, so he wasn't exactly an expert at knowing what he needed to get done before he became inaccessible. 'Inaccessible' also wasn't a thing Arthur was most of the time.

Arthur had tried not to bring that stress into life at home with Max. Max was *so* excited about the holiday, and Arthur didn't want to ruin it by complaining about how much he had to do before leaving work. He didn't want to give Max the impression that he didn't want to go on the holiday, because he did. And he also recognised that it was unhealthy of him to be feeling this way, that he should be able to get away more easily.

So mostly Arthur let himself focus on the packing when he was home. Arthur had to have *something* to stress about, and Max was never going to be practical about packing, Max never was. For their honeymoon, they had gone to Greece, and Max had packed a single T-shirt with plans to buy whatever else he needed when he got there. Arthur had been a little appalled at what he'd got into, marrying someone who thought that way. But he had to admit it had made luggage very easy to deal with.

At any rate, because Arthur dealt with change by burrowing into stress, he hadn't given a lot of thought to what he expected from France. But if he had given thought to it, he wasn't sure it was going to be this picture-perfect rambling house in idyllic French countryside.

Arthur sat in the car and blinked around him and said, 'Wow.'

Max grinned at him, then grinned at Sam. 'I have heard him sound like that very few times in my life, so this is already a fabulous holiday.'

'But it's *beautiful*,' Arthur said, getting out of the car. Max was already chasing Charlie down, as he was attempting to find a way to fall into the water cistern, with Jack barking excitedly behind him. Arthur watched Max safely corral Charlie and then tipped his head back to take in the blue sky above him.

'Isn't it?' said Sam. 'I think Libby is actually in heaven.' He slung an arm over Libby's shoulders.

'We're so honoured to be the first to arrive,' said Max. 'We'll get to be the exclusive guests until everyone else shows up. Hello, Jack! We've missed you! It's good to see you again! How are you enjoying France?'

'He's done lots of investigating,' Teddy said. 'And he's met some *kittens*.'

'Did you know it would be so beautiful?' Arthur asked Libby. He was astonished by how much prettier it was than he'd anticipated.

'No,' Libby admitted. 'I just hoped.'

Max said, 'Oh, hello.'

Because a woman neither one of them knew had just wandered out of the house.

'Oh, yes,' Libby said. 'This is my friend Isla who I was telling you about. Isla, this is Max and Arthur and Charlie.'

'The artist, the insurance agent, the baby,' Isla said, as she greeted all of them.

'And the wanderer,' Max said, indicating Isla.

Isla laughed. 'That's a nice way of putting it. You've got stuck out here in the garden when there's so much to see inside.'

'Yes, we've heard about the stray kittens,' said Max.

'And also the ghosts with the ghost offering,' said Isla.

'The ghost what?' said Arthur.

Isla grinned and said, 'Welcome to the old Bernard farmhouse.'

The room they were given had a gorgeous view but the house was filled with gorgeous views. Arthur leaned against the window and stared out at it. Charlie was downstairs being fussed over by Libby and Sam, who had apparently missed the added chaos of having a Charlie in their lives. Max was behind him, opening every drawer and wardrobe in the room in a fit of investigation.

'What exactly are you looking for?' Arthur asked, not taking his eyes off the view, which was clearly more important than the contents of a dusty wardrobe.

'Something ghostly,' said Max. 'I'm very excited about the ghost story.'

Arthur shook his head, smiling fondly, and stayed focused on the view.

'What are *you* looking at?' asked Max, and came up behind him to rest his chin on Arthur's shoulder.

'I'm looking at the view. I feel a little like I could get drunk on this scenery.'

'You *must* like it here,' said Max. 'That's not a very you thing to say.'

'Maybe we should go away more often,' said Arthur thoughtfully.

Max slid his arms around Arthur. 'I'm very happy to be in France.'

'Me, too,' said Arthur.

'You have some spectacular wine here,' Max remarked at dinner, swirling a glass of it around in his hand.

'Oh,' said Sam. 'That all comes from the local vineyard. Château Laurent. You should go. I don't have to work tomorrow, Libby and I could take care of Charlie.'

'Oh,' Libby said, sounding surprised. When everyone looked at her quizzically, she said, 'Right. Yes. Of course. We can watch Charlie for you.'

'Not if it's too much trouble,' said Arthur, sounding confused.

'It's no trouble,' Libby said, and forced a smile. 'No trouble.'

Her eyes flickered towards Isla. Libby still clearly had not mentioned her pregnancy to Sam.

Max said, 'Would you like some wine, Libby?'

'No,' Libby said. 'Thank you.'

'No?' Sam said.

'I'm doing a cleanse,' Libby said.

Definitely still hadn't mentioned her pregnancy, thought Isla.

'A cleanse?' echoed Sam. 'In *France*?'

'Well, I went those few days not drinking while I had that headache and I felt so great, I thought I'd keep doing it,' said Libby.

'But you didn't feel well the other day,' said Teddy frankly.

'Right, so I'm hoping backing off wine will let my stomach settle better,' said Libby.

'It's a good idea,' Isla said, because Libby was clearly flailing around and needed a little bit of help. Libby sent her a grateful smile. 'I've done a few no-wine stretches during my travels and I really feel like they were a great reset.'

'Sure,' said Sam. 'I just think people don't usually decide to give up wine while they're in *France*.'

'Well, you know me,' said Libby. 'I love to be different.'

Sam was surprised when Libby came up to bed with him. 'No chat with Isla tonight?'

Libby managed a smile. Sam had always loved Libby's huge, wide smiles, and he felt like they'd been rarer here than before. 'Too tired. I'm too old for these late-night chats any more.'

Maybe she *was* just tired, Sam thought. 'Hey,' he said, as Libby pulled down the blankets.

Libby looked at him expectantly.

'You're not upset I volunteered us to take care of Charlie for Max and Arthur, are you?'

'No,' Libby said. 'Why would I be upset?'

Sam tried to study her closely but she was focused on getting the bedsheets just so. He said, 'I don't know, you seemed ... odd. I was thinking that, well, it's their holiday, and they only have a few days here, and they might like some time alone. And Charlie's a sweet baby. I'm sure he won't give us any trouble. He is vastly entertained by Teddy and Jack, so we can just let them run wild and he'll watch them all day.'

'No, I know.' Libby finally looked up at him and smiled dazzlingly. 'I love Charlie. I'm excited to spend time with him. And it was sweet of you and clever of you to give Arthur and Max some alone time. They deserve it.'

Sam caught Libby's hand and tugged her in. 'I don't want you to think that I've forgotten that it's *our* honeymoon.'

Libby grinned. 'Good to know.'

'I'll get us some alone time, too,' Sam promised.

'And I am looking forward to it,' said Libby, and smiled at him for a moment, soft and small.

Sam enjoyed the smile. With a sense of relief, he nudged her closer and kissed the terribly soft skin behind her ear and listened to her sigh. And he murmured, 'I want you to know, if you don't like it here, we don't have to stay here. Don't feel compelled just because we have people coming to stay, or because you made a big deal about all of us coming out here. I'm really okay if you want to go somewhere else, or even back home, and let our neighbours rotate through this place.'

Libby tipped her head back, dislodging Sam enough that she could see him. 'Do you want to leave?'

Sam shook his head. 'I'm growing kind of fond of the quirks of this place. It's a weakness I have. I grow fond of quirks. It happened with my wife, too.'

This coaxed a smile out of Libby, which had been Sam's intention.

'You've been smiling less,' Sam said soberly. He wanted Libby to know he meant this. 'I'm rather dependent on your smiles. If it's something I'm doing that's making you unhappy, then—'

Libby reached out and laid her fingers over Sam's mouth. 'It's not you,' she said softly. 'I promise. I'm just tired.'

'Yeah,' Sam agreed. 'You have been. I can tell. This adrenalin crash is brutal.'

'Absolutely,' said Libby ruefully. 'Apparently it can take a while to get over one.'

'Hmm,' said Sam. 'Well. Take it easy. Don't overdo it with Isla.'

'I sense Isla is about to grow very distracted with Brooke and we'll see her less and less,' said Libby.

Sam chuckled. 'Well. At any rate. Feel free to sleep in tomorrow as late as you want. I'll take on the lion's share of watching Charlie for us.'

'I'm looking forward to watching Charlie,' Libby said. 'I really am. It's going to be a lovely day.'

Sam wasn't sure if Libby was trying to talk herself into it but he decided to leave it. He'd pried as much as he could for the moment. If something was bothering Libby, he had to trust her to tell him in her own time.

In the morning, Arthur presented Sam with a bag full of items and a checklist of questions and possible answers to those questions: why Charlie might be fussy, what Charlie might like to eat, which toy Charlie might like best to play with.

Sam, impressed, said, 'Wow, I never once documented Teddy this extensively.'

Arthur hesitated, and Sam felt guilty for giving him pause about his thorough parenting. 'I just want to make sure he doesn't give you any trouble—' Arthur began.

'Of course,' Sam interrupted hastily. 'It's very kind of you. I'm sure Charlie will be a perfect little fellow to hang out with all day.'

'He's getting a tooth, I think,' Arthur said. 'He was up in the middle of the night last night and he almost never does that any more.'

'Or he's just thrown by sleeping in a strange place,' suggested Sam. 'I keep waking up in the middle of the night, too.'

'Or it's the ghosts waking you up,' Max said, coming into the kitchen with Charlie in his arms, and he fluttered his hand in a way Sam supposed he meant to be spooky.

'It's not the ghosts. That's not their sort of prank. Trust me, I know these ghosts very well by this time.'

'Young master Teddy,' Max said, as he handed Charlie over to Sam, 'what's on your agenda for the day?'

'Dad says Jack and I have to entertain Charlie,' Teddy said glumly, picking a croissant apart for breakfast.

'By playing lots of raucous games outside,' Sam said drily. 'It's hardly a hardship.' Sam looked at Arthur, who looked concerned about leaving Charlie, and said, 'Ignore him, it's nine-year-old sulking.'

'Almost ten!' protested Teddy, who was clinging tena-
ciously to the nearness of that double-digit birthday.

'Nearly-ten-year-old sulking,' Sam corrected himself.
'Turns out to be startlingly similar to nine-year-old sulking.'

'Good morning, all,' Isla said cheerfully as she walked into
the kitchen. 'Where's Libby?'

'Sleeping in. I told her to. I wanted to steal alone time with
Charlie.' Sam poked Charlie in the belly and earned himself a
toothy giggle, which made him grin. Few things in the world
were better than a baby giggle.

'We're off to see your girlfriend now,' said Max.

'Stop,' Isla said, unable to fully suppress the smile twitch-
ing around her lips. 'She's not my girlfriend.'

'Any messages you'd like to pass on to her?' continued
Max. 'Perhaps you'd like us to tell her that her eyes are like
sparkling—'

'Leave her alone,' Arthur said, and looked at Isla. 'Ignore
him. He's incorrigible. I could only marry him because I shut
him up with kissing long enough that I forgot how terrible he is.'

Max laughed, delighted, and said, 'Come along, darling, to
the romantic vineyards with us.'

They left, and Sam looked at Isla.

Isla said, 'You Christmas Street lot are never a boring bunch.'

Max whistled when he saw Château Laurent. 'Now, *that*,'
he said, 'is a house.'

'No, it's not,' Arthur said, peering at it through the wind-screen of the car Sam had let them borrow. 'That's a palace.'

Max laughed. 'It's all a matter of perspective.'

Arthur frowned at the house in front of them, not really seeing it.

Max said, 'What's up? You look thunderous.'

'Is it unusual that I gave Sam that checklist for Charlie?' Arthur blurted out all at once. 'Am I a ridiculous father?'

Max blinked, looking startled, and said, 'What?' with an incredulity that made Arthur feel a little bit better. 'Darling, of course you are a ridiculous father, and that's what makes you such a wonderful father. Charlie's very lucky he's got you. If it were up to me I'd forget to ever feed him a vegetable or keep him from tumbling down the stairs.'

'No, you wouldn't,' Arthur retorted. 'You're an excellent father. And I'm just . . . ' He lifted his shoulders in a shrug.

Max was watching him closely. 'You're just what?'

'I don't know—'

Someone tapped on their car window, startling both of them. It was a man wearing a straw hat who waved at them cheerfully.

'Do you know this person?' Max asked.

'No,' said Arthur, and put the window down. 'Hello?'

'*Bonjour,*' he said pleasantly. 'Are you Arthur and Max? Here for a tour?'

'Oh,' said Arthur. 'Yes. That's us.'

'Brooke told me to expect you. Perhaps you'd like to get started?'

The alternative was to stay and continue to have this conversation that Arthur wasn't really very sure he wanted to have, so he said, 'Yes. We would.'

Max was enchanted by the vineyard. The landscape was gorgeous and there was something about the *sound* of it that really got to him. London was so noisy, in a way that Max barely even noticed any more, because that was just *home*, constant background buzz. The French countryside wasn't exactly quiet. There were birds twittering, and cicadas humming, and other nature-y sounds Max couldn't place. They were noises that made Max feel a contentment deep down in his soul. He felt like he could hear the *sunshine* here, hear the vines growing through the soil, hear the clouds drifting across the sky. He wanted to paint the noise of this place.

But Max was also thinking about Arthur, as they followed Raphael through the vines, along the spectacular hallways of the chateau, along the winding cellars and through to the tasting room. Arthur looked engaged in the tour, asking intelligent questions, but Max knew Arthur could ask intelligent questions in his sleep, so that didn't mean he wasn't still fretting over being a ridiculous father.

They bought some wine in the tasting room, Max paying while Arthur thanked Raphael for the tour.

'My pleasure,' Raphael said. 'How are the ghosts doing?'

'I think the same,' said Arthur. 'We've got an offering out but the electricity still hasn't come on.'

'They haven't tried any more pranks, though?' said Raphael. 'That seems unlike them. They're usually very active ghosts. We've had many reports of them over the years, whenever someone was at the house. I showed them all to the woman who was here before you.'

'We were regaled with the tales,' Max said, and tucked the wine against him. 'Can we wander the vineyard a bit with our wine?' he asked, as he reached for Arthur's hand.

'Please do,' said Raphael, making an expansive gesture. 'In fact . . . ' he reached for a corkscrew and pulled the cork out of the wine for them with a flourish. 'Let me find you glasses . . . '

Max said, 'Not necessary. Let's reconnect with our profligate youth and drink straight from the bottle.'

'That was *your* profligate youth,' Arthur said, but there were dimples in his cheeks, so Max just smiled at him.

They ended up finding a spot on the hillside, slightly dusty but with a commanding view of the vineyards stretched below them and the rest of Provence beyond that. They sprawled out together and passed the wine between them, and Max let them just be for a little while, in companionable silence.

Max looked over at Arthur, his eyes closed as he basked in the sun, with that gorgeous backdrop behind him, and said, 'I could paint you, exactly like this. It would be glorious. I *should* paint you. We should do some *en plein air* painting. We can take Charlie along. He'd love it.'

Arthur spoke without opening his eyes. 'Being a model

for you? It doesn't sound like the sort of thing Charlie would love. He never sits still.'

'I'd paint him as a dash of energy,' Max said. 'A swirl of colour.'

'That would be appropriate,' Arthur agreed.

Max let silence fall again, and then he said, 'You are a natural father, you know. You're stunningly good at it. Charlie worships you.'

Arthur said, 'You don't have to try to make me feel better.'

'I'm not.' Max wriggled over so he could lie right next to Arthur. 'I'm telling you the truth.'

Arthur sighed, and said after a moment, 'I just envy you sometimes. No, forget that – I envy you *all* the time. You're so able to just take things as they are. To go on holiday. Think of grabbing a bottle of wine for us to share in a vineyard together, straight from the bottle. I'd never think of that. I'd never even *consider* it.'

'But here you are doing it,' Max said.

'Who wouldn't do this?' Arthur countered. 'You always have the best ideas. I wish I had ideas like that. I wish my ideas weren't "Write a checklist for Sam for our child."'

'I don't,' said Max seriously.

Arthur turned his head to look at him. 'You don't?' he said drily. 'You don't wish for a more spontaneous and romantic husband who would sweep you off your feet every once in a while?'

'I mean,' said Max, 'of course I wish for that. And lucky me, because that's exactly what I got. I don't wish you had my ideas, because you have *your* ideas, and I love those

225

ideas. Those ideas are very romantic to me. A husband who worries about grocery shopping is *heaven* to me.'

Arthur shook his head and said, 'You're so *weird*,' but he looked appeased.

Max said, 'Would you have me any other way?'

'No,' said Arthur.

'See?' Max beamed at him. 'That's my point.'

Sam left Libby sleeping and took Charlie and Teddy and Jack for a wander around the property. Teddy was complaining because they still hadn't found the key.

Charlie was being thrilled by every rock he could overturn, which was really very charming. Sam remembered when his son used to be that easy to entertain.

'I was hoping to at least find something mysterious by now,' said Teddy. 'Pari's going to be so disappointed when she gets here and I haven't found anything *at all*.'

'We live in a house with ghosts,' Sam pointed out. 'We literally have a ghost offering on our steps.'

'Yeah, but those ghosts haven't done anything interesting,' said Teddy glumly, kicking at the ground. 'We have boring ghosts.'

'I thought you were terrified,' Sam remarked.

'No,' Teddy denied firmly.

Sam bit down on his smile. 'Okay,' said Sam. 'Well. *I* find them terrifying, how about that? Let's not taunt the ghosts, hmm?'

'Are you out here looking for the ghosts?' asked Victor, and Sam jumped a mile.

'Jesus,' he gasped, holding a hand to his chest. 'You scared me to death.' Charlie, also clearly startled, came running back to Sam, arms held up to be swept into an embrace.

'Sorry,' said Victor, not looking at all sorry. 'I thought you would hear me approach. Then again, it makes sense that you would not, as you were thrashing about like giraffes.'

'There aren't any giraffes around here, are there?' asked Teddy, with a little bit of hope in his voice.

'No,' said Victor. 'But there used to be werewolves.'

'Oh, God,' groaned Sam, as Teddy perked up.

'*Werewolves?*'

'This was many years ago,' said Victor. 'Centuries ago. Before the ghosts. So there probably aren't any around any more. Probably.'

'Thanks, Victor,' Sam said sarcastically. 'Was there something we could do for you?'

'No, no,' said Victor. 'I was just checking up on the playhouse.'

'The playhouse?' said Teddy.

'There's a playhouse by the river over there.' Victor pointed. 'You didn't know? It's a ramshackle thing but I check up on it every so often. How is your electricity coming?' he asked Sam.

'Not well,' said Sam. 'I guess the ghost offering isn't good enough.'

'They have not shut off the rest of the electricity,' said Victor wisely, 'so it must be good enough for *something*.'

'You always make me feel better, Victor,' remarked Sam, 'I really cherish our little chats.'

Victor gave his Gallic shrug and said, 'Well, enjoy the rest of your day,' and then wandered off.

'There's a *playhouse*,' said Teddy, practically jumping for joy.

'Let's not expect much from the playhouse,' Sam warned. 'Given the state of the house itself, I'm not sure Victor's caretaking is terribly effective.'

But the playhouse, when they found it, was unexpectedly charming. It was much bigger than Sam had expected it to be, consisting of several rooms with a surprising amount of old wooden furniture scattered through it. The house seemed almost big enough to live in, much bigger than any playhouse would have been. It didn't have a kitchen or a bathroom but its variety of rooms included something like a library, with mostly empty shelves lining the walls; and something like a lounge, with a few questionable chairs clustered around an old, filthy fireplace; and something like a bedroom, with an abandoned iron bed shoved up against a wall. The windows had all been shuttered in the way the farmhouse's windows had been closed but Sam could tell that the view would be lovely. The 'river' Victor had mentioned was more accurately a little brook that went gurgling merrily, slipping over stones with that particular musical laughter of a brook.

Teddy, after they had finished, said, '*Wow*. Who do you suppose played here?'

'I have no idea.' Sam recalled the story everyone had told

him about the prior inhabitants of the farmhouse. 'Maybe Great-Aunt Clarissa, when she was a girl. She used to spend her summers here, remember?'

Sam sat on the banks of the brook, watching Charlie carefully as he leaned over to splash in the shallow water. Jack waded into the brook, splashing up a storm, and Charlie clapped in glee even as he simultaneously squeezed his eyes shut and recoiled against the water flying at him. Teddy sat beside Sam with the heavy sigh of a nine-year-old. No one could be as abjectly disappointed by life as nine-year-olds, thought Sam.

'What's up?' Sam asked. 'I thought you'd be excited to have discovered this. It's a pretty cool playhouse. I can help you fix it up a bit for when Pari gets here in a couple of days.'

'Yeah, Pari's going to love it,' said Teddy, and heaved another sigh.

'And that's a bad thing? Aren't you excited about Pari coming? I thought that would help make France bearable for you.'

'Oh, yeah,' said Teddy. 'I'm super excited for her to come. And, you know, France hasn't been *all* bad, I suppose.'

'High praise,' said Sam drily, 'thank you.'

'I'm just ... The mama cat's going to leave eventually, isn't she?'

Sam hesitated, absorbing the question. 'Eventually. When the kittens grow up, and don't need her any more.' He studied Teddy's profile. He was frowning, and it was small on his little face but intense. Sam thought about

Teddy's own mum, leaving her little kitten well before he was ready, and took a deep breath. Most of the time, he knew that he and Teddy were doing well, but that didn't mean there weren't still times when Teddy missed his mum, no matter how great Libby was. Sam said gently, 'But they won't be alone.'

Teddy plucked at the grass underneath him. 'Do you think they'll miss her?'

'Probably. They might not ever stop. But they'll have other people to love them, and they'll be happy most of the time, and that's life. Some kittens learn that sooner than others.'

'Well,' Teddy said. 'The kittens will be okay because everyone on Christmas Street will adopt them and then they'll always have all of us and each other.'

Sam sighed. 'I don't know if everyone on Christmas Street wants a kitten. Least of all Arthur and Max. They're pretty busy with Charlie.'

'But Charlie really wants a kitten,' Teddy said. 'Don't you, Charlie? You want a kitty?'

'Yeah!' exclaimed Charlie enthusiastically, and 'Meow!' and then he giggled in delight.

'See?' Teddy said.

Sam chuckled. 'You don't have to convince me. It's not my decision. You've got to convince Arthur and Max.'

'I'll ask them at dinner tonight,' Teddy decided. 'They won't say no to *me*.'

'Hello, Jack,' Libby said, patting him. 'Back from your walk?'

'There you are,' Sam said, coming into the room holding Charlie.

'Hi, Libby!' Teddy shouted as he ran into the room, much louder than was necessary. 'Hi, Isla!'

'How are you feeling?' Sam asked Libby, looking down at her with concern. 'Well rested?'

Libby smiled. 'Yes, actually.' She looked at Charlie. 'How has your day with Charlie been?'

'Oh, fantastic,' Sam said. 'We found a playhouse.'

'A playhouse?' said Isla.

Teddy nodded. 'It's pretty brilliant.'

'Quite the discovery,' Sam said. 'Victor stopped by to point us in the right direction. And to tell us we still haven't found the right offering to make to the ghosts, but at least they haven't shut any more electricity off.'

'Oh, dear,' said Libby. 'I'm glad they haven't done that, yes.'

'So I guess the ghosts like us a little bit,' Sam finished.

'Let's be grateful for that, I suppose,' said Libby, picking herself up off the dusty floor with Sam's assistance.

Charlie, with his fist in his mouth, gave her a shy smile that was so sweet that Libby's heart totally melted. She couldn't help but reach for him.

He came willingly, still smiling sweetly, and Libby pressed her nose to his head, breathing in his lovely baby scent. At just that moment, the fact that one of these was growing inside her didn't feel so huge and unmanageable. It felt like a perfectly sized package of cuddly wonder.

'Hello, Charlie,' she said. 'What a busy day you've already had. What else shall we do until your dads come back?'

'Lunch and then a nap,' Sam said.

'Sounds doable,' Libby said with a grin.

Arthur and Max returned from their day at the vineyard practically walking on air.

'Did you have a good time?' Sam asked them.

'How dare you ask them that,' said Libby, smiling. 'It's obvious they had a splendid time.'

'We did,' Max said, taking Charlie and allowing himself to be cuddled hello. 'It may have been exactly what we needed.'

'Thank you so much for watching Charlie,' Arthur said, leaning over to give the baby a kiss. 'How was he?'

'A dream,' Libby said honestly.

'No trouble at all,' said Sam. 'We went for a walk, and ate, and took a nap, and played some games. Teddy kept him entertained.'

'Teddy was lovely,' Libby said. 'Everyone got along so well.' She had been paying close attention to all of the interactions, knowing how soon Teddy would have to face the prospect of a baby around all the time, and Teddy had been at least tolerant of Charlie's foibles and at times even

232

seemed somewhat charmed by them. Maybe he would be excited to have a baby brother or sister.

'Oh, good,' said Arthur, sounding pleased. 'Well done, Charlie. There are the manners I've taught you.'

'He's nineteen months old,' Max said. 'He doesn't have manners.'

'Don't be silly,' Sam said. 'Any child of Arthur's had manners practically immediately.'

'Thank you, Sam,' said Arthur primly.

'I'm not sure it's a compliment,' remarked Max.

'It's definitely a compliment,' responded Arthur.

'Honestly,' Max said to Isla, 'you don't know us but this is us being very romantic with each other.'

Arthur grinned at him. 'It's actually true.'

Libby looked between them and thought they seemed very relaxed and happy. She caught Sam's eye and couldn't help but smile at him. Really, it was the sort of day when everything seemed doable. Maybe she could tell Sam about the baby that very night.

Libby sat in bed waiting for Sam to come to bed, which was the reverse of how things had been going for them in France.

Sam came in eventually, yawning and rubbing at the back of his head in a way that mussed up his hair adorably. It made him look like Teddy, and she couldn't help but smile.

233

'Sorry,' he said, as he crawled into bed with her. 'It's not an outrageous time in America.'

'It's fine,' she assured him.

'I'm exhausted,' he said, eyes already closed as he settled against her. 'Babies are exhausting. I'd forgot.'

'Oh,' Libby said uncertainly, after a beat.

'I'm reminding myself that Teddy was once that much work. It seems impossible.'

'I thought Charlie was really good,' Libby ventured carefully.

'Oh, he was a dream,' Sam agreed. 'He was lovely. As perfect as a baby could be. Still exhausting.'

Libby considered, looking up at the ceiling.

Sam said, 'It's just a relief to be through that with Teddy. To be reminded how easy Teddy is now. I mean, there are definitely other challenges, but, by and large, I'm happy Teddy can use words to communicate what he wants and also doesn't make me change nappies any more.'

'Right,' said Libby thoughtfully. 'Right.'

'Mmm,' murmured Sam, snuggling closer and brushing a kiss over her shoulder, apparently totally oblivious to all of her inner turmoil. 'Good night.'

'Yeah,' Libby agreed over the lump in her throat. 'Good night.'

She stared up at the ceiling long after Sam had started lightly snoring beside her.

Chapter Twenty

The ideal mille-feuille will have countless layers of complexity but still feel light as air!

Max had difficulty sleeping, and only a little bit because Arthur had taken a fussy Charlie into bed with them and he was on a dedicated schedule of kicking them at least once an hour in his quest to sleep in as many unique directions on the bed as he could achieve.

Really Max was thinking of the way the light seemed to glow and dance around the vistas, the way the olive trees seemed to catch it in their silver leaves, the way the lavender fields looked gilded in it and the sunflowers seemed to glitter with it.

Max wanted to paint.

As dawn crept its way through the window and into the room, Charlie finally seemed to grow tired of kicking and fell into a deeper sleep, curled up right up against Arthur. Max looked at them and smiled and leaned over and kissed both of their cheeks. Then he slid out of bed.

Nobody else stirred as he pulled out of the luggage the small canvases and sets of paints he'd packed. Arthur liked to joke that Max, when packing, always prioritised impractical things like painting paraphernalia over things like clothes. Max thought this was very clever of him.

He texted Arthur *Gone painting, be back later*, and Arthur's mobile dinged with the text coming in. It made Arthur turn over with a little mutter, but he didn't wake, and Max tiptoed out of the room.

He'd expected to find the rest of the house still asleep, but he was startled to find Isla in the kitchen when he got there.

'Oh, hello,' he said.

'Hi,' she said. She was sitting at the table looking out over the back garden, with her hands closed around a mug. 'Didn't mean to startle you.'

'Couldn't sleep?' Max guessed.

Isla made a noncommittal sound. 'I made coffee.'

'Is this about Brooke?' Max asked, as he poured himself a cup.

'No, not really. Not entirely. It's mostly about me, and, like, am I just a disaster?' Isla sighed. 'I might be just a disaster.'

Max smiled at her. 'I doubt it. Most people are disasters, which means that none of us are, because we can't all be disasters.'

Isla tipped her head and considered. 'That's interesting logic.'

'My speciality.' Max sipped his coffee and snagged a

croissant, which had been his initial reason to go to the kitchen in the first place. 'I'm going to paint *en plein air*. You're welcome to come along.'

'I don't want to interrupt your creative process,' Isla said.

'Unless you're going to babble nonstop, you won't,' said Max. 'If you're just going to sit around staring wistfully into space, you might as well do it somewhere with a dazzling view.'

'You make a good point,' agreed Isla.

Watching Max paint was oddly soothing. He chose a patch of meadow on a gentle slope and she watched with interest as he set himself up. There was a view laid out below them that was stunning, and he somehow applied paints in a way that suggested the landscape while not mimicking it.

By the time he stepped back from the easel with a self-satisfied smile, the sun was high in the sky and Isla couldn't believe how quickly the morning had passed. She had been so caught up in her own head, worrying about all the things she kept doing wrong in life and how she might just keep doing them, for ever, and now she'd spent the morning not worrying at all.

Max was magic.

'What do you think?' Max asked, gesturing to it.

'You're magic,' Isla told him.

Max laughed. 'Let's tell Arthur that.'

'Your painting is beautiful,' she said honestly.

'Thank you. And I'm feeling better about everything.'

'Were you not feeling good?'

'I don't know,' said Max, as he packed up his supplies. 'I had this really successful exhibition and I've been worried about replicating the success. I've had some insights into my painting process but I'm still working my way through them. It's hard to trust in your own creativity. Or so I've found.' He looked over at Isla. 'How about you? Are you feeling better?'

Isla took a deep breath. 'I think so. I don't know. Meeting Brooke has made me feel like ... like I don't want to keep making the same mistakes I've made in life so far. Do you know what I mean?'

'I do, yes,' said Max, and she believed him. 'I think the first step is recognising that what was happening were mistakes. But also, they brought you here, so they couldn't be all bad.'

'You're both magical *and* wise,' said Isla, as they began walking back to the house.

Max laughed. 'And you're very good for my ego, I might hire you to just follow me around.'

Arthur woke because Charlie kept poking at him. He opened one eye and looked at his son sternly.

'Ba,' Charlie said to him, which was his all-purpose sound of demand.

'I suppose you want breakfast.' Arthur rolled onto his back and stretched and looked at the light in the room. 'And it's morning so I can't even be angry with you for being awake. Where's your other dad? Max?' Arthur lifted his head, but the bedroom wasn't big, and Max clearly wasn't in it.

Arthur frowned and looked back at Charlie and said, 'Hmm.' Then he reached for his mobile and saw Max's text and smiled, because that was good. It was always good when Max felt painterly impulses kicking in.

'Okay,' Arthur said to Charlie. 'It's you and me for the morning. How's that tooth you're working on?'

Charlie was gnawing so hard on his fist that Arthur felt compelled to point out, 'You know you shouldn't actually eat your own hand, right?' He pulled Charlie into his arms and kissed his head and said, 'You're so dramatic. You get that from your other dad. He's giving you drama lessons during the day when I'm not around.'

Arthur got out of bed and went downstairs. There was a pot of coffee, but no other sign of life. Arthur supposed Max had made the coffee before he'd gone out to paint and was grateful for the thoughtfulness. He poured himself a mug and then found Charlie breakfast before he started shrieking and woke the whole household.

Teddy came down next, with Jack heralding his arrival by bounding into the kitchen. Charlie delightedly forgot all about breakfast in his desire to get down to the floor to play with the slobbering Jack.

Arthur said, 'What can I get you for breakfast, Teddy?'

'A chocolate biscuit?' Teddy asked hopefully.

Arthur gave him a look. 'You think I'm that easy?'

'Max would have been that easy,' grumbled Teddy.

'Don't I know it,' Arthur agreed, and tried to coax Charlie into eating his breakfast instead of flinging it to the floor.

Libby came into the kitchen and stood for a moment, sighing as she gazed at the stove.

'Libby?' Arthur asked gently. 'You okay?'

'Oh, yes,' said Libby, visibly shaking herself out of it. 'I'm just . . . contemplating cooking. I'm the cook in the family now, you know.'

'Yes,' said Arthur. 'Cooking by osmosis. Where's Sam? Still asleep?'

Libby nodded. 'He let me sleep in yesterday so it's his turn today. He had to work late last night so I think he was worn out, and then there was of course this little fellow.' She tweaked at Charlie's chubby cheek.

Charlie giggled and tried to throw oatmeal at her.

'It's a sign of love,' Arthur told her.

Libby laughed and sat at the kitchen table with her hands cupped around her mug.

Arthur studied her, thinking that she looked a bit tired. And maybe a bit shadowed, like her mind was preoccupied with something. He decided against saying anything in front of Teddy.

But then Teddy announced, 'I'm going to go check on the kittens. Come on, Jack!' And he and Jack dashed off.

Which gave Arthur the perfect opening.

Charlie squawked in protest but was distracted when Arthur handed him a wooden spoon to bang.

Arthur said to Libby, 'So how are you? I know watching Charlie can be a bit of a handful.'

'Why do you think I'm not able to watch Charlie?' Libby asked defensively.

'No, no,' Arthur corrected hastily. 'I didn't mean to imply that. I just . . . know he's a lot. He routinely runs us to exhaustion. I was just . . . being sympathetic, if you're tired. Because of Charlie.'

'I'm not tired because of Charlie,' Libby insisted. 'Charlie was lovely.'

Arthur had no idea what to make of this. He'd clearly trodden on some sensitive topic he hadn't known was there. 'It wouldn't offend me if he hadn't been,' he said slowly, 'but I'm glad to hear he was lovely.'

'Sorry,' Libby said, and sighed and rubbed her temples. 'I've . . . got a bit of a headache. I woke up with one.'

'France has been rough on you,' Arthur said, watching her closely and worrying a little bit, because Libby looked like she was approaching the end of her tether.

'Not really. I mean . . . I just haven't felt well. But it's fine. Sam thinks it was an adrenalin crash.'

'You were running around a lot before you left,' Arthur allowed, trying not to sound as dubious as he felt.

'It isn't that I dislike France. I actually love it here. I love this house and I love the area around it and I love the whole *lifestyle* represented by this place. I wish I felt better so I could enjoy it.'

Libby sounded so painfully wistful that Arthur wanted to bundle her up in a hug. Maybe he should have a talk with Sam, although that was definitely not his thing. Maybe he'd suggest that Max ought to have a talk with Sam.

'Well, I'm sure you'll start feeling better soon,' Arthur said, hoping to improve Libby's mood a little bit.

Libby managed a smile and said, 'Yes. Absolutely. Me, too. Now where's Max? Did you let him sleep in like Sam?'

'No, actually,' said Arthur. 'He off painting *en plein air*. He's feeling very inspired here, I think.'

'I don't blame him,' Libby said. 'It's a pretty inspiring place. I can't wait to see what sort of art comes out of it.'

'Me, too,' said Arthur.

Isla thought that the thing to do was to be honest with Brooke about what a disaster of a human she was. Once Brooke understood that Isla was a scatterbrained commitment-phobe terrible at keeping the things that were important to her, then she would know not to do things like flirt with Isla or smile at Isla or kiss Isla. Isla had to talk to Brooke about this. Isla would feel better once she knew, without a doubt, that Brooke knew everything about her and wasn't going to be interested in her any more. That was a storyline Isla was well familiar with.

Isla sat in her bedroom mulling this over and trying to recapture the way she'd felt that morning watching Max paint: settled and calm and ... *rooted*. In a way Isla never felt. But it was no good. She just felt more jittery than ever. She had to find a way to find Brooke to talk to her.

Isla left her room and paused at the top of the staircase, looking at Mary and Adélaïde, who smirked smugly out of their portraits.

'I wish you two were ghosts who could give me some tips,' Isla sighed. 'Like, helpful ghosts. Not haunting tips, romantic life-experience tips. I figure ghosts have seen a lot of love stories. A lot of happy endings.' She considered for a moment. 'Then again, maybe not. How many love stories even have happy endings?' She sighed heavily, feeling sorry for herself, and walked down the stairs.

And ran directly into Libby. 'Oh, good,' Libby said, linking her arm with Isla's. 'I've been trying to make lemonade. I mean, surely lemonade can't be that difficult. I must have some sort of instinct for lemonade, right? Come and taste my lemonade and tell me why you're looking so reflective.'

'I don't know.' Isla heaved a sigh, following Libby out to the garden. 'I feel like I really need to talk to Brooke. I really want to talk to her about ... about *me*.'

'Hmm,' said Libby, pouring the lemonade. 'Then you should go and see her?'

'That's what I was thinking. Do you think it's a good idea? Do you think it's too ... clingy?'

'I don't think it's clingy, I think it's romantic,' Libby said consideringly, handing Isla the glass.

'I don't know, is it romantic to go and tell someone you're too much of a mess to be with them?' said Isla dubiously.

'Isla,' Libby chided. 'You're not too much of a mess to be

243

with her. You're an amazing catch and everyone can see that. Everyone who's not you. Trust me. Brooke would be so lucky to have you. And I'm pretty sure Brooke knows that.'

'You're required to say things like that to me,' Isla said, 'you're my friend.'

'I promise I'm completely unbiased, I would tell you if you were awful. Just like you'd tell me if my lemonade was awful.'

Isla tried the lemonade. It was quite awful. She said, 'It's delicious.'

Libby narrowed her eyes and said, 'Hmm.'

'I do think I should talk to Brooke,' Isla said, partly to get the conversation away from the topic of the lemonade, 'but I don't even know how I would get to her. Sam took the car.'

Just then the doorbell rang.

Libby and Isla exchanged a look.

'I'm going to consider that a sign,' said Libby.

Libby answered the door. Isla, worried it might be Brooke, had decided to hide for a few minutes as she got ready to face her. But it wasn't Brooke at the door. It was Victor, who said, *'Bonjour! Bonjour!* I have come to check on the ghosts.'

'Oh,' said Libby. 'I suppose they're the same as they've always been. Still dead.'

Victor gave her a disapproving look. 'Do you say such things about the ghosts? That's rude.'

'Is it?' asked Libby. Why couldn't she find a way to get

along with these bloody ghosts? 'I didn't realise that. I thought it was just fact.'

'May I come in and look at the electricity?' Victor asked politely.

'Please do,' Libby said, holding the door open wider for him.

Instead of going into the older part of the house, Victor went up the staircase and stood in front of the portraits.

After a moment of contemplation, he hmph'd at the ghost offering, nudging it with his foot. 'You know what you need here?' he demanded. 'Alcohol. Some sort of spirit, eh? Ghosts like to drink as much as the rest of us.'

'Of course,' Libby agreed. 'Did you want to go to the other part of the house, though?'

'Why would I?' asked Victor blankly.

Libby pointed out, 'Well, you said you wanted to look at the electricity.'

Victor gestured to the portraits. 'I just did.'

'Oh,' said Libby, who knew better than to question. 'Okay. Are you done here, then?'

'I think so,' said Victor. 'Is there anything else happening? I do like to be of assistance if I can be.'

You could fix the electricity, Libby thought drily, but didn't say. Instead, she thought suddenly of the assistance they needed. 'Wait,' she said. 'Actually. How did you get here?'

'I just appeared,' Victor said. 'I'm magic.'

Libby stared at him for a very long moment.

Then Victor started laughing. 'I am only joking, of

course. Of course I am not magic. But you were willing to believe me, no?' He wagged his finger in Libby's face.

Libby wanted to point out that Victor thought the electricity was going to be fixed by leaving a bottle of champagne out for some ghosts, but she refrained because she wanted to ask Victor for a favour. 'So you drove here?' she asked politely.

'*Mais oui*,' said Victor, with a little shrug. 'What else would I have done?'

'Could you do us a favour?' Libby asked, and decided to really embellish the situation, relying on Victor's Frenchness. 'In aid of a great romance?'

'But of course!' exclaimed Victor, looking almost eager. 'What can I do?'

'You could drive Isla up to Château Laurent.'

'Victor what?' said Isla, staring at Libby.

'Take Victor up on his offer and let him drive you to see Brooke,' Libby urged her.

'I . . . ' Isla didn't want to do that. Isla didn't want to go to Brooke and tell her all the terrible things about her. But Isla also knew she *had* to. She'd been living in a fairy story and it had to stop. 'Yeah,' she said. 'Okay. I guess so.'

'Don't worry,' Libby told her as she ushered her out of the kitchen. 'Your hair looks great.'

'I wasn't worried about my hair until just now,' said Isla.

'You look beautiful,' Libby assured her. 'Brooke won't be able to resist you.' She nudged her out of the front door.

Victor was waiting by his car in the farmyard, with his straw hat tipped back on his head. He gave her that wide smile of his when he saw her. *'Bonjour, mademoiselle.* I am told you need to go to the vineyard.'

'Yeah,' Isla said. 'I guess. Kind of. I think so.'

Victor said, *'C'est la vie,'* and shrugged and ushered Isla into the car.

Isla tried to plan out what she was going to say to Brooke. *You should know that I'm a disaster. I'm really bad at relationships. I don't want you to think I'm going to be good at this. I think you must have the wrong impression of me.*

Any of those statements would work and get her point across pretty succinctly. And probably the conversation would be done after that, so she didn't need to think of what else she ought to say.

Which was good, because she was too busy focusing on not dying. Victor's driving seemed to regard roads as mere suggestions, and traffic laws as non-existent. Isla clutched the handle of the door for dear life, hoping it would keep her from careering all over the car inelegantly.

Eventually he came to a stop in the courtyard of Château Laurent and said cheerfully, 'Here we are.'

'Merci,' managed Isla, as she half-staggered out of the car.

'Tell Raphael I said hello,' Victor said. 'And that he still owes me money from that last poker game.'

'Okay,' Isla said, even though she wasn't really there to talk to Raphael.

Unfortunately, Raphael was who she met first. He came up behind her as she was watching Victor skid his way out of the courtyard and thinking that she hadn't thought this through. Now she was stranded at the chateau, about to disclose to Brooke what a terrible girlfriend she would be.

'*Bonjour*,' Raphael said behind her, and made her jump.

'You scared me,' she said as she turned to him, pressing her hand against her racing heart. She might be a little on edge.

'Ah,' said Raphael. 'My apologies. Was that Victor?'

'Yes. He says hi, and something about money from a poker game?'

'He lies,' said Raphael laconically. 'Did you enjoy his driving?'

'It's very ... *laissez-faire*,' Isla said diplomatically. 'I was hoping to talk to Brooke.'

'She is not here,' Raphael said.

Isla paused. 'She's not here, or she doesn't want to talk to me?'

Raphael looked perplexed. 'Why would she not want to talk to you?'

Isla was projecting, she thought. There was no reason for Brooke not to want to talk to her. Yet. Isla shook her head. 'Never mind. I'm being ... Never mind.'

'You seem very troubled about Brooke,' Raphael said kindly.

'No,' Isla said. And then, 'Yes.' And then, 'It's just that ... I don't know. Maybe she doesn't know enough about me.'

Raphael shrugged. 'Maybe you don't know enough about her.'

Isla drew her eyebrows together thoughtfully. 'Should I know more about her?'

'Of course,' Raphael replied. 'You should always know more. Is that not what love is? To always know more and more and more?'

'I . . . ' said Isla, feeling a little out of her depth, with all this talk of love and what it might and might not be.

'Mademoiselle,' Raphael said, smiling at her, and took her hands in his. 'You are getting yourself into a dizzy, no?'

'A tizzy, I think,' Isla corrected faintly.

'When there is no need,' Raphael continued. 'Brooke is a lovely lady who is just as alone and unsettled as you, just seeking some solid ground, like you. Trust me on that.'

And . . . Isla did. She wanted to know more, of course, but she also trusted the idea that she and Brooke were perfectly matched in that regard. Maybe – could it be possible? – she and Brooke could be *each other's* solid ground.

'How are you getting back to the farmhouse?' Raphael asked.

Isla looked around and realised. 'Oh, oops. I'm stranded here.'

Raphael smiled. 'It's no trouble at all. We can send you back to the farmhouse with a better driver than Victor.'

'I do appreciate that,' Isla said, 'although I hate to trouble anyone.'

'No trouble at all. Jeanne doubles as a driver, and she will be delighted to take the car out. It doesn't get as much use as Jeanne would like.'

Jeanne turned out to be the other woman who worked

at the vineyard, and the car turned out to be some utterly gorgeous old vehicle. Isla didn't know anything about cars but this looked like some classic 1950s Rolls Royce type that Grace Kelly would have driven in.

Isla drew to a halt upon seeing the car. 'Hang on,' she said. 'There's a mistake.'

'*Oui*,' Jeanne agreed shortly, as she leaned over to rub at a non-existent spot on the bumper. 'Raphael does not keep this car as well as he might. I am forever telling him. Big mistake, letting a man who doesn't appreciate cars take care of this lovely creature.' Jeanne crooned to the car as if it were a tiny baby animal. If the car had had a chin, she would have scratched underneath it.

'Er,' said Isla. 'Not that mistake. The mistake that I can't possibly take that car back to the farmhouse.'

Jeanne looked at her blankly. 'Why not?' And then her expression hardened. 'Don't you like it?'

'No, no,' Isla corrected hastily. 'I love it. It's beautiful. It's much too beautiful for me.'

'*Mademoiselle*,' Jeanne said, and took Isla's hands in her own. It was a gesture so familiar that it startled Isla into being able to do nothing but stare. Jeanne met her gaze solemnly. 'I do not know you very well, but I give you advice that is very important to your life, and you will listen.'

'Okay,' Isla said, because it was unthinkable to say anything else.

'You must believe that you deserve beautiful things like Etienne.'

'Who's Etienne?' asked Isla.

'The car,' said Jeanne.

'Oh,' said Isla.

'You must think better of yourself. You are beautiful, and you deserve beautiful things.'

Isla thought of her mission here today, her determination to tell Brooke exactly the opposite of that, and found herself inexplicably with tears springing up in her eyes. 'Thank you,' she said to Jeanne, her voice choked. 'I don't believe you, of course, but thank you for saying that. I haven't heard that in a long time.'

Jeanne looked dubious, and Isla thought she was going to protest that Isla should believe her, but instead she said, 'Please don't cry inside Etienne.' And Isla laughed.

Just after Sam arrived home, Isla arrived in a gorgeous car.

Sam gaped at it as it came up the driveway. 'That is . . . wow.'

'A nice car?' Libby guessed.

'A *nice car*?' Sam echoed. 'That's putting it mildly.' He practically ran out of the farmhouse to greet it. Libby, amused, followed somewhat more sedately, meeting Max and Arthur and Charlie and Jack and Teddy in the front hall.

The woman from the vineyard was explaining about the car to Sam, although Sam seemed not to need the explanation.

'No, no,' he said. 'I know what it is. I've just never seen one in person before. Can I get in?'

'I didn't know you were a car person,' Max remarked, looking bemused.

'I mean,' said Sam, *'everyone* should be a car person when faced with a car like this.'

'Exactly,' said the vineyard woman, who Isla had introduced as Jeanne, fervently. 'You understand, *monsieur*. It is a relief.'

'I think we are disappointing her,' Max murmured to Libby. 'None of us are as appreciative of the car as she wishes us to be.'

'Excuse me, *messieurs*,' Jeanne called out, 'do not allow the baby to drool upon Etienne.'

'Who's Etienne?' asked Max blankly.

'The *car*,' Jeanne snapped.

Charlie babbled in protest as Arthur tucked him away from the car.

'Also, the dog must be put in the house.'

'What?' exclaimed Teddy in outrage.

Libby ignored all the drama around Etienne in favour of trying to corral Isla as she slunk out of the car.

'So?' she asked eagerly. 'How'd it go?'

'Brooke wasn't even there,' said Isla morosely.

'Well,' said Libby, trying to put a positive spin on things. 'Then you got to drive home in Etienne, so it couldn't have been all bad.'

'Jeanne drives Etienne like she's a museum piece,' Isla said.

'Well, I think Sam would agree with you that Etienne *is* a

252

museum piece.' Libby gestured to where Sam was ooh-ing and aah-ing over everything on the dashboard, pointing out the features to Teddy. Libby had never seen Teddy take much of an interest in cars – probably natural, considering they didn't own one – but he was clearly soaking up his dad's enthusiasm, and it was sweet to see.

'Yes,' Isla said. 'But you don't understand: apparently museum pieces cannot drive more than ten kilometres an hour. It took us for ever to get back here. And every time a car passed going in the opposite direction, Jeanne cursed the dust it kicked up and pulled over and got out and rubbed the car down.'

Charlie was fretful in the evening. Arthur was fairly sure this was because he was getting another tooth in. He walked with him through the garden, trying to distract him with the sights and sounds, but Charlie wasn't in the mood. Jack followed behind them, whining out of concern for Charlie.

Arthur said to Jack, 'I appreciate the gesture, but really, one of you crying is enough.'

Jack abruptly went bounding off away from Arthur, and returned barking with glee as an advance guard for Max.

'Hello, darling,' Max said. 'Still not feeling any better?' He frowned in concern at Charlie, who crankily pushed him away.

'It's his tooth,' Arthur said.

'Teeth are hell,' Max said sympathetically. 'And honestly,

once they're in, you have to deal with the dentist, so it's not like teeth ever get any better.'

'Going to the dentist isn't that big a deal,' Arthur said. 'Ignore him, Charlie.'

Max looked at Arthur, uncharacteristically solemn. 'I'm sorry about our cranky baby.'

'Don't be,' Arthur said. 'To be honest . . . it feels perfect. This entire holiday has been lovely. Charlie's fussiness and all. It's just . . . been a thousand times nicer than I thought. It's not at all what I expected.'

Max looked amused. 'Did you think it was going to be torture?'

Arthur laughed. 'Well, travelling with a small child. Wait, I mean *two* small children.' Arthur gave Max a meaningful look.

'Ha,' said Max. 'Very funny.'

'In all seriousness,' said Arthur, wanting to make sure Max knew how serious Arthur was about this, 'I've had an amazing, wonderful holiday. Thank you so much for suggesting this. I honestly could never thank you enough. I feel revitalised.'

'You don't need to thank me,' Max said. 'It's obviously been my pleasure to whisk you off to a French paradise. And I'm hoping this means you'll be open to taking more holidays.'

'I think I will be,' Arthur said. 'I think it was good to really remind myself of all the life beyond work.'

'You're good at remembering that anyway,' Max said. 'I have no complaints. And I appreciate that you work so hard to give me the luxury of being able to fling paint onto a canvas every so often.'

'I don't mind,' Arthur said. 'I've never minded that. I don't view you as a burden I need to carry.'

'I know,' said Max.

'Speaking of flinging paint onto a canvas, I'm very glad you had an omen that we ought to come to France. You've seemed excited about painting while we're here. I feel like you're out of your usual post-exhibition funk.'

Max laughed. 'I suppose I do go through that every time. It just feels new to me every time.'

'I know,' Arthur said.

'But yes, I'm feeling much, much better. I mean, how can you help but feel anything but inspired here?'

'Because of how beautiful it is.'

'Because of how beautiful you and Charlie are.'

Charlie began crying in earnest, hiccupping through the fat tears rolling down his cheeks.

Arthur said, 'Terribly beautiful.'

Max looked at them and said, 'You have no idea.'

Sam had planned an evening at a patisserie. A baking demonstration. A complement for Libby's cooking classes. Libby was feeling oddly nervous about it, a flutter in her stomach. She thought the presence of Arthur and Max was making all of them feel like they needed to up their romantic game. Sam had planned this date and Libby was feeling nervous like it was the very first days of their courtship.

'You know,' Isla remarked, fastening Libby's necklace for her. 'You should take some of your own advice.'

'Which is?' said Libby.

'*Tell him*,' said Isla.

Libby met Isla's eyes in the mirror.

Isla rubbed Libby's shoulders in a little hug. 'You told me to be honest with Brooke. Don't you think you should be honest with Sam? I mean, at least you know Sam loves you already.'

Which was true. But Libby had been a coward for this long. It was hard to stop being a coward now.

But then they were in the patisserie, and the baker was demonstrating *mille-feuille*, and Libby was thinking, *I know how to do that*. Pauline had taught her. Everything this baker did in front of them, Libby already knew how to do. Not as well and not as expertly, but she was familiar with it. It didn't seem astonishing and intimidating any more, it seemed prosaic and everyday: eminently conquerable, eminently doable.

Libby stood in the patisserie, and Sam whispered into her ear, 'This is just like our first date,' and *everything* suddenly seemed eminently doable. Look how much Libby had accomplished this summer, while she had been convinced she was being a coward. She had learned how to make *mille-feuille*. She could handle a few million more layers to her life.

After the baking class, they walked hand in hand through the village. Sam was talking enthusiastically about the baking class, but Libby was thinking of other things entirely.

Sam noticed. 'You look like you're a million miles away from here.'

Libby opened her mouth, closed it, looked at Sam. And thought, *Here's your chance. Here's what you've really been learning how to do all summer.*

She said, 'I'm in our future.'

Sam lifted his eyebrows and smiled. 'Our future?'

Libby nodded.

'And what does that look like?' asked Sam, still smiling.

And just like that, Libby said it. Just like that, it seemed like the easiest thing in the world to say, looking at Sam beside her, smiling and easy and *hers*. 'We have a baby,' she said.

Sam looked at her, his expression somewhere been puzzlement and joy. 'Do we? Do you want to have a baby?'

'Yes,' Libby said. 'In fact, it's not only wanting at this point.'

Sam went still next to her. His eyes flickered down to her stomach.

Libby nodded and lifted his hand and pressed it against her abdomen.

'Wait,' Sam said, shaking his head a little, looking dazed. '*Really?*'

Libby nodded again.

And then Sam gave a little shout and swept her into his arms and swung her around in a circle.

Libby laughed delightedly and clung to Sam and wondered why she'd ever been worried about any of this.

'Oh, *Libby*,' Sam said, setting her down, and then kissed her.

'You're happy?' Libby said. 'You're really happy?'

'*Yes*,' Sam said, and then tipped his head quizzically. 'Did you think I wouldn't be?'

Libby was embarrassed now over how worried she'd been. 'Yes.'

'Why?' asked Sam, looking bewildered.

'I don't know. You'd made . . . You'd said things, at different times, that made me think you didn't really want any more children. And we'd never talked about this. Believe me, I know. This just sort of happened. I suppose . . . I was a little terrified myself, so I couldn't imagine how *you* were going to feel.'

'Well,' said Sam. 'No offence, but I have the easy part of this whole thing. You're entitled to be more terrified than I am. How are you feeling?' He smoothed a hand over her hair and looked at her with concern.

'So much better now,' Libby said. She couldn't believe how well this had turned out. 'I'm feeling so much better now.'

'I'm sorry you were feeling unwell,' said Sam, and kissed the tip of her nose. 'I'm sorry I said careless things that made you nervous. I know I'm the sort of person who's bad at handling change, but I promise you, I am going to be a *rock* during all of this.'

'I know,' Libby said, and wondered how she could have been so blind. She looked at Sam's dear, beloved face and said, 'I know, because you're such a great dad.'

Sam grinned. 'Teddy is going to be over the moon.'

Teddy was not over the moon.

'What,' he said flatly, staring at Sam and Libby.

Sam didn't know what to make of this reaction. 'Didn't you hear what we said? We're having a baby.'

'A *baby*?' said Teddy. 'Like ... Like Charlie?'

'I mean, yes, the same basic concept.' Sam was perplexed. 'Teddy. This is good news! Congratulate Libby!'

'Great!' Teddy flung his hands skyward in frustration. 'This is just *great*!'

'What?' Sam blinked.

'You're replacing all of us with new models. First Mum and now me.'

Sam was taken completely aback. '*What?* That is not what's happening.'

'Isn't it? You're going to have a brand new baby and no one's even going to notice me any more. I've seen what Charlie's like. No one even has time to look around when they're taking care of Charlie.'

'Teddy,' Sam said, bewildered. 'This is ridiculous—'

'It's not!' Teddy shouted. 'It's *true*! First you made me

259

come to this horrible place, and then you – go and do this – and you might as well just *leave* me here.'

'This is ridiculous and absurd,' Sam bit out. 'How dare you behave this way when you—'

'Sam,' Libby said, laying a hand on his arm. 'Maybe don't—'

'No, Libby. I let him throw his tantrum and have his sulk about going to *France*, of all things, as if he isn't the most privileged child in the universe to get to spend this summer doing this, and now he's acting like this.' Sam turned back to Teddy. 'I understand why you're upset about the new baby, considering that having a new baby means you won't be able to act like a baby any more.'

Teddy's face went furiously red, and then he turned and went running out of the garden.

'Teddy!' Sam called after him.

'Sam, he's—'

'No,' Sam said to her. 'This is ridiculous of him. I'm going to talk to him.'

Sam started out of the garden, entering the house through the kitchen and meeting Arthur coming through.

'Everything okay?' Arthur asked. 'Teddy just went running through here—'

'Everything's fine,' Sam said shortly.

'Okay,' Arthur said slowly. 'Maybe now's not the best time—'

'Not the best time for what?' asked Sam.

'I just got off the phone with Pen. She . . . Bill fell.'

This broke Sam out of his preoccupation. 'He fell? Is he okay? Was it serious?'

'It doesn't seem like it was that serious, but, you know, he's older, and he's fragile, and every fall is serious in those circumstances.'

Sam swore, tearing his hands through his hair. Here was Bill with serious bad things to be distressed about, and instead Teddy was throwing a fit over the good news of a new baby. 'Poor Bill. Christ.'

'We're not sure if he's going to be able to come,' said Arthur.

Chapter Twenty-One

Dear Pari, Some things have happened here. I don't
think I can write them all down. I'll have to tell you
in person.

Teddy, standing at the ghost offering on the landing, heard
Arthur in the kitchen. *Great*, he thought. Another awful
thing. Mr Hammersley wasn't coming. Mr Hammersley
was getting older. Dad was never going to let him move
in with Mr Hammersley, which was clearly the pref-
erable thing to do, since Dad was going to have a new
baby and not care about Teddy any more. At least Mr
Hammersley wasn't going to have any new baby. At least
Mr Hammersley would always care about him, was never
going to *replace* him with a more adorable model.

'Everything's terrible,' Teddy told Jack, as he flung himself onto his bed.

Jack, with a sad wag of his tail, agreed.

Teddy stared at the ceiling above him. It had damp
marks on it, and peeling plaster, and it was probably about

to fall down on him. That would suit him well: the entire ceiling falling down on him.

There was a brisk knock on the door and then Sam opened it. 'Teddy—'

'Go away,' Teddy commanded, turning his back to the door and curling up into a tight ball.

'Teddy, we have to talk about this,' Sam said. 'You're being ridiculous.'

His dad had just announced he was being replaced, and was now saying he was ridiculous for feeling hurt over it. That, Teddy thought, was what Mrs Dash would have called 'adding insult to injury'. Teddy sniffed hard.

Sam said, 'Teddy . . . '

'I'm fine,' Teddy insisted. 'Go away.'

After a moment, he heard the door close.

Teddy lay there, as the house grew quiet all around him, as the adults eventually went to bed, and he thought about how no one was even noticing he was holed up in his room, nobody even *cared*.

They already didn't care.

No one would even notice if he left.

So he left. He got out of bed and walked out of the dark, silent house. Just like that. No one even tried to stop him. No one noticed.

No one was ever going to notice him ever again.

He was going to drift through his life like a ghost. Like the ghosts haunting their house. He should just stay right here in France with all the other ghosts. He was going to fit right in.

'He's a little boy,' Libby said to him.

'That's no excuse.' Sam leaned up against the open door leading to the terrace. In the distance, he could make out lightning flashing across the hills. A storm was rolling in.

'It is an excuse. It's the only really valid excuse,' said Libby. 'You yourself said that he's had a lot of change. A lot of upheaval. I mean. It took me a while to get used to the idea of a baby, and I'm a grown-up. I can't imagine what it's like to be him.' She wrapped her arms around Sam, leaned her chin on his shoulder.

Sam took a deep breath and let it out. When she put it that way, that did make some sense. 'I just . . . ' He turned to face her. 'I never think of it the way he said, and it made me feel so . . . It made *us* feel so . . . This is a wondrous thing. What we have. What we're getting. These are miracles. These are rare, and they are precious. You are not a replacement for Sara, you never have been, that would have been impossible. That's not how it works. I just got to have two rare loves in my life, and that makes me so lucky, and I think every day I'm worried I won't be grateful enough and something in the universe will happen to take that away from me. You asked me why I believed in ghosts, and to be honest there's a superstitious streak a mile wide, and I'm always worrying I will take a step wrong, somewhere, and not be grateful enough. Like, maybe I wasn't grateful enough the first time around, maybe I didn't notice the

264

rarity of ... Anyway. I am the luckiest person on the planet, that I have Teddy, and that now I'm going to get to meet another child, and how dare he act like he's not lucky, too. Like he's not lucky to have you, and this little baby inside of you.'

'Oh, Sam,' Libby said, softly, gently, and cupped her hands around Sam's face.

Thunder rumbled and lightning flashed and she leaned her forehead against Sam's. 'You know these things because you learned them with the wisdom of age. He hasn't learned them yet. We need to be patient with him. We need to give him time to get here with us. He's just a little boy.'

'Yeah.' Sam took a deep breath. Libby was so calm, and so grounded, and if anyone should be upset, it ought to be her, hearing her stepson so blatantly unhappy about her pregnancy. It gave Sam the ability to take a breath and settle down himself, find that calming groundedness.

'Give him time,' Libby murmured. 'Isn't that what you kept saying to me while he was sulking? Give him time, and he'll come round. He's a good kid who loves us a whole lot. He's just feeling overwhelmed.'

'Yeah.' Sam straightened away from her and kissed her forehead. 'You're right.'

'I'm very wise,' she said.

'I hope our baby inherits your brain.'

'If we're lucky,' she grinned. 'Now, come to bed and watch the storm with me.'

Sam fell asleep to the crack of thunder and the lashing of rain against the windows, the storm being violent enough that they had to close the doors. And he awoke to the sound of Jack, barking furiously.

From outside.

It took a second for that to penetrate through his sleep, but once it did he sat bolt upright in bed. Jack. Outside. Jack had been on Teddy's bed the last time Sam had seen him.

Why would Jack be outside?

Sam leaped out of bed.

'Sam?' Libby said sleepily. 'What—'

Sam ignored her, racing out of the bedroom. He met Max and Arthur coming out of their room, Max holding a squalling Charlie.

'Is that Jack outside?' Arthur asked.

Sam threw open Teddy's bedroom door and punched the lights on. Empty. The room was empty. 'Oh, my God,' he breathed.

'What is going on?' Max asked.

'Teddy's gone,' Sam said.

'What?' said Libby, coming out of their room, rubbing sleep out of her eyes.

'He's gone. He left. He ran away. And there's a huge storm. And Jack is out there barking.' Sam shouted this up towards everyone as he ran down the stairs.

'Sam!' he heard Arthur call behind him. 'Wait!'

'We'll help you look!' added Max.

But Sam didn't have time to wait. Who knew how long Teddy had been outside, all alone, lost, without Jack?

The rain was coming down in sheets that took Sam's breath away when he stepped out into it, and his son was caught somewhere in this. His heart clenched in his chest at the thought. Jack leaped up at him and then bounded away, still barking furiously.

'Yes, I'm here now, let's find him,' Sam said breathlessly, and followed Jack.

Jack was moving at a punishing pace, and Sam hadn't stopped to put shoes on, and it probably wasn't wise to just be dashing around like this barefoot but also Jack was freaking out and that made Sam freak out. Sam knew Jack now; Jack never panicked unnecessarily.

Jack only panicked like this when it was a matter of saving someone's life.

Sam stumbled over the terrain as Jack wove them through the trees, barking and barking. Surely Teddy would have been able to hear Jack's barking, but Sam added his voice, hoping Teddy would hear it and know help was coming. 'Teddy! Teddy, I'm coming, hang tight!' He tripped over a tree root and reached a hand out to scrape against the trunk, then kept going, pushing through. He thought he could maybe hear the rest of the house calling his name as they pursued him, but he focused on getting to Teddy.

Jack stopped running, standing in one spot, pacing and barking, and Sam, reaching him, caught his forward momentum just in time to realise that he was staring down into what looked like possibly an old well. Teddy, at the bottom of it, looked up at him, and a flash of lightning illuminated the sheer terror in his eyes.

'Dad?' he said, lower lip trembling.

'Teddy,' Sam gasped. 'Hi. Okay. I'm here. Are you hurt? What hurts?'

Teddy shook his head desperately. 'Nothing. I'm fine. I'm not really hurt. I mean, a bit scratched but I didn't break anything, I just . . . can't get up.'

'Right,' Sam said, and tried to lean over to grab him. But the well was too deep, and even Teddy on his tiptoes, straining for him, couldn't reach him.

'Hang on,' Sam said, and sprawled onto his stomach, hanging over the edge of the well and reaching down with all his might. Still not close enough.

'Dad,' Teddy said, tears soggy in his voice.

'It's okay,' Sam said. 'We're going to—' Then he became aware of everyone else calling for him. He leaned away from the wall to call back, 'Here! We're over here! I need your help.'

Max and Arthur both appeared out of the trees.

'He fell into this well,' Sam said. 'It's not that deep but it's deep enough I can't reach him.'

Max and Arthur peered over the side.

Max said jovially, 'Not to worry, Teddy. We're going to get you out.'

Arthur said, 'Sam, if Max and I hold onto you, you can get yourself further over the edge without falling in your-self. I think you'll be able to reach him then.'

'Right,' Sam said. 'Right. That makes sense.'

He stayed sprawled out on his stomach, and Max and Arthur took up position behind him, holding his legs, and inched him forwards with a gentle nudge.

'Almost,' Sam said, straining for Teddy as Teddy strained toward him. 'Almost—'

And then Teddy's fingers brushed his, and then his whole hand, and then Sam clasped him firmly and pulled upwards with all his might.

Sam ached from head to toe, his muscles were knotting up in protest, he had a million bruises, the scrapes on his hands from the tree trunk were still oozing droplets of blood, and his feet were so torn apart he could barely walk, but it was only Teddy he was focused on, bundled in blankets on his bed, shivering, while Libby thrust hot chocolate into his hands and Arthur brusquely looked over his head for any injury.

'No harm done, really,' Arthur said. 'You seem fine to me.'

'You've got one tough kid,' Max told him.

'*Lucky*,' Sam said. 'We're so lucky.'

'Plus there was Jack,' Teddy said.

'Thank God for Jack,' said Sam.

'Well. Now that we know you're okay, maybe we should all try to get some sleep,' said Libby, tactfully clearing the room.

Which Sam appreciated. He had a million things he wanted to say to Teddy, and one of them was *What the bloody hell were you thinking?*, but instead he said none of them. He just stared at him, whole and alive and there. *Teddy.*

Teddy put his hot chocolate aside and then looked back at him hesitantly and said, 'I'm sorry, Dad, I—'

'I'm so glad you're okay,' Sam said, choked, and then he clambered onto Teddy's bed and pulled him into his arms like he was a much smaller child.

Teddy clung to him, trembling against him.

'Teddy, Teddy, Teddy,' Sam breathed against him. 'I'm so glad you're here. And okay. And here. I'm so, so glad.'

'I wasn't sure you'd notice,' Teddy said. 'When I fell into the well, I . . . I wasn't sure anyone would ever come looking for me.'

'*Teddy*,' Sam said, anguished. 'What have I ever done that would make you think that I wouldn't notice you were gone? That I wouldn't come looking for you? I would look for you for the rest of *time*, Teddy. I would miss you with every breath I took until I found you. I have done something terribly wrong that you don't—'

Sam cut himself off, took a deep breath, and forced himself to let go of Teddy a little bit, make Teddy look him in the eye.

'Teddy. This new baby is not about replacing you. Any more than Libby is about replacing your mum. That's not how it is at all. Love isn't finite. You're not given a set amount and that's all you get to spend in your lifetime.

270

Love just keeps filling up, spilling over. When I met your mum and fell in love with your mum, I thought I could never love anyone as much, that that was it, I'd made my quota. And honestly I was happy with that, because your mum was amazing and I considered myself lucky. But then you were born and I realised I was kidding myself: I hadn't met my love quota. There was so much more inside of me. There's always going to be so much more inside of me. I will always love you the most impossible amount. I would love you that way if I had ten children, but, I'm not going to have ten children. And I'm not going to love you any less. I'm not taking love away from you to give to the new baby. I will keep loving you more, every day, the way I always have. I will keep being amazed, every day, by *you*. And I will keep, every day, being *so grateful* that I get to know you, and love you, and raise you. You have already made me the luckiest person in the universe. And now we get to be the luckiest people *together*. I already had a baby alone. I don't want to do it again. I want to have a baby with a big brother around.'

Teddy's eyes were wide, and he looked very young, but at least not quite as pale as he had been. And not nearly as angry, or despairing, or hopeless.

Sam ruffled his hair. 'What do you say? Want to do this thing with Libby and me? We desperately want you to. We can't imagine life without you.'

Teddy swallowed thickly. Then he said, 'Big brother.'
'Yeah.'
'I didn't think about that.'

271

'Yeah.' Sam smiled. 'Big brother. That's you. Now, instead of just having Libby and me to adore you, you'll have another little person, too.'

'Big brother,' Teddy said, and swallowed again. 'Okay. Maybe that could work.' Sam kissed his forehead.

Chapter Twenty-Two

An Evening under the Stars at Château Laurent!

Join us for food, music, dancing, and, of course, wine from our fabulous vineyards!

More Christmas Street people were beginning to arrive.

Isla had heard quite the earful about Pari from Teddy. Pari this and Pari that and Pari was an excellent dog trainer and Pari was a genius spy and Pari was a good planner and once Pari had broken a vase just to prove Millie was a ninja.

'Was Millie a ninja?' Isla asked.

'No,' Teddy admitted. 'But it was a good plan.'

Isla smiled.

Teddy's excitement was infectious, and it took Isla's mind off Brooke.

Bill had no interest in going to France. He told everyone on Christmas Street many times that he had no intention of going. And then he fell, and it looked as if he wasn't going to be able to go to France, and then he was *determined* to go to France, it was the only thing he wanted to do. He wasn't going to be so old as to be told that he couldn't travel to France. Pen insisted on coming along as a babysitter even though that wasn't necessary, but maybe it was nice to have some company to keep him from thinking too much about Agatha.

At the train station, Teddy shouted, 'Mr Hammersley!' and came running up to him, and Bill realised why he'd been so determined to come to France, and it wasn't anything to do with proving he could still do it.

Jack came up, bouncing around, barking excitedly.

'Hello, Jack,' Bill said. 'Hello, Teddy. Really, no need to make such a fuss, goodness.'

'We didn't think that you were coming! You fell! How do you feel? Are you okay?'

'I'm perfectly all right,' Bill said gruffly. 'Goodness, so much fuss for no reason, honestly. Pen's been hovering over me the entire time, it's been ridiculous.'

'Sorry you've been so suffocated with love and care,' Sam said good-naturedly, prising Teddy away from him a bit. 'How are you? You look excellent.'

'I'm fine,' Bill grumbled. 'I cannot believe how much everyone keeps *fussing*.'

'See?' Pen added, smiling. 'He is absolutely *fine*.'

'How do *I* look?' Teddy asked.

'Er,' said Bill, not sure what he was supposed to say. Teddy looked like Teddy.

'Good?'

'I'm almost ten now!' Teddy exclaimed. 'Don't I look older?'

'Oh,' said Bill, still not knowing what he was supposed to say.

'You look *much* older,' Pen said. 'Have you started going grey?'

'Funny you should mention that, we found a grey hair on Teddy's head yesterday,' Sam said.

'Did you?' asked Bill.

Sam laughed. 'No, I'm joking.'

'Look at what Jack can do,' Teddy said. 'Jack, what's two plus two?' Jack barked four times.

'See?' Teddy said. 'Jack can do maths!'

Bill blinked at Jack, impressed. 'Jack, what's one plus one?' Jack barked four times.

'He can only do maths if the answer is four,' said Teddy.

'That's how I do maths,' remarked Pen.

'Hello, Bill,' Libby said, leaning forward to hug him. 'We're so excited you're here.'

'Well, it's silly,' Bill grumbled. 'I don't know what you expect to do with an old man around for the next few days.'

'And you were just so determined to come on this holiday,' Pen pointed out, with the gall of sounding amused.

Bill mumbled nonsense under his breath that he hoped sounded disapproving.

'We've got a lot planned,' Libby said, smiling. 'My mother's already arrived and is looking forward to taking some nice long rambles.'

'We're going to enter you in a pétanque tournament,' said Sam, as he took Bill's luggage and directed them to the car. 'We think you'll win.'

'Oh, stop,' said Bill, 'you're so foolish.'

Sam laughed. 'It was a joke, don't worry about it. Although, if you'd like us to . . .'

Bill harrumphed.

Sam laughed again and then said, 'Oh, wait, Pen, how silly, let me help you with those bags,' and moved off to where Pen was wrestling their luggage into place.

'We've got a huge secret!' Teddy exclaimed. 'Wait till you hear it!'

'Is it about this tournament thing?' Bill asked suspiciously.

'No, no, it's way better than that.' Teddy cast a suspicious eye toward Pen and his dad to make sure they weren't listening, then leaned closer to Bill. 'But you can't tell anyone else,' Teddy hissed at him. 'They don't know yet.'

Bill was in that state of utter bewilderment that he always had when dealing with the Bishops.

He'd never actually tell any of them this because he'd never want to encourage their tomfoolery, but he may have missed that particular Bishop-inspired bewilderment. Just a bit.

'What do you mean, there's no electricity?' said Bill.

'The house is haunted,' Teddy said.

'Haunted?' barked Bill. 'What nonsense is this? The house isn't haunted.'

'I tried to tell them the same thing,' Rebecca, Libby's mum, said, shaking her head. 'They're obsessed with the idea. Look at the ghost offering.'

'*Offering?*' Bill repeated in disbelief. 'You're making an offering to ghosts?'

'Victor said we had to,' said Teddy.

'Who's Victor?' asked Bill.

'He comes with the house,' said Teddy.

'Is he a ghost, too?' demanded Bill.

Sam laughed. 'No, he's the caretaker. Such as it is. Took much better care of the garden than the house, as you can see. Anyway, here in France, we believe in ghosts.'

'I love everything about this place,' Pen announced.

'Well, I've never heard such flim-flam in all my life,' said Bill. 'This bloke won't fix the electrics because he's lazy. It obviously has nothing to do with ghosts.'

'It's all right,' Sam said. 'We turned out not to need the other part of the house, so we've got along okay.'

'And the ghosts have let us keep electricity in the rest of the house,' said Teddy.

'That is a ridiculous statement,' said Bill.

Teddy apparently ignored him. 'Come see the kittens!' he said instead.

The kittens were admittedly cute little things. They were tumbling all over each other, their feet getting in each other's way.

'Everyone gets to take one home!' Teddy said. 'You'll have to pick one out, Mr Hammersley. And Pen. Oh, and you, too, Rebecca, they're not just Christmas Street cats.'

'You know,' Libby said, 'you'd better stop and count the kittens. You've given more away than we have.'

'Oh, Brooke said we could have some of hers, too,' Teddy said.

'It's true,' Libby's friend Isla confirmed.

Bill had no idea who Brooke was or what her kittens were. He was preoccupied with what Teddy had said. 'I'm not taking home a kitten. What will I do with a cat?'

'Play with it,' said Teddy.

'Cuddle it,' said Rebecca.

Bill stared at her.

Rebecca said, 'Actually, I think I rather like the idea of a kitten. There are always mice to chase out in the country.'

'Exactly,' Teddy said, and then thought. 'Although, you'd have to bring your cat to Christmas Street a lot to visit all the other cats. I don't want them to get lonely. In fact, maybe you'd better take two.'

Rebecca laughed. 'Maybe I'll take Bill's, too.'

They had dinner outside, in the back garden, and it was casual and boisterous and Bill didn't mind it as much as he might have.

He'd been given a bedroom at the front of the house. There weren't enough rooms for everyone and Pen was going off to stay at the inn in town, but Bill had been urged to stay right in the farmhouse with them. Bill told himself this was a dubious honour, as he walked up the stairs past the ridiculous ghost offering. He made sure to scoff at it on his way past but he didn't disturb it because, well, he didn't want to be accused of upsetting the house's ghosts.

And, with the sound of the rest of the party downstairs drifting up to him, he had to admit he wasn't truly dubious about how lovely this all was. His room was large and airy, the windows standing open to the sort of gorgeous Provence view Agatha would have loved. Jack trotted into the room after him and wagged his tail and jumped up on the bed.

Bill smiled at him. 'Spending the night with me, are you? I hope Teddy won't be too heartbroken, but I do think it's my turn for a bit of Jack time.' He rubbed behind Jack's ears and Jack wagged his tail.

He slept astonishingly well, which he credited to travelling the day before and the fresh country air coming in through the window. Bill loved London and would never live anywhere else, but the air in London was nothing like the air out here, it had to be admitted.

Agatha had noticed very much the same thing, all those years earlier.

In the morning, Bill went downstairs bright and early. No one else in the house seemed to be up, so Bill got Jack some breakfast and then poked around for something suitable for him.

Rebecca, who had also been given a room in the farmhouse, came into the kitchen and said briskly, 'Oh, lovely. There was no one up for ages yesterday and breakfast was a very lonely affair.'

'Oh,' said Bill, because that seemed like a sufficient response, and then he gestured vaguely to the kitchen. 'What have they got for breakfast round here anyway?'

'I can whip something up,' Rebecca said cheerfully.

'Oh, you don't have to,' said Bill, feeling awkward at making Rebecca go to work for him.

'Nonsense. I made myself breakfast yesterday, at least today I'll have someone to share it with. Everything here is so delightfully fresh. Libby says they go to one of the local markets virtually every day. I think that's such a healthy way to live, don't you? I've often thought that Libby and Sam might give some thought to moving Teddy out of the city. It's such an unhealthy place to raise a child, don't you think? I keep reminding Libby what a lovely, joyous childhood she had, out in a village with a bit of room where you can breathe. The air out here is just incredible, isn't it?'

Bill had been thinking much the same thing the night before but he bristled at the idea of Sam and Libby and Teddy moving away. He said, 'Children can be raised in London just as well as anywhere else. Teddy has a little village all his own that he has full run of.'

Rebecca paused, then allowed diplomatically, 'True.'

The entire time she'd been talking, Rebecca had been gathering ingredients, and now she was pulling together a proper fry-up. Eggs were sizzling in the pan and the smell of bacon was gathering in the little kitchen. Bill couldn't remember the last time he'd had a proper fry-up for breakfast. His mouth was watering. He glanced down at Jack, who looked just as eager for the fry-up as Bill felt.

Rebecca eventually put breakfast on the table and sat opposite Bill and said, 'I've never actually been to Provence before like this. Libby said there's a local vineyard everyone always takes a tour of. I've never been to tour a vineyard before. I'm looking forward to it. Surely you'll come along?'

Bill, with a fry-up in front of him and a good night's sleep behind him, felt decidedly less glum. If ever there was a time to be more adventurous, maybe this was it. If you couldn't be adventurous whilst on holiday in France, when could you?

Bill said, 'Yes, that sounds lovely.'

Libby said honestly to Rebecca, as she walked with her through the back garden, 'It's lovely to have you here, Mum. It's just lovely.'

Rebecca's face glowed with pleasure. 'It's lovely being here. Thank you for the invitation.'

Libby thought of the baby inside her. The knowledge that she was about to embark on this new journey made her feel even more grateful that her mother would be there through all the confusion. She said, unexpectedly choked up, 'I'm really glad you could come.'

Rebecca looked at her, startled. It wasn't like Libby to start crying like that. 'Oh, dear, is everything okay, Libby?'

Libby nodded and swiped at her eyes. 'I'm fine. Sorry. It's just been an emotional summer.'

'France can have that effect.'

'I guess so,' Libby said, and sniffled and got herself under control.

She was about to say something else even more sentimental when Rebecca said, 'I'm so glad you and Sam and Teddy took this holiday. I think it was a good idea, to start your life off like this. I think it will be a memory you cherish as you go through the rest of your life together. The rest of your adventure.'

'And I think it is definitely going to be an adventure,' Libby remarked. And then she took her mother's hands in hers and said softly, 'I'm having a baby, Mum.'

Her mother's face was still for a moment, and then joy began dawning on it. 'Oh, *Libby*,' she said, and pulled her into a fierce, close hug. 'Oh, darling! That's such wonderful news!'

'It's taken me most of the summer to come to terms with it,' Libby admitted. 'But I think I've finally got there.'

'It's *wonderful*,' Rebecca said. 'Having a baby is terrifying, of course. But you'll face it all together, and that will be the best part about it.'

And Libby believed it. 'We'll face it all together. Yes.'

Rebecca was silent for a moment, then said, 'I think I shall have to move closer. Are there any openings on Christmas Street?'

Sam found Bill in the hall, studying the carvings on the staircase balustrade, and he said, 'I hope you're enjoying your stay here.'

'Very much,' Bill said, and Sam hadn't exactly expected an honest response, so he didn't know what to say for a moment.

Bill straightened away from the staircase, brushing a hand over it reflectively, and said into Sam's silence, 'It's beautiful work.'

'It is,' Sam said. 'Jasper's coming soon, and I'm really looking forward to what he thinks about the whole place.'

'Oh, I think he'll be impressed. It's impressive. Ghost offering nonsense aside.' Bill waved his hand to where the ghost offering still sat.

Sam chuckled. 'Yes, well, that aside, this house has been lovely to stay in. I'm sorry to see it coming to an end.'

'You've still got a bit of time,' Bill said.

'You know,' Sam said, 'your carving is just as beautiful as anything in this house.'

'You do say the most ridiculous things,' Bill said.

'No, I don't. You're an artist. You could be an artist, like Max. Max has already said you could have a show. Maybe it's time to start thinking about that. You're still alive, you

283

know. You've got plenty of time for more adventures. Look how well this one is turning out.'

Bill's hand rubbed up and down and over the balustrade, and Bill watched it reflectively, quiet.

Sam waited him out, aware that just to have Bill mulling this over was a triumph.

And then Bill said, 'I don't know. Maybe you're right. I don't know.'

Sam smiled. 'We'll talk about it more. I bet we can talk you into it. Just like Teddy talked you into that kitten.'

'I'm only taking the kitten if no one else wants him,' Bill insisted. 'I don't want him to get left behind without all his mates.'

Sam smiled. 'Noted.'

Millie's first glimpse of the farmhouse was akin to glimpsing heaven. Then again, she'd been feeling that way ever since she left London. Everything she saw was incredibly, impossibly beautiful. Jasper seemed able to continue to carry on conversation, making small talk with Sam as he drove them from the train station, but Millie was far too distracted by everything.

'There's the tree that looks like Winston Churchill,' Sam said, which made no sense, but Millie didn't even care.

The house was everything a French farmhouse should be, and Millie was rapturous over it but trying not to be. But she couldn't believe she was *here*.

284

Jasper smiled at her and took her hand and squeezed it, and Millie amended that thought: she couldn't believe she was here *with Jasper*.

And so much of the rest of Christmas Street, who greeted her happily like they hadn't just seen her a few days ago and then led them on a tour of the house.

'I hope you've brought party clothes,' Libby said, as they settled in the back garden all together. 'We have a very special vineyard experience. We've been invited to a *party* there.'

'A party?' said Millie.

'Isla's got a special in,' Libby said.

Isla rolled her eyes. 'I don't have a special in.'

'She's dating one of the vineyard workers,' Libby said.

'Aw,' said Millie. 'Is that true? That's so romantic.'

Isla said, looking a little embarrassed, 'I don't know. I guess. Sort of.'

'It's totally true,' Libby said. 'It was love at first sight.'

'I don't even believe in love at first sight,' Isla said.

'It was totally love at first sight,' Libby said. 'Don't mind Isla, I'm going to have to correct everything she says.'

Millie smiled. Libby and Isla were sweet together. Millie liked the dynamic. When she had been with her ex-husband Daniel, he had isolated her from all of the friends she had had before, and while she had tried to reconnect with some of them, she felt like their relationships faltered, like they were always looking at her wondering how she'd got everything so wrong. It was nice to be in the presence of an easy friendly relationship born of years of knowing each other.

Millie may have lost that, but also maybe she was

gradually rebuilding that. Here she was, on holiday, with friends who had invited her. Maybe, in a few years, it would be her and Libby, knowing each other that well.

Isla said, 'Okay, enough about me, tell me about you and Jasper. Was it love at first sight?'

Millie looked for Jasper, finding him down in the olive grove, with Sam and Teddy and Max and Arthur and Charlie, Jack racing in circles around all of them. She said, 'Maybe it was. It feels now like it was.'

'I get exactly what you mean,' said Libby with a smile. 'And Isla will be saying exactly that about Brooke in a few months' time.'

The Basaks and Pachutas arrived together, in a flurry of activity, and Isla was introduced to everyone. As with everyone else Isla had met from Christmas Street, they seemed like pleasant people, except that Anna Pachuta was a trifle preoccupied with the ruins of her luggage.

'I *told* you it wouldn't survive the journey,' her teenage daughter was saying, and shaking her head at the state of it.

'Oh, dear,' said Teddy, examining the suitcase. 'Did everyone see your underwear hanging out like that?'

'This is the worst moment of my life,' announced Emilia.

'Well, at least everyone who was going to see your underwear has now seen your underwear,' Teddy pointed out. 'You can go put it away and it'll be like we never saw your underwear.'

Emilia gave him a look. 'Will it?'

'I feel like you shouldn't mention Emilia's knickers like that,' said Pari.

'I would like to go up to my room,' said Sai, looking mortified. 'Is that possible?'

And then there was the jangling of a bicycle bell, and Brooke came into the farmyard.

Teddy said, 'Oh, look, another person's going to see your underwear.'

'Oh, no,' moaned Emilia. 'Just kill me now.'

'Don't worry,' said Teddy. 'That's Brooke. She's Isla's girlfriend.'

'I don't think you're helping anything,' Sam told Teddy, 'so why don't we stop talking about Emilia's knickers and just all go inside?'

'Except for Isla, of course,' said Teddy, with the frankness of youth believing adult interactions to be childishly uncomplicated.

Libby gave Isla a querying look, as if to ask if she was going to be all right alone with Brooke. Isla hadn't filled Libby in on exactly everything that had happened in Isla's brain, but Isla felt like Libby had a good idea that Isla had been in a bad headspace.

Isla shook her head a little, to indicate to Libby that she was going to be fine.

Brooke said, 'Oh, my, look at the crowd.'

Emilia scurried over and pulled a pair of obvious knickers out of sight, tucking them in her pocket.

'Brooke,' Isla said, because she felt the introduction

burden should be on her, 'these are more Christmas Street neighbours.'

'More?' said Brooke, sounding amused.

'There's a lot of them,' said Isla.

Teddy said to Pari, 'Do you want to see the kittens?'

Anna said, 'Do you have kittens here? How lovely. What does Jack think of them?'

'He loves them and they love him. Come see them. They've opened their eyes and are really starting to be *kittens* now,' Teddy said.

Pari and Teddy raced off, and Sam said, 'Come on, I'll show you to your room, stop worrying about the luggage, it's fine,' and reached for the luggage.

Libby looked at Brooke and said, 'Brooke, did you want to come in for a glass of wine or something?'

Brooke hesitated, and Isla said, 'That's okay, I think Brooke and I are going to go for a walk,' and felt very brave as she said it.

Brooke smiled at her and said, 'Good idea.'

The day was hitting that endless twilight time that seemed to make the air all around them glow golden, and they struck out in an aimless direction together, away from the house. Isla wanted as much privacy for this conversation as possible.

Brooke said, looking around as they walked, 'I've always admired this parcel of land. It's so beautiful. And the history of it is quite something.'

'Yes, the rivals,' Isla said. 'Raphael told us all about it.'

'Rivals?' Brooke echoed, frowning.

'Yes. Mary and Adélaïde.'

'Were they rivals?'

'That's what Raphael said. I mean, not to me. The day we learned about all of that, I was . . . with you. In the vineyard. But that's what everyone else said later. Mary and Adélaïde were rivals.'

'Rivals for what?'

'This house. It belonged to Adélaïde's brother, and she didn't approve of his British wife.'

Brooke smiled wryly. 'Trust the French to tell a story about mistrusting the British.'

'Why? Isn't that how the story goes?'

'The idea that throughout history women had to be rivals instead of friends is a special pet peeve of mine,' Brooke said. 'I didn't hear that Mary and Adélaïde were rivals. I heard they liked each other very much. They were friends. After Mary and Clarissa moved back to England, Mary sent her daughter here every summer to visit.'

Isla frowned. 'Right, but not with Adélaïde. I thought Adélaïde went away when Mary's daughter came to visit.'

'Adélaïde wanted her to have a relationship with her father. But she didn't stay away the whole time. And Mary very much wanted Clarissa to have a relationship with Adélaïde, too.'

'This story's very different. Where did you hear it?'

'From a real estate agent,' Brooke said. 'They all know the gossip about the properties around here.'

'But why would Raphael tell us they were rivals?'

'Because it's a more dramatic story.'

'If they were friends, why would they be haunting the house?'

Brooke cast her an amused glance. 'That presupposes they are haunting the house. It presupposes that the house is haunted at all.'

Isla realised that she had just come to accept it as a given that the house was haunted. She said slowly, 'Yes, I suppose that's true,' and noticed that they were coming upon a small, weathered structure perched next to a little stream. 'Oh!' she exclaimed. 'This must be the playhouse Sam found the other day.'

'Playhouse.' Brooke looked at it in wonder. 'A bit big for a playhouse.' She looked at Isla and grinned mischievously. 'Maybe it's a playhouse for adults.'

Isla had been distracted throughout their walk by the new story about Mary and Adélaïde. But now she felt all of her nerves rush back into her system, looking at Brooke smiling at her like she expected her to flirt back. *Tell her*, Isla screamed at herself.

Brooke said gently, 'I'm sorry I've been a bit . . . I know I wasn't around when you came to see me and that maybe it seems like I . . . I know I could have texted you and . . . I'm worried I'm giving you the impression that I don't want to talk to you, when the opposite is true. I would like to talk to you for many hours on end. I'd like to whisk you somewhere and just . . . talk. A lot. About anything and everything. For instance. Here we have this handy playhouse, perfect to curl up in and talk. I'd like to talk and so much more. I'd like everything. Partly I've been trying to come to terms with how much I would like everything. But if you would like everything, too, well, then, I think we could ... maybe ... try to have everything? Could that be arranged?'

It was the sweetest, most beautiful speech anyone had ever made to her, and Isla had no idea what she was supposed to do in the face of it. People didn't *speak* to her like that.

People didn't say such nice things to her. Isla blurted out, 'You should run away from me.'

'Run *from* you?' Brooke repeated quizzically. 'That is not at all what I want to do. That's what I'm saying.'

Isla shook her head. 'No, but it's what you *should* do. You should run away from me before I run away from you.'

Brooke was looking at her closely, with those unerring eyes that seemed to see right through her. 'Why would you run away from me?'

'Because I just *do* that,' Isla said in anguish. 'I'm always mucking everything up. I'm terrible with relationships. All relationships. I've never had any successful relationship in my life. I don't do people well. People don't like me. I don't love them well enough.'

'That's not true,' Brooke said.

Isla shook her head again. 'You don't know me. You don't know how true it is.'

'I know you're spending the summer at the house of a friend of yours from college. Libby likes you a lot. She seems to think you love her well enough.'

'I didn't even go to her *wedding*,' Isla said. 'She got married, and I didn't even come home for it. I . . . ' She trailed off helplessly.

Brooke's gaze was still unerringly on her. 'What were you doing?'

Isla uttered a laugh that was more like a sob. 'I don't even know! I mean, I was travelling. I've always been travelling. I've been travelling since university ended.'

'Why?' asked Brooke.

It was such a straightforward question, asked so simply, that Isla didn't know what to say, momentarily thrown. 'What?'

'Why were you travelling?'

Isla considered, seriously, for the first time in a long time. 'I said I wanted adventure. I said I wanted to see the world. I'm bad at putting down roots. I'm always restless. I've always just wanted to *move*. So I moved.'

'But *why*?' Brooke asked again. 'I mean . . . ' She looked out at the stream trickling by them. 'In my experience, restlessness is usually there for a reason. Either this feeling that you're not doing enough, that the world needs more out of you, that you need to . . . be more than you are.'

Isla looked at Brooke curiously. 'Is that why you're here in France?'

Brooke took a deep breath and let it out in a whooshing exhale. 'Yeah. I think it is. I felt like . . . yeah, I felt like there was more I needed to do. More I could be. More I could give. I had this job that was supposed to be everything in my life, it was supposed to make me fulfilled and happy, just this job . . . But it didn't work like that for me. I couldn't just have that job. I came here because I felt like I needed . . . *something*. Something more. I couldn't articulate it. Everyone made fun of me for dropping everything for a vineyard, like I'd find truth at the bottom of a wine glass. But the truth is . . . I found much, much better than that. I found . . . I would never have predicted what I've found. I had no idea. But . . . look at it. You're my *something*.' Brooke looked from the stream back to Isla and smiled a little. Normally Brooke's smile was so wide and confident, but now it looked small and hesitant and hopeful, like it was asking a question. *Tell me that's okay*, it seemed to say. *Tell me I'm okay.*

And that was so exactly what Isla wanted to ask Brooke to do for her. 'I think that's a great reason to be here. That's not why I went travelling.'

'Why did you go travelling?'

'Because I run away. Because I always run away. Because I sabotage the things that are good about my life, and when people get close to me I push them away, and I run.'

Brooke looked at her for a long moment. Then she said lightly, 'Who told you that?'

Isla blinked. That was not what she had been expecting Brooke's reaction to be.

'What?'

'Someone told you that. Someone told you that you do that. Who told you that?'

Isla swallowed and looked away. 'It doesn't matter.'

'I think it does,' insisted Brooke gently. 'Because for some reason you believe the person who told you that.'

'Because they were right!' Isla said. 'I mean, here I am, still flitting about, while everyone I went to university with is getting married and having babies and I'm ... alone.'

Brooke reached out to take Isla's hand and squeezed it. 'You're not alone,' she said softly.

Isla stared down at their joined hands.

'And maybe you were running away from the people you ran away from because they weren't right for you. Not all of us find what we need in the first place we look. That doesn't make us broken. That doesn't mean there's something wrong with us.'

Isla kept her gaze on their hands. 'But what if it's true about me? What if I am like that?' She forced herself to look up, to be brave and meet Brooke's gaze while she said this. 'What if I poison everything I touch? What if I'm about to break your heart?'

Brooke didn't look horrified, the way Isla had thought she would. She didn't look wary, or concerned, or angry. She looked unaccountably *enchanted*. Isla didn't even know what to make of it, watching in astonishment as the corner of Brooke's mouth tipped up into an unmistakably fond smile. She lifted her free hand up and cupped Isla's cheek tenderly. 'I've had my heart broken before, by people not nearly as worth it as you are, because they weren't people who ever *worried* about breaking it before it had happened. You're preworried about hurting me. That makes me feel a lot better about my chances of not being hurt, frankly.'

Isla uttered a little squeak, that she intended to be protesting but probably sounded more charmed, because *really*.

294

She said, 'I wanted you to understand who I am. I wanted you to understand what a disaster of a human I am. And I don't think that's really happening right now.'

Brooke, unbelievably, *laughed*. 'Maybe it's happened but I just think you're still incredible.'

Isla shook her head. 'Maybe I'm worried about you, not because I'm going to break your heart but because you have no sense of self-preservation.' Brooke just laughed again.

Isla took a deep breath and said, 'I wanted ... I wanted to make sure that you were falling in love with *me*. Not a better version of me. *Me*.'

Brooke said, 'But, Isla, I'm pretty sure you *are* the better version of you.'

'Wait, wait, wait,' Brooke said, laughing. 'Time out. Hang on.' She waved her hands around in a *stop* sort of gesture. 'I'm going to need more explanation on how you ended up *accidentally* becoming a monk.'

'I mean,' said Isla primly, trying not to grin too hard, 'that's a story that you need more alcohol in me to get out of me.'

'I see,' said Brooke, 'the alcohol goes in and the story about monkish transgressions comes out.'

Isla laughed. 'Something like that.'

'Let me ask you a question. Did accidentally becoming a monk involve alcohol going into you?'

'No, actually. *I* was perfectly sober.'

'Hmm,' said Brooke. 'Let me guess. Can't say the same for the guy who made you a monk?'

'Maybe,' said Isla, and tried her hand at a Mona Lisa smile. She wasn't sure how successful she was but Brooke looked delighted and charmed, so Isla thought she wasn't doing too badly.

They were sitting on the bed in the playhouse, which was much more comfortable than either of them had supposed it would be, and all around them darkness had fallen, such that they could barely make out each other's faces, the endless twilight finally seeming to gleam into full-on night, and Isla had never had as much fun in her life as she had curled up with Brooke just talking about everything. Isla wasn't sure she'd ever spent time like that just ... getting to know someone. She felt like every relationship she'd ever had had been so dedicated to spontaneity that she had jumped in, feet first, and all the getting-to-know-you part happened later. Upon reflection, that had probably caused many of the problems with the relationships.

Maybe she hadn't been sabotaging things, so much as they were things she should never have been involved in in the first place.

And maybe she was doing a better job with things this time around.

'It's late,' Isla said, because it was. 'I should be getting back. They'll be wondering where I am. Lib'll send a search party out for me.'

'See?' said Brooke, with a gentle teasing smile. 'She loves you a lot.'

'Yeah,' said Isla, and nodded. 'She does.' And maybe Isla hadn't always felt deserving of that love, but she was going to work harder on that. She was going to work harder on letting herself feel worthwhile of love. Since she felt like she'd worked so hard on letting herself feel unworthy of it, of letting herself feel like she destroyed it whenever she encountered it.

They clambered off the bed together and tiptoed their way out of the playhouse. The stream babbling by outside seemed somehow louder in the darkness than it had in the daylight.

'Careful,' Brooke said. 'Let's not fall into it. How will I ever explain to Libby if I haven't taken good care of you?'

'You've taken excellent care of me,' Isla replied, smiling. 'Trust me. Libby's seen much worse when it comes to me.'

Brooke frowned. 'I don't like the sound of that at all. Who are all these people you met who didn't absolutely adore you?'

'They seem very unimportant right now,' Isla admitted, and maybe that was a terribly sappy thing to say but Brooke put her in a terribly sappy mood. Isla felt like she might be incapable of saying anything other than terribly sappy things for the next little while.

'Good,' Brooke said, looking satisfied, as they walked back to the house together. 'Then my work here is done. That was exactly what I hoped to achieve.'

They fell into a companionable silence, and the house looked silent and sleepy as they reached it. Some lights were still shining, but it was wrapped in such quiet solitude that Isla stopped and just looked at it, gleaming peacefully in the moonlight. She was feeling very fond of the house.

And then something stirred in the doorway all the way to the right. Some horrible amorphous shape and ever afterward Isla's only excuse was that they did so much talking about ghosts in the house that naturally she should think, upon seeing an inexplicable dark shape out of the corner of her eye in the quiet of the night, that it was a ghost. And so she screamed bloody murder.

'What?' Brooke asked in alarm, and Isla pointed wordlessly, at where the shape, seemingly made of shadows, kept growing out of the darkness.

And then Brooke said, 'Oh. Just go this way and don't bother it.'

'Don't bother it?' Isla practically screeched, because they'd been running around making ghost offerings and still the ghost seemed bothered.

But then the shadow finally moved into the light and Isla realised it ... was a pig.

'It's only a wild boar,' Brooke said, nudging Isla towards the house. 'It's fine. They won't bother you if you don't bother them. We get them around here; it probably came snuffling in here looking for food.'

'Blimey,' Isla said, trying to catch her breath, clutching her hand to her chest. 'I thought it was a ghost!'

Brooke started laughing.

Meanwhile, the door opened and everyone blinked out at her, in various states of sleepiness. Her screaming had plainly woken the entire household.

'It's nothing,' said Isla, trying to be dignified about it. 'Just a wild boar I thought might be a ghost.'

'It could have been the ghost of a wild boar,' said Pari instantly. 'Did you get a good look?'

'Okay,' Sam said. 'Now that we know Isla's all right, we're all going back to bed.'

Everyone shuffled off, the teenagers especially giving Isla dirty looks for waking them, while Libby just winked at her, and Isla turned back to Brooke.

'Quite the finish to the evening,' Brooke said, obviously struggling not to keep laughing.

'Let me give it a better finish,' Isla suggested, and kissed her.

Libby made a rhubarb pie, all by herself, and she was amazed by it. She took a slice out to Isla, who was sitting in the garden on a picnic blanket, and said, 'Look at this amazing pie I've made. You must try it.'

Isla tried the pie and made an appropriately rapturous noise over it. '*Libby*. Did you make this pastry?'

Libby, beaming, nodded. 'The recipe comes from Pauline. I am prohibited from writing it down, but I can share it with you through osmosis.'

Isla laughed. 'It's awfully quiet. Where is everyone?'

'A massive outing to a village. Christmas Street likes to travel *en masse*.'

Libby arranged herself on the blanket next to Isla and fixed her with a look. 'Tell me *all* about it.'

'What?' Isla asked, feigning innocence.

'Well,' said Libby, 'for starters you can tell me how you came to be outside in the farmyard after dark screaming about a ghost wild boar with Brooke by your side.'

Isla laughed, embarrassed. 'Everyone's always talking about ghosts around here! I was on edge! Who expects a wild boar to just be hanging out in a doorway? I didn't mean to wake everyone up like that.'

Libby laughed as well. 'It's fine. It was our excitement for the evening. Christmas Street has to have some excitement, even when Christmas Street has moved itself to France.'

'I will say, it did make me feel reassured for if I ever am attacked by a ghost in the farmyard, everyone showed up *very* quickly.'

'Another thing Christmas Street is good at,' Libby said. 'So, anyway, the fact that you disappeared for hours I'm going to assume is a good sign.'

Isla smiled, probably a terribly sappy smile, because she was stuck in a terrible sappiness. 'It went so well. I told her everything.'

'Everything? Everything like what?'

'About what a disaster I am.'

Libby said, 'Isla. You're not a disaster.'

'Oh, I'm totally a disaster, Lib. Look at me. Look at you, and look at me. Look at what you've accomplished, and I've only—'

'You've travelled the world. That's an enormous accomplishment. And isn't that what you wanted? Not everyone needs to settle down right away. It's okay to be a free spirit.'

'But it's not okay if you feel like you're sabotaging every

relationship you could ever have, like you're driving people away. I didn't even come home for your wedding, Lib.'

Libby stared at her. 'And I already told you that you didn't have to! That wasn't something you did *wrong*.'

'But I felt like I did. I felt like I was doing everything wrong. And then there was ... I had this relationship, that didn't go well, and they maybe said something to me that kept ... that kept ringing in my head, that maybe I was never going to be able to have a good relationship, because there's just something *wrong* with me that I keep running away.'

'*Isla*.' Libby reached for her hand. 'That is *not true*,' she said fervently. 'Whoever these people were, they were wrong to tell you that. I've known you way longer than any of them, and you're a wonderful friend, and you've never been running away from us, you've been trying to find out who you are, and that's an admirable thing to do. It's not something you should feel like you have to apologise for, do you understand me? Ever.'

Isla nodded, blinking back tears. 'I know. I know. Brooke said kind of the same thing. Without the bit about knowing me for a long time. But Brooke was ... Brooke was so wonderful. She didn't treat me as if I'm a disaster, she didn't believe that I'm a disaster, she made me see that maybe I just haven't found the right thing for me yet. Maybe I haven't put down roots yet because I haven't found the place I want to put down roots yet. Or the person. Which sounds weird, but you know what I mean.'

Libby nodded with a smile. 'I do know what you mean.

301

And I'm glad Brooke didn't treat you like a disaster. You don't deserve to be treated like a disaster. I'd have to go and give her a piece of my mind if she'd let you say these things about yourself. I'm glad she didn't.'

'Me, too,' said Isla.

'So do you think she could be the person who makes you want to put down roots?' Libby asked.

'I don't know. Maybe? It's too soon to tell. But ... she makes me want to stay longer.'

Libby smiled.

Isla smiled back, and they lapsed into silence for a moment.

Isla said, 'So. Do you feel better about being pregnant?'

Libby groaned. 'I don't know. I'm glad that Sam knows now but ... You are much braver than I am. I just keep thinking in my head ... How am I going to be as a mother?'

'You're going to be an exceptional mother. I promise. I think maybe the waiting is the hard part.'

'You are definitely wrong about that. Definitely the hard part happens once the baby is outside your body.'

'Okay, that's probably true,' Isla allowed.

Libby sighed and sipped from her mug again and said, 'I have to say, though, I am already heartily sick of herbal tea.' Isla laughed.

Isla found Brooke between the vines, floppy straw hat on her head shielding her from the sun.

Her nose still had freckles over it anyway, and Isla loved them.

She also loved the way Brooke broke out into a wide smile upon seeing her. 'Hello there! What a pleasant surprise!'

'I thought I'd come and see you,' Isla said, and accepted the kiss Brooke gave her in greeting.

'And I'm glad you did. I was going to have to swing by the house to see you later, but this saves me the trip. I have to go out of town.'

Isla frowned. 'Out of town?'

'Don't worry. I'll be back next week. Trust me, I know the timing is poor, and I tried to put it off, but it can't be helped. There's a lot of stuff that has to be managed, and I should just get there and do it.'

'Really?' Isla said, trying not to be too disappointed.

'Yeah.' Brooke did look properly chagrined by this development. She didn't look like she really wanted to run away.

Isla still wanted it verified. 'You're not . . . Look, if you want to not do this any more, then—'

'*No*,' said Brooke firmly. 'I was worried you'd think that, and that is absolutely not what's happening here. I've honestly had business come up that has to be dealt with.'

'It's just that the summer's almost over,' Isla pointed out.

'Do you have somewhere else you need to be?' Brooke asked.

'No,' Isla admitted. She never really did.

Brooke gave her a crooked, irresistible smile. 'Then I'm

hoping to convince you you might have a reason to stay after everyone else leaves.'

Isla couldn't help the fact that she felt like her eyes literally turned into hearts at the idea. 'I might be persuaded.'

Brooke's smile was curling and satisfied as she fitted Isla into her arms. 'Yeah?'

'Possibly.' Isla tried to play coy but knew she was failing entirely. She decided to try to shift the subject a little bit. 'I had no idea vineyards were such demanding places to work.'

'Oh,' said Brooke. 'Yeah. It's madness. You've no idea. Let me show you this, though.' She tugged Isla over to look at a cluster of grapes, fragrant and sun-warm, and Isla thought, *Maybe we can just do this indefinitely.*

It sounded like a lovely thought.

Isla didn't really want to let Brooke go, but she gave herself an internal pep talk and told herself to be grown-up about the whole situation. Grown-up, and trusting Brooke: that's what she was striving for.

'Jeanne can drive you back, if you like,' Brooke suggested. I'm sure everyone would enjoy that.'

'You have no idea,' Isla said, 'but I don't want to get you in trouble for taking the car out or something.'

Brooke shook her head. 'It's fine. The car should be driven. I'll tell Jeanne.' She hesitated, studying Isla's face.

'What?' Isla asked.

More head-shaking. 'Nothing. I'll be back next week, and we can talk.'

'Yeah,' Isla agreed, perplexed. 'Is there something we need to talk about?'

Brooke grinned now. 'You spending as much time here as possible.'

Isla couldn't help but grin in return. 'Oh, yeah. We should talk about that.'

Brooke gave her a quick kiss, and then said, 'I'll go tell Jeanne. And I'll see you next week.'

'Can't wait,' Isla said, grinning from ear to ear.

Isla watched Brooke disappear inside the chateau, and then she caught sight of Raphael, apparently having just finished giving a tour. Isla hadn't realised people who weren't them also took tours of the chateau.

Isla waved to Raphael.

Raphael wandered over to her. 'I am happy to have met you. We're having a soirée here at the chateau. Hmm. How would you say? A garden party? Pretty dresses, a bit of wine, in the courtyard here. And *poker*. Everyone should come. All of the nearby villages are invited. It's going to be a grand time.'

'Yes, we heard. Like a village fete?' Isla said. 'We'll be sure to come, and see Victor beat you at poker.'

'That is not what happens,' Raphael insisted.

Isla laughed, as Jeanne came outside and indicated that she was getting the car ready.

Raphael waited beside Isla, apparently content to just stand in silence with her.

Isla thought of how they'd first met, and said, 'The story you told, about Mary and Adélaïde.'

'Yes?'

'And how they were rivals?'

'Yes?'

'How do you know they were rivals?' Isla asked.

Raphael looked blank, like he didn't know what else could be said.

'As opposed to something else?' Isla suggested. 'Like friends?'

Raphael said, 'Stories about friends don't tend to survive into legend. There must be more to it, no?'

Chapter Twenty-Three

Pari and Teddy's Ghost Plan:
Make ghost traps!
Look in dark wardrobes
Attic????
Secret tunnels!!!

Isla didn't expect to see Brooke at the vineyard garden party. Brooke, after all, was away on business. They'd texted a bit, but Brooke had clearly been busy, and also in a different time zone, given the times that the texts were coming in. So Isla was generally trying not to bother her. She believed Brooke, and when she got back they would talk about Isla spending the rest of the summer at the vineyard, maybe the rest of the year, maybe the rest of her *life*.

That was how Isla was feeling.

And then, at the garden party, from across the court-yard, Isla caught sight, unexpectedly, of Brooke. Which was odd in and of itself, because she had assumed she was still out of town. But what was extra-odd was how Brooke was dressed. Isla had got used to Brooke being, well, Brooke, in casual jeans and worn-out trainers and that silly, floppy straw hat. This Brooke, on the other side of the courtyard, was dressed in some kind of ridiculous bright yellow concoction that floated and frothed all around her. Her hair had been slicked back, and pinned precariously to one side of it was a huge, curling yellow feather that bobbed around behind her whenever she moved. And from across the courtyard Isla could see the sun glinting on bright, dazzling jewels around Brooke's neck.

Isla could do nothing but stare, because that was Brooke but that was . . . not at all Brooke.

'Is that Brooke?' Libby asked from beside her, sounding honestly perplexed.

'I don't know,' Isla said. 'I can't tell. I think it is, but it's—'

Then Brooke happened to glance her way, and clearly caught sight of her. Her eyes widened, as if she hadn't expected Isla to be there, and Isla thought sardonically, *Bingo*. That was definitely the look of a Brooke caught in a lie.

Isla didn't even know what to think. What was the lie? Had she ever gone out of town? Was the lie that she liked to dress like this in her free time? Was the lie that she wore diamonds? Isla didn't know the extent to which she should feel betrayed, just that she *did*. Something had happened here that had made her feel like a rug had been swept out from under her, and that it had been unfair for Brooke to do that to her.

Isla wanted to flee. That was her first instinct. She wanted to run away. Of course she did. She wanted to run away from Brooke, she wanted to run away from France, she wanted to grab the first train or plane going anywhere but here.

And then feedback squealed across the courtyard. A woman had mounted the small stage set up on one side, and she said in French into the microphone, 'Thank you all for coming to our little party. We are so grateful to have these beautiful surroundings for our gathering, and we cannot thank enough Mademoiselle Brooke Demesne for loaning us her beautiful chateau courtyard.'

There was applause all around the courtyard, and Isla continued to stare at Brooke, who kept snatching glances back at her in between talking to other people who kept coming up to her. Did Brooke *own* this chateau?

'What did she just say?' Libby hissed to Isla. 'She was talking way too fast for me.'

'I think Brooke owns this vineyard,' Isla said, never taking her eyes off Brooke. 'Like the vineyard, the chateau, the . . . lot. I think she owns *the lot.*'

Brooke was now ascending the stage, and stood in her ridiculous outfit and said to the crowd in beautiful, fluent French, 'I am happy to have been welcomed so thoroughly into your community.' She looked out over the crowd and met Isla's eyes. 'My time here has changed my life, and I hope all of you have as magnificent a time tonight as I have had during my time here in Provence with you.' She used the plural *you* but Isla felt like she was talking just to her.

There was another smattering of applause, and then Brooke got off the stage, and started heading straight towards Isla. Her yellow outfit was like a beacon in the crowd.

Libby said to Isla, 'Did she say something devastatingly romantic to you?'

'No,' Isla lied. 'Not really.'

And then Brooke arrived at them. 'Hi, Libby,' she said, without taking her eyes off Isla.

'Hi, Brooke,' Libby said. 'I like your feather.'

'Can we talk?' Brooke asked Isla.

'I think we should,' Isla agreed.

Brooke smiled tightly, and then she led Isla out of the courtyard and into the chateau. And she didn't even stop there. She went up the stairs, and Isla followed, and she went down the hallway, and Isla followed, and then she opened a door and went into a bedroom and finally stopped and turned back to Isla.

Isla cast her eyes around the room and looked back at Brooke. 'This is your bedroom, isn't it?'

Brooke took a deep breath.

'You own this chateau,' Isla accused.

After a second, Brooke said, 'Yeah.'

'Is that *couture* you're wearing?' Isla realised.

Brooke looked down at her outfit. 'The French really love for you to wear couture. Like, always.'

'And yellow diamonds,' Isla said, feeling a little

hysterical. 'You're *drenched* in yellow diamonds. How rich *are* you? Are you some kind of French royalty?'

'No,' Brooke said ruefully. 'Not at all. I'm actually just a lowly computer programmer who happened to work for the right start-up and, oops, now I'm a billionaire.'

Isla stared at her. '*What?*'

'So,' Brooke said, and started pacing around the room, trailing chiffon and ribbon in her wake, her feather bouncing along on her head. 'I made a lot of money, but I was miserable. It was awful. It was the worst environment, and what was I even doing, was I even doing anything to help the world, I didn't deserve all this money, I should be doing something more important with it. So I quit. I cashed out. I had been here on vacation, they told me to go on vacation to sort my head out, and I just ... bought the place. Why not own a vineyard in France? I thought. And then I could figure out what other good I could do in the world. Which I've been trying to figure out. I've had lots of meetings with different foundations and charities and stuff, trying to get ideas. That's where I've been. That's why I've been so busy. But then, in the meantime, I was here, and I ... met you.'

Isla kept staring at her. 'Why didn't you *tell* me?'

'It isn't the sort of thing you lead with, right? I don't introduce myself to people: "Hello, I'm Brooke, I'm very rich." And then by the time I ... by the time I realised I was falling in love with you, I realised that I'd never told you who I was, exactly, but it ... it seemed so unimportant to me, in comparison to how amazing *you* are. It's not like I've done a lot of dating since becoming rich. It's not like

I've done *any* dating since becoming rich. I wasn't exactly sure how to navigate ... And then you told me everything you told me and I didn't ... I didn't want to make you run. I didn't want to give you a reason to run by telling you that I hadn't been telling you the truth about myself. I thought, once I got back from this business trip, and I got through this party, then I'd tell you. I'd ... ask you to stay in France with me, and I'd tell you. That was my plan.'

'That was your plan?' Isla echoed. 'And what were you going to say?'

'I was going to say ... ' Brooke trailed off and stopped pacing and looked at Isla. 'I was going to say ... ' She walked up to her and held out her hand. 'Hello. I'm Brooke. I'm very rich, but I hope it's more important to know that I fell in love with you the first time I saw you, and I've been falling more ever since, and I'm hoping, if you'd like to run away, you'd let me run away *with* you. I'm hoping that neither one of us has to run away alone any more. We can do it together. What do you say?'

Isla studied her for a long moment, and then said, 'That's a nice speech,' and then she used Brooke's hand to pull her forward and kiss her.

Pari, playing with the kittens, said, 'Oh, my goodness. Do you know what this means?'

'That everyone on Christmas Street can have a cat?' said Teddy.

'That they're so young that we can train them! We can have cats who do tricks!'

Teddy was dubious. 'Are cats like that? I don't think cats are like dogs. The Pachutas' cats don't do any tricks.'

Pari waved a hand airily. 'That's because Mrs Pachuta never bothered to train her cats. But kittens are totally trainable if we start early. By the time I have to go home, we should have a *whole show*. Jack will do tricks and we'll introduce the kittens at the end. We could maybe have a *travelling circus* eventually.'

Teddy frowned, thinking. 'Do they still have circuses?'

Pari didn't seem worried about that. 'Just a dog and some kittens aren't good enough for a circus, really, so we'll have to make sure the tricks are really good.'

'The kittens *just* opened their eyes,' said Teddy, trying to be practical about all of this.

'Oh, yeah, of course it'll take them a little while to be as good as they're going to be,' said Pari. 'We can be patient. In the meantime, tell me more about the ghosts!'

'You know what I've been thinking?' Pari said to Teddy, as Jack failed to bark four times in response to their *what's two plus two?* question.

'That maybe dogs can't do maths?' said Teddy.

'That there might be secret passages in the fireplaces,' replied Pari.

Teddy looked from Pari to the fireplace they were sitting near and back again. 'What?'

'Look,' said Pari, 'doesn't this seem like the kind of house that would have a secret passage or two?' She scrambled to her feet and scooted into the fireplace. Luckily it was big enough that she fitted comfortably, but, even though Libby and Sam had made them all clean the house, it was still pretty dirty in there. Pari was black with soot almost immediately.

Teddy wrinkled his nose and said, 'I mean, I guess so, but you're going to get in trouble. You should see how filthy you are.'

Pari waved her hand around. 'That doesn't matter when we're *discovering* things.' Jack went to jump around in the fireplace with her, barking happily. 'Jack, do you see any hidden passages? I bet Jack is aces at hidden passages.'

Teddy looked at the soot Jack's wagging tail was spreading all over the room, and at the sooty pawprints Jack was leaving all over, and said, 'Oh, boy.'

'I told you the fireplace was a bad idea,' Teddy said, with a sigh, as he and Pari entered hour three of scrubbing at the soot that had ended up *all over* the room.

'It would have been a great idea if we'd found a hidden passage,' grumbled Pari. 'Maybe the fireplace in the next room has a hidden passage.'

'I don't think we should look in any more fireplaces,' Teddy said.

Pari sighed heavily.

'We've been going about it all wrong,' Pari announced. 'If there are secret passages for the ghosts, I don't think they're *in* the house.'

'But why would the ghosts need secret passages?' asked Teddy.

'I mean the people who the ghosts *were*,' said Pari. '*They* needed secret passages. Think how old this house is. People definitely needed to sneak in and out. So. That's where we have to look.'

Teddy just looked at her.

So did Jack.

Then they looked at each other.

'Jack and I are lost,' Teddy said. '*Where* are we looking?'

'Outside the house,' Pari said. 'Clearly all of the secret passages leading to the house have been boarded up. We're never going to find them. But probably they still exist outside the house.'

Teddy thought it over. 'Probably the playhouse would be the best place to start looking.'

The fireplaces in the playhouse weren't quite as sooty as in the main house. Teddy had been worried about creeping into them, but it turned out that they just had to brush out a lot of fallen leaves and twigs.

'Maybe we'll find some kind of wild animal living in here!' Pari exclaimed. 'And then we can make it a pet!'

Jack gave Teddy a concerned look.

Teddy said, 'We're going to have a lot of pets, between Jack and the kittens and some kind of wild animal.'

'It's going to be perfect,' Pari said. 'Perfect for our travelling circus.'

Teddy wasn't sold on the idea of a travelling circus – it seemed like a lot of work – but that seemed like a conversation for another day. In the meantime, Pari was trying to see if there were any secret doors in the back of the fireplace.

'So how do you think this would work?' Teddy asked, sitting on the floor and watching her with interest.

'I don't know,' she answered, clearly thinking hard. 'I feel like you should be able to, like, I don't know, lean on a brick or something, and something opens. I see them do it in the movies all the time!'

'And then you think it would tunnel all the way back to the house?' Teddy said. 'It just seems like a long way to go.'

Pari shrugged. 'I don't know. Maybe.'

Teddy looked around the room they were in. 'Maybe the controls are somewhere out here.'

'They could be,' Pari said enthusiastically.

So Teddy started crawling all over the floor, tapping on the floorboards, looking for anything that might look like a secret passage handle.

And that's how they found the little hollowed-out bit under the floor that held all the letters.

They gathered them up and ran gleefully back to the house with them, Jack barking for joy behind them, and when Teddy tumbled inside he shouted, 'Dad! Dad! We didn't find the key but we did find *these*!'

Teddy woke the following morning and immediately felt different. He was ten years old now. That changed *everything*.

'Happy birthday!' Sam told him at breakfast, and Libby gave him a kiss, and then they set a gift on the table in front of him.

Teddy tore the wrapping paper off to reveal the latest videogame in the Extinction Event series. 'This is so cool!' Teddy exclaimed. 'Just what I wanted!'

'A massive extinction event,' Sam said. 'Do I know my son or what?'

'Actually,' said Pari. 'You already got the best birthday gift anyone could ask for.' Teddy looked at her.

'The letters!' Pari said.

'Oh, yeah,' said Teddy, and looked at Isla, who everyone said spoke the best French out of all of them and so had offered to translate the letters. 'How's the translating going? Any luck?'

'Oh,' said Isla. 'Not really.'

'You only gave them to her last night,' Libby said. 'You need to give her time.'

'I just know that those letters are going to unlock all of

the mysteries of this house,' said Pari. 'And then we'll get to tell Mrs Dash how we solved all of the mysteries! She'll be so impressed. Wait until we tell her everything there is to know about the ghosts haunting this place.'

'I'm curious about that as well,' said Isla. 'There are unexpected layers to this whole ghost story.'

'Really?' said Libby. 'What have you found out?'

'Brooke had a different version of the story, that's all. She said a real estate broker told her that Mary and Adélaïde were great friends. No rivalry at all.'

'That would make sense,' Sam said. 'Rivalries are too exhausting to keep up. I'm sure they got along. And that's probably why they're such relatively benevolent ghosts. Too much work to fully haunt us. They're probably just hanging out somewhere gossiping about us.'

'What is there to gossip about with us?' asked Diya. 'We're all very boring.'

Millie sat at the window of their bedroom and looked out over the countryside. She knew she couldn't stay up for a second night in a row, but she *wanted* to, because she didn't want to close her eyes and miss even a moment of this place.

Jasper said behind her, 'You should come to bed,' and kissed her shoulder.

Millie said, 'I'm somewhat worried if I fall asleep here, then I'll have to wake up and realise it's all been a dream.'

Jasper slid his arms around her and rested his chin on her shoulder. 'None of it's a dream,' he murmured. 'I promise.'

'It seems like it should be,' Millie admitted. 'I could never have imagined something like this—'

'Shh,' Jasper said, and kissed her ear.

'I'm just saying, that now I have ... I have you, and this life, and these friends, and baking, and everyone's so nice to me—'

'Everyone should always have been nice to you,' Jasper said seriously. He nudged Millie to make her look him in the eye. 'Do you hear me? Everyone should *always* be nice to you. That is no less than what you deserve.'

'I can't believe I'm here,' Millie said, her voice trembling. 'I can't believe I'm here *with you*.' She cupped her hand around Jasper's face. 'I never dared to believe that I would find someone who ... I can't believe I'm here.'

Jasper gave her a crooked smile. 'And here I've been working so hard to get you to believe exactly that. I guess I just have to try harder.'

It was the last night that they would have at the farmhouse as a full family. Isla was going to go to the chateau with Brooke the next day. All of the visitors were going back home with Teddy, and Sam and Libby would have a few days together before locking everything up and putting the house back into its sleeping state.

They worked together to turn out a dinner of ratatouille, made entirely from fresh produce they all picked together on the property, with creamy fresh goat cheese on the side that they spread onto the last pillowy soft bread of their summer. They ate in the back garden, where they lit candles and talked into the night, reluctant for it to end. Millie brought out an amazing tray of sablés and they praised all of the French food extravagantly.

Sam said, 'So, this is our last real night all together in this house, huh?'

Pen said, 'Feeling nostalgic?'

'Actually,' Sam said, 'I am feeling very optimistic about the future. Considering there's going to be a baby in it.'

There was a moment of silence, and then there was a cacophony of enthusiastic reaction and a flood of people engulfing Sam and Libby and Teddy in hugs and congratulations.

Brooke gave Isla's hand a squeeze, and managed to say, 'That's wonderful news,' when she could get a word in.

'Oh, that's a reason to drink more wine if ever I heard of one,' exclaimed Pen. 'Except for you, Libby. Sorry, I'll have your share.'

'How generous of you,' Libby laughed.

'A friend for you!' Max said to Charlie, who was up way past his bedtime and wide-eyed at the turn of events. 'How wonderful!'

'We're going to have our very own memory of our time in France,' Sam remarked. 'The best souvenir anyone could ask for.'

'That, and a kitten,' said Teddy.

Sam laughed.

'Well, I am going to miss all of you Christmas Street people,' Brooke said. 'Is there room for more people to move in on that street?'

'Oh, I would *love* that,' said Libby.

'Hmm,' remarked Marcel Pachuta. 'Maybe we could just trade places. I would be very interested in running a vineyard.'

'An exchange programme,' Brooke laughed. 'That could be fun!'

'I think,' said Isla, 'that the idea of settling down doesn't sound so bad if it's on Christmas Street.'

'I think it doesn't sound so bad if it's *together*,' said Brooke.

And then, suddenly, every light in the dark part of the house came on at once, blazing through the darkness. They all exclaimed as illumination flooded the garden.

'The electricity!' cried Libby. 'It came on!'

'Huh,' said Sam. 'Look at that. I guess we must have finally appeased the ghosts.'

'Well,' said Isla. 'I have to admit that makes some sense.'

'Hey,' Teddy said, 'did you ever finish reading the letters?'

'I did,' Isla replied. 'And knowing what I now know about Mary and Adélaïde, well, it makes sense that they are now appeased.'

'Why?' Libby asked. 'What do you know about them?'

'They were in love,' Isla said simply. 'All those letters? They were love letters. There was no rivalry between them. They loved each other deeply and profoundly. That's why

Mary eventually left, because of the scandal it caused with her English family. She couldn't handle it, so she went home. Adélaïde begged her not to. Adélaïde wanted to run off somewhere else together. Somewhere no one knew who they were. Somewhere it wouldn't have mattered who they were. But Mary had Clarissa, and Mary never ran off with Adélaïde. Mary had ... too many roots.'

Isla could feel Brooke's eyes on her. 'They needed to find a balance,' Brooke said.

'Yes,' Isla agreed. 'And they never reached it. Their story was tragic. Their ghosts are here because they're trapped in death as they were trapped in life. At least, if I believed in ghost stories, that's what I would say. But it makes sense they're appeased now, because I think, finally, they got to see all the happiness in this house they always wanted, and never got to have.'

'That is so beautiful,' Pen said, sniffling and wiping at her eyes.

'Poor Mary and Adélaïde,' Libby said, and looked at the brightly lit house. 'I hope, wherever they are, they're happy now.'

'I think,' said Isla, 'that they definitely are.'

Epilogue

As summer ended, Jack returned to Christmas Street. A lonely farmhouse in France was closed up again, and Christmas Street rang with the sounds Jack loved best, with rather more applause and exclamations greeting Sam and Libby wherever they went. But Jack liked being home, liked the London squirrels and his familiar bed and his multiple dinners every night.

As the year swung towards Christmas, the kittens appeared on Christmas Street. So did toys, and new furniture, and the house smelled like paint, and then eventually, they brought home a tiny person who made a lot of noise.

And then, when summer came, and that tiny person was slightly larger, they went back to the farmhouse with all the land and the French squirrels and the vines that smelled rich like grapes, and all of the lights went on the first time they tried.

Acknowledgements

Thank you to all of my usual suspects!

Maddie West, Thalia Proctor, and the entire team at Little, Brown UK, for coaxing this little story along to make it better;

My agent Andrea Somberg, for always being an excellent cheerleader;

Sonja L. Cohen, for going above and beyond with editorial support;

Larry Stritof, for dealing with all my tech wizard issues;

Kristin Gillespie, Erin McCormick, Jennifer Roberson, and Noel Wiedner, for putting up with all the venting;

Aja Romano, ditto;

Everyone at my day job, for being endlessly supportive;

Everyone on the internet, for being my friends;

BTS, for putting out a large number of albums to keep me company while I wrote this;

And, as ever, Mom, Dad, Ma, Megan, Caitlin, Bobby, Jeff, Jordan, Isabella, Gabriella, and Audrey, and Peyton, for making life fun.

Visit Christmas Street

On a little street in a big city, everything is changing

Everything eight-year-old Teddy loves is in America. But his widowed father, Sam, has brought them both back to England to be closer to their family. Sam's one wish is for Teddy to be happy again.

As Teddy and Sam settle into their new life, and Sam has an unusual meet-cute with the delightful Libby, a very special four-legged neighbour is determined to make them feel at home. Jack, the Christmas street dog, is welcome in everyone's house – but will it be in his power to help a little boy remember the true meaning of the season?

As the snow sparkles on the ground, one small act of kindness will give a whole street a happy Christmas . . .

Sam is about to propose to his girlfriend Libby, and his neighbours in Christmas Street all think they know the right way to do it. With their help – and sometimes hinderance – Sam gains a fiancée and the wedding planning begins.

Meanwhile, Sam's nine-year-old son Teddy and his friend Pari – with their constant companion Jack the street dog – are fascinated by the arrival of a mysterious new neighbour on the street who has rented the empty, run-down house. Their attempts to spy on her are thwarted by her staying indoors with the curtains drawn most of the time. But soon Christmas Street begins to work its magic and Millie is reluctantly drawn into street activities.

As Millie starts to relax into thinking she can have a different life, maybe even with Jasper, the local carpenter, someone turns up from her past to threaten that. But with all of the street looking out for her, Millie's Christmas will be filled with hope and promise.

'Heartwarmingly festive – if only all streets were like Christmas Street!' Ali McNamara

Join us at

For competitions galore,
exclusive interviews with our lovely
Sphere authors, chat about
all the latest books
and much, much more.

Follow us on Twitter at
@littlebookcafe

Subscribe to our newsletter and
Like us at /thelittlebookcafe

Read. Love. Share.

Printed in Great Britain
by Amazon